a SONG *for*
NETTIE JOHNSON

a SONG *for*
NETTIE JOHNSON

GLORIA SAWAI

COTEAU BOOKS

WWW.COTEAUBOOKS.COM

Edited by Edna Alford.
Book and cover design by Duncan Campbell.
Cover image, "Woman Dancing in Meadow" by Gary Isaacs / Photonica.

Printed and bound in Canada at Houghton Boston, Saskatoon.

National Library of Canada Cataloguing in Publication Data

Sawai, Gloria, date-
A song for Nettie Johnson

ISBN 1-55050-223-9

1. Title.
PS8587.A3894S66 2001   C813'.54   C2001-911221-1
PR9199.3.S392S66 2001

  3   4   5   6   7   8   9   10

AVAILABLE IN CANADA & THE US FROM

401-2206 Dewdney Ave.   Fitzhenry & Whiteside
Regina, Saskatchewan   195 Allstate Parkway
Canada   S4R 1H3   Markham, ON, Canada, L3R 4T8

The publisher gratefully acknowledges the financial assistance of the Saskatchewan Arts Board, the Canada Council for the Arts, the Government of Canada through the Book Publishing Industry Development Program (BPIDP), and the City of Regina Arts Commission, for its publishing program.

For my parents, Gustav and Ragnhild,
my brothers, Donald and Robert,
my children, Naomi and Kenji

CONTENTS

"Look to the rock from which you were hewn,
the quarry from which you were dug."
— Isaiah 51:1

"Grace is everywhere."
– GEORGES BERNANOS

A Song for Nettie Johnson

FROM HER CHAIR AT THE EDGE OF THE QUARRY she looks down at the bottom of the pit – as wide and long as a garden, as big as a front yard with grass, or the sunny porch of a white mansion somewhere far away.

She looks. But she doesn't climb down anymore. Doesn't slip on loose gravel and cascading sand or, reaching the dry floor of the pit, kneel on pebbles to see the beetles scramble to their little houses under the stones. She could, she's not old, not yet fifty, but she doesn't. Nevertheless, she remembers: stones and beetles, and the lonely space below the wind.

She feels for the buttonhole on her sweater, searches for a button to secure the garment more tightly against her chest. But the button isn't there, hasn't been there for as long as she can remember, wasn't there even when her mother was alive a long, long time ago.

Her mother is an angel of light. She is slim and golden and wears a pale blue dress and plays a harp. She holds the silver harp on her lap, and her thin fingers slide over the strings, and the music lifts the stars.

But her mother isn't here, the small black harp she used to play on winter nights inside the trailer is in a box at the back of the closet, and the sweater has no buttons, not one. Tomorrow she will look for a pin. Somewhere in the trailer there is a safety pin. She will find it tomorrow.

She glances at the blue book lying on her lap, strokes the cover with her fingers, and rocks in the chair, back and forth slowly. The chair's rungs move easily in the deep grooves they've made among the stones. In the sky above the quarry a magpie squawks.

She opens the book and examines the words. They are printed in two straight columns down the page, but the print is faint, the paper smudged, some of the letters gone entirely. She presses her finger on the top word in the first column.

"Stone," she says softly to the word under her finger.

"Stone," she says again, loudly, as if it were a cry to someone she can't see, someone beyond the quarry.

"Stone," she calls, and her voice echoes above the prairie.

"S-t-o-n-e." She spells the word slowly, each letter distinct, melodic. She lifts her finger from the page and looks closely at the printed word.

"That is correct," she says.

She places her finger on the second word.

"Dust," she calls. And the magpie swoops down

from the sky into the branches of the willow tree.

"D-u-s-t," she spells. She removes her finger and examines the spelling.

"Ha," she says. "Right again."

She closes the book, rests her hands on it, and rocks gently in the chair. Dry wind blows against her face, against her skin, tight and hard and darkened by the sun. It lifts her hair, the colour of ripe wheat, swirls it in front of her, pressing the strands against her cheeks, her chin, her bare neck. She loops her finger into the buttonhole of the sweater, looks up, and says quietly, "Sometimes it helps, sometimes it does help, just to spell."

Behind her, in the tiny bedroom of the trailer, he is sleeping, his lean body curved under the blanket, his weathered face sunk into the pillow. He's dreaming of rain, of the creek bed below the quarry hill once more filled with water, of robins splashing, sparrows drinking. He sighs in his sleep, and a long procession of people march across the prairie to the creek. One by one they step into the stream, splashing their feet and singing, *Oh thou that tellest good tidings to Zion....* The room's one small window lets in a rectangle of light that rests on the grey blanket covering him.

He awakens, blinks his eyes against the light, and sings, mumbling, the rest of the line, *get thee up into a high mountain.* He raises one hand above the covers, moves the melody through the air with his fingers. He stops. Can't remember the rest of the song. How could he forget something he's known so long? Since university days? And heard so often? "Get thee up into a high mountain," he says, his voice scolding. "Get thee up," he repeats, more firmly. "Get thee up right now, Eli, and get moving."

But first, he turns on his side, reaches under the bed with his long arm, scrunches his body closer to the edge, stretches his arm farther under the springs, and farther still, circling his thin arm over the dusty linoleum, his fingers searching. Then he remembers. It's not there. He's thrown it out. Thrown them all out. Every bottle. He's not drinking any more. He's sober. The realization comes as a shock so early in the morning and just awakened from a gentle dream.

He retrieves his arm, swings it across the bed to the empty space beside him. She's gone too, her pillow cold. He lies back, thin and chilly under the blanket. It's not fair, having to start the day with two such losses.

Outside, the wind rolls and dips and touches the land, bending the stems of thistles, pushing their brittle leaves to click against each other, moving the little stones and hard kernels of sand to sift and scrape and clatter softly in their tiny houses in the pockets of the earth.

He opens the trailer door. Fully dressed now, he stands on the steps and watches her for a moment.

"My Lady of the Quarry," he says – to the back of her head, to the back of the rocking chair that faces the quarry, to the back of her, Nettie, rocking.

"Eli," she says. "You're up." She does not turn to him.

"My Lady of the Word," he says.

"Oh stop that," she says.

"I'm going now," he says.

"Oh?"

"To town. I've got an important errand."

"Oh sure."

"It's October. It's time."

She doesn't answer.

"I'll be back," he says.

"Ha."

"I said I would and I will."

"Tell me another one."

"This afternoon when I'm finished."

"Finished at the Golden West?"

"I'm not going to the Golden West."

"Oh sure."

He walks the few steps from the trailer to her chair, stops behind her and touches her hair with his fingers.

"I always come back, Nettie."

Her face listens. Eyes narrow, lips tighten. Her gaze moves from the book on her lap to the ground at her feet, to the quarry in front of her, to the pasture beyond the quarry, to the horizon's edge and up, more, still more, neck stretching, to the blue dome directly above her. She's measuring his words.

"That's what you say." She opens the book again, face sour.

"Come with me," he says.

"Never."

"Leave the damn pit for awhile." He slides his hand across her slim back, feels its firmness. "And come."

"Don't try any of your tricks," she says. "I'm not going anywhere."

He walks away from her, around the quarry to the hill's edge, where he turns, facing her, and says, "I'll wave to you below the hill, beside the willow tree. Will you watch for me?"

"You mean look at you?"

"Something like that."

"It's tiring to do that all the time," she says.

He stands there for a moment. And she sees his body tall against the sky. Then he turns and steps over the hill's rim and down through gravel and small rocks to the bottom. Here he walks into the dry creek bed, the soles of his shoes slippery against the dusty pebbles, and crosses to the other side.

By the willow tree he stops, turns, looks up, waits for her to appear at the hill's edge. He wants to wave to her. He wants her to wave back. He waits for this desire to manifest itself in the air above him, to change the nature of the space between them, two simple movements, his wave, her response. But she doesn't appear, so he turns his face toward town and steps out into the broad pasture that lies before him.

When she knows he's gone – across the creek and into Jacobson's pasture – she drops the book, stands up, and goes to the ridge of the hill.

"Well, be careful then," she calls. "Watch out for cactus."

The tiny particles of her voice flow over the hillside, over the creek bed and the willow tree, and into the pasture.

She calls louder. "Keep your eyes open. Don't step in a gopher hole." And the little pieces of sound speed through the air and almost touch him.

She sees him in the pasture leaning forward as if pressing against a strong wind, his steps slow. "You're not that old," she says, "so stop pretending." She leans her own thin body out toward him. A breeze blows against her, moving the cloth of her long skirt, the colour of fallen leaves, against her legs, and pressing against the faded green sweater that has no buttons.

"Look at him," she says finally. "Away he goes. So far. Thousands of miles. He'll never come back, I can count on that, that's one thing I can count on."

She kneels beside the quarry, digs among the stones with her fingers, and picks up a smooth grey pebble. She lays it in the palm of her hand and curls her fingers over it. Small and snug, it fits in her palm like a baby in its basket.

"Would you like to go for a little walk?" she asks.

"Yes, I would," she answers.

She takes the long way around the quarry, holding the pebble. She stops, looks down at some wild oats, creamy yellow, swaying a little at her feet, and a single purple vetch beside a rock. She sees a grasshopper crouched on the ground, wings folded, then sees it leap up into the small circle of light around it. "Ho," she says and moves on. When she gets to the chair, she sits down and puts the stone on her lap, the small blue book beside it. And she says to the dry and moving air in front of her, and to the clouds and the one beyond the clouds, "I can do something too, you know. I can spell."

In the golden chair above the sky, her angel mother in a pale blue dress moves her fingers over the harp strings, and the melody falls down like rain.

And Nettie gathers the song in her arms and folds it against her heart and holds it there. She rocks back and forth in the chair. And her voice when she sings is full of longing.

> *My bonnie lies over the ocean,*
> *My bonnie lies over the sea,*
> *My bonnie lies over the ocean,*
> *Oh, bring back my bonnie to me.*

IF YOU WERE A FARMER or rancher or one of the town men who drank at the Golden West, and if you were taking a shortcut from Nettie's place, through the pasture and into the town of Stone Creek, you would, just south of the creamery, cross a shallow ditch lined with thorny clumps of thistle, and step onto the narrow road running north and south. Walking north on this road you would pass the creamery, once alive and smelling thick of milk and butter, once noisy and wet, water running from hoses and taps, splashing over the concrete floor, gurgling into drains, down pipes, and into sour sloughs behind the building, once busy with men come to deliver battered cans of cream, come to talk awhile with Eric Sorenson in white smock and black boots, the town's only Dane, who tasted of every can, spitting the white liquid onto the wet floor where it flowed in creamy rivulets over the concrete.

But it hasn't rained for several months. The fields are bare, pastures dry, the creamery closed. And Eric has retired to his large brick house in town.

If you were to continue a short distance past the creamery, you would come to the big hill, its incline long and steady, packed with dirt, sprinkled with dusty gravel. Eli stands at the foot of this hill and looks up. Then down at his feet. His shoes are old, the soles thin; he feels the rigid thrusts of earth through the leather. He waits a moment, takes a deep breath, moves one foot forward, then the other.

Halfway up he stops, gazes at the hill's crest; the hardest part is left, but he can't quit now. He hunches his shoulders and steps forward, watching his feet as he climbs, observing their slow and careful movements on the road, how, at each step, at each small resting place, they make a niche for themselves in the dust.

If you were an insect, a beetle perhaps, or a black ant, and if you'd stopped on this road to rest awhile, to sit at the road's edge to catch your breath, you would see, with your bulging insect eyes, huge whorls of dust approaching, and emerging from dust like ships in fog, the shoes of Eli Nelson, up, down, up, down. And you would feel the movement of his steps on the ground beneath you, the heaviness pressing on the earth around you, the sharp weight of his sorrows piercing the earth's crust and moving slowly in long thin streams toward the world's centre.

Then the shoes disappear and he's gone. He has reached the top, has already passed the elevators and crossed the railway tracks, and is standing at an intersection of roads, one road going east to Regina and west to Alberta, and the other, the one just travelled, leading north and becoming the main street of town.

IF YOU WERE A BIRD, a large bird say, or better yet an
angel, a young angel sent from the north of heaven, and
if you were flying south this day, over the town of Stone
Creek, and if your muscles were strong and the sinews
of your wings sturdy so you could balance above the
town, resisting winds that could blow you past Regina
and into Manitoba, and if you were looking down as
you paused in your flight, you would see below you a
huddle of ragged buildings beside thin and dusty roads.

In the northwest corner, the two-storied school; in
its treeless yard, a metal swing creaking; and nearby,
attached by ropes to a long pole, a torn flag whipped
and flapping. In the southwest corner, the yellow
Russian church, its roof a silver onion glittering in the
sun. In the southeast, Sorensons' house, with leafless
vines climbing the brick walls and hanging, coarse and
tough, over the windows. And up from Sorensons', past
Gilmans' and Munsons', past the tin-roofed warehouse,
the parsonage of St. John's Lutheran Church, where at
this moment Christine Lund in a blue apron is stirring
leftover potatoes in a black skillet. Then next to the parsonage, at the northeast corner of town, the church
itself, silent now and empty, except for many sparrows
swooping in and out of their home in the belfry.

And in the middle of town, Main Street.

At noon the siren whistles from the town hall at the
north end of the street, and Morris Gilman, in the back
room of his drugstore next to the hall, splashes water on
his hands and scrubs them with soap that smells faintly
of iodine. Across the street Tom Wong gazes over the
oilcloth-covered tables in the café – the pink cloth

faded, edges frayed – and waits for his noon customers: Louie from the furniture store and funeral parlour three shops down, who prefers the company of the restaurant to a silent lunch by himself in his room above the store; Steve Boychuck from Imperial Oil; Sam Munson, who prefers nearly any place to that of his own home next to Sorensons', where his wife Hilda at this moment is fluttering the lace curtains of her front window, looking out, waiting, her arthritic fingers nervous on the lace. Maybe he'll want lunch with her today after all, it could be. At the centre of Main Street, three women in hats stand on the steps of the United Church of Canada, considering the sky. Down from the church, past the post office and Cutler's Dry Goods, in the Golden West Hotel, Doctor Long lifts a glass with Sigurd Anderson, forgetting for awhile his wife Nora, who's raking brown and yellow poplar leaves in their yard across from the school.

Then, just as Gilman turns the key to lock the door of the drugstore, and Sam Munson steps into Wong's Café, and Mrs. Long leans her rake against the garage door, and just as the old doctor gurgles over his glass, "You are a *very very* good friend, Sigurd," just then, Jacob Ross, principal, standing in the doorway of the Stone Creek School, makes an extraordinary announcement to the children lined up in stiff rows in the dark and musty hall: "There will be no classes this afternoon," he says. "I will be in Swift Current at the doctor's."

Down the steps they go, past swing and flagpole, feet crunching gravel, across the road, into the alley behind

Longs', around the corner, speeding past Grace Olson's, hollering, no school, not now, not ever, barely hearing the music seep out of the window of Grace's little house sunk in a dip of land among lilac bushes, now bare, and stiff hollyhocks, where Grace is sitting in front of the varnished piano, her thin foot pressing the silver pedal, her thin body leaning forward toward a faded sheet of music, playing and singing tenderly, *Last night I lay asleeping, there came a dream so fair, I stood in old Jerusalem beside the temple there.* And the dry stems of the hollyhocks under the half-opened window click and rustle against the house. *I heard the children singing....* Grace, with no children, no husband, not now or ever.

Peter Lund and Joe Boychuk are the first to reach Main Street – grade sevens get a head start. And when they lurch to a stop in front of the United Church, missing the ladies in hats, they see him down the block gazing at the wooden door of the Golden West Hotel, Eli Nelson, thin and worn and very still, standing as though suspended in the dry Saskatchewan air.

They whip their bodies around and run back to the small troupe that has been following. Peter reaches them first.

"He's back," he says, panting for breath.

"Who?" asks Elizabeth, his sister in grade four.

"Eli. He's back in town."

"Tell us another one," says his brother Andrew, who's eleven.

"It's true," Joe says. "He's standing in front of the Golden West."

"Is he drunk?" asks Mary Sorenson.

"Is he throwing up?" asks Mike Downey.

"Puking in the ditch?" asks Ivan Lippoway.

"Pissing his pants?" asks Gussie.

"No, he's all cleaned up and walking straight."

They ponder this a moment, standing on the road's edge above a ditch of thistles.

"It must be Christmas," Andrew says. And they all race over to Main Street to see this thing for themselves.

And there you are, the young angel, hill-high above the Golden West, and you see Eli too, and you flutter over him, dipping your feet in the prairie wind. He is standing on the sidewalk, examining the letters on the door, Golden West Beer Parlour, and for a long time he doesn't move a muscle. Then you notice him shrug his shoulders, turn sharply, and walk on up the street. And you call down to him in that melodic, bell-toned voice of angels, "Good for you, Eli," and whirl on south, over the tracks, the creamery, the pasture, and over the quarry, where Nettie is rocking beside the pit. And you hover ever so briefly above her and shake your golden sun-tanned face and sigh and coo gently, like a sweet and sorrowing dove, "Poor Nettie," then soar off to the United States, because some things are too hard for angels to endure, too human and incomprehensible.

NETTIE PICKS UP THE BOOK, opens it, and examines the words, bending her head to the left of them and to the right, trying to see them from every angle. She touches a word with her finger, presses on it hard. Maybe if her skin and the bone under her skin can reach beneath the print, dig under the letters, press together the parts of each letter, crumble the parts into tiny pieces, discover the ingredients of each piece, then, maybe, she will be able to tell exactly what the words are saying, what each word means.

IN THE KITCHEN OF ST. JOHN'S PARSONAGE, Christine Lund glances at the clock beside the stove. 12:20. Jacob lets his pupils out at twelve sharp and the Lunds' back door usually bangs open at ten after. Peter is first, Andrew next, and then Elizabeth, who dawdles. Why are they late? The potatoes in the skillet are crisp and golden brown, the meatballs smell rich of onions and meaty gravy, and string beans she canned in September are steaming in the pan. The table is set, bread and butter, a jug of milk. Jonathan will be hungry, will be wondering why she hasn't called him. She looks out the square window over the sink, sees only sparrows flitting among the dry branches of the caraganas.

Upstairs in his attic study, Jonathan sorts through sermon notes he's written on half sheets of paper ("He knows our frame, he remembers that we are dust") and arranges them in a pile, sets the pile in the middle of the desk, and leans back in his swivel chair. The attic door is open; he smells the dinner below. He gazes out the small triangle of glass above his desk, the room's only window, sees a sparrow dart past, hears the wind seep into the cracks that edge the glass. He gets up and stretches. Usually she calls, but maybe he'll go down regardless. Why not?

Except for the three Lunds and Ivan Lippoway, all the children have gone home to eat, Mary to the vine-covered house on the corner, Mike to the big house north of town, Joe to the café to eat with his dad, Gussie to the tiny shack below the railroad tracks. Peter, Andrew, and Ivan follow Eli from a distance; Elizabeth trails behind them.

Eli has reached the town hall, turned right and crossed the street to the north corner of Wong's Café. Here he stops for a moment as if considering his next step, then walks past the café, past the vacant lot behind it, toward St. John's church. He cuts across the church-yard and shuffles toward the Lund house. The children run to catch up to him, but when they reach the vacant lot, they stop, wait for their next move. Beside the cara-gana hedge, Eli pauses briefly, then walks the short dis-tance to the back door.

Christine hears the scraping sounds on the step, then the knock. She opens the door and sees him standing there, bent forward, his sandy hair blown in tufts from the wind, his jacket worn, shoes dusty. His cheeks have deep wrinkles in them, his skin is hard. He looks older than fifty.

"Eli," she says.

"Eli," she says again. "It's you. I wasn't expecting you." She stands by the table and looks at him. Thin, gaunt. She's glad she has never seen him drunk. She's glad when Jonathan opens the attic door and steps into the kitchen. He stops abruptly.

"Well, Eli," Jonathan says. "You've come. October, right?"

Eli looks down at the floor.

"So let's go upstairs and have this chat that's waiting for us," Jonathan says.

"No," Eli says. "The cellar's fine. It's always been the cellar."

"Suit yourself," Jonathan says.

Christine sees Eli's skinny neck above his collar, his thin wrists stretching out from the sleeves of his brown jacket.

"Why don't we eat first," she says. "Why don't we all sit down and have a bite."

"No no," Eli says. "None for me. I want to get this thing settled."

When the two men have disappeared down the cellar stairs and Christine has closed the door after them, she goes back to the window and looks out. She sees the children in front of the caraganas. They'll come in when they're hungry, she thinks, and covers the food on the stove and goes into the living room. She sits down in the soft chair beside the piano. Sits under a bouquet of roses in pink and red needlepoint, flowers stitched by her mother and framed in a soft wood frame.

OUTSIDE, Peter scrambles from the hedge to the small basement window at the side of the house. "They'll go to the cellar," he says. "That's where they go." He kneels on the ground and peers into the window. The glass is dirty, splattered with bird droppings; he can see nothing. Then a light comes on, and he can see figures moving, dim and indistinct. "I told you," he says.

Andrew and Ivan creep up behind him, peer over his

shoulder. Elizabeth remains by the caraganas.

"I know someone who wouldn't quite approve of what you're doing," she says.

"Shut up," Peter says, "I can't hear."

Ivan presses closer to the glass.

"How can you see with all this bird shit?" he says.

JONATHAN sits down on a wooden bench in front of the furnace, Eli on a backless chair facing him. The cellar is dim. One bare bulb hangs from the ceiling. The pale light falls on Eli's head, on Jonathan, on the cement floor, chipped and dusty at their feet.

"So," Jonathan says, "who'll begin?"

"You," Eli says. "The pelicans, remember?"

"Again?"

"You can't beat it," Eli says. He rests his elbows on his knees, his chin cupped in his hands.

ELIZABETH steps away from the caraganas.

"I'd stay a little farther from the window if I were you. I wouldn't bump that glass. Someone we all know would not like this."

"Why are they in the cellar anyway?" Ivan asks.

"They're praying," Andrew says.

"Eli's repenting," Peter says.

"What's repenting?" Ivan says.

"You don't even know what repenting is?" Peter says.

"How should I know?"

"It's what you do if you're a sinner," Peter says.

"Do what?" Ivan asks.

"Put your head between your knees and say how awful you are, and how you wish you were never born, and you are a real miserable sinner," Peter says.

"Do you repent?" Ivan asks.

"Me? I don't drink whisky."

Ivan strains at the glass to try to see repentance.

"Do you have to do it in a cellar?" he asks.

JONATHAN'S voice is soft in the dim room.

"My days are consumed like smoke. My bones are burned as an hearth..."

"Ohh," Eli says, as if there were a small pain under his rib.

Jonathan's voice rises. "My heart is smitten and withered like grass. I forget to eat my bread..."

"Yes, yes..." Eli sighs.

"...my bones cleave to my skin..."

"True..." Eli says.

"I am like a pelican of the wilderness. I watch. A sparrow alone upon the housetop." Jonathan sounds passionate, and Eli hears the passion.

"Pelican in the wilderness," Eli repeats, "sparrow on a housetop, magpie on a rock, lark on a dry and thorny branch."

IN THE LIVING ROOM, Christine rests her head on the back of the chair. Why did Eli do that anyway, leave town just after his huge success, everyone raving about him, doors opening up to welcome him, and all that respect? And why would he leave his room in Peterson's basement, not fancy but safe and warm, to trudge out there, that December day after the concert, when the drifts were high, and all that blowing snow? And then stay there? Live there?

It was Nettie, of course. She had a strange pull with her spelling and rocking and men coming and going, but now only Eli of course. Everyone's talked about it. They've heard the story from delivery men who bring her water, from Peterson who's repaired her heater. And they wonder how the two of them manage out there. What do they actually do all day? Does she cook for him? Clean and sew for him? Does he read to her? And sing? He is a musician, after all.

And at night when the sky is black above the quarry, does she lie beside him in their dark bed and spell to him, crooning the alphabet into his ear, the letters of love soft against his earlobe, as the wind whistles in the chimney and rattles the window?

IN FRONT OF THE COLD FURNACE, Eli stretches his thin neck forward and looks into Jonathan's face.

"You haven't finished," he says.

"You never want to hear the rest," says Jonathan.

"I want to."

"All right then. Listen." Jonathan lowers his head, clasps his hands together. "But thou oh Lord shalt arise and have mercy upon Zion, for thy servants take pleasure in her stones and favour the dust thereof." He peers up at Eli. "There it is. That's the rest of it."

Eli says, "But you missed the most important line." He raises his finger toward Jonathan and directs the words up and down, agitating the tiny particles of dust floating in the grey air between them. "'Thou hast lifted me up and cast me down.' Up. Down. There. That's it in a nutshell."

IVAN GETS UP and heads for the gate. "I'm leaving," he says. "What's so great about repentance?"

Peter, Andrew, and Elizabeth go in for dinner.

IN THE DIM LIGHT under the bare bulb, Jonathan prepares Eli for bad news.

"It's thanks to you, Eli, that we've had wonderful concerts for the last five years. You get the very best out of the singers. No one can top you. And no one can top the *Messiah*. Imagine, Handel in Stone Creek. But this year, well, I think you've tried people's tolerance a bit much; we're considering other possibilities."

"But I threw out the last bottle," Eli says. "I quit."

"It's not the liquor I'm referring to. We've handled that before."

"What then?" Eli says.

"Do you even need to ask?"

Eli is silent for a moment. Then he says, "Nettie?"

"Men have been coming and going out there for years."

"I'm not coming and going. I live there."

"And how do you think that looks?"

Eli leans forward, looks up into Jonathan's face. "Looks? How it looks?"

Jonathan stumbles, answering. "Well, we both know that Nettie is not like other women," he says. "Should you be taking advantage?"

"Advantage? I cook for her, and clean, and shop for groceries. And she sings to me. And spells. We get on fine. No one's taking advantage. And no men are coming and going."

Jonathan shakes his head. "I'm sorry," he says.

CHRISTINE sits at the table with the three children. She asks about Jacob Ross: Why is he going to Swift Current? Is Beverley sick again? How serious is it? How long will he be gone?

The children inform her that Beverley is always sick, hardly ever comes to school, and when she does she stays in for recess, and she smells bad. But not as bad as Annie Levinsky. Annie is in the same grade as Elizabeth, but Christine has never met her. Elizabeth has never brought her home to play after school.

"Annie smells real bad," Elizabeth says.

"She smells like something died inside her," Andrew says.

"Like when the cat died under the steps," says Peter.

"Annie Levinsky stinks," Andrew says.

"Enough," their mother says.

ELI FEELS A TIGHT KNOT in the middle of his spine, a pain that spreads up his back, pulls at his skin. He was not expecting this, not after he prayed, not after he confessed and repented. Jonathan Lund has been his ally for years. He stares at the furnace door, digs his heel into the crumbling cement.

"No *Messiah?* No Handel?" His voice is high and thin. "Or have you got someone else to direct it?"

And he thinks. It's Hilda Munson. Hilda, who moves her arms when she directs, as if she's scraping beans out of a tin can.

Jonathan, wishing he were someplace else, wishing Eli were someplace else, explains that it probably will be Hilda who'll direct the Christmas concert, but it won't be the *Messiah*. It will not be Handel. And surely there's nothing wrong with a break in tradition for a change.

Eli groans. "Hilda Munson. It's come to that." The two men are silent. They do not look at each other.

How can Eli put into words how he feels? How can he make Jonathan understand? How can he describe how his fingers even now are alive and moving, flicking this way and that, directing the notes inside his head; how his ear is alert, skin and cartilage taut, how those three small bones, shaped so delicately, hover there in that narrow channel, waiting; and his feet, planted here on the dusty floor, how they're shaped in just the right way to balance his body leaning toward the sound, to hold him steady while the music soaks into his bones and nerves and muscles and alerts them that he, Eli Nelson, is alive and on this planet, affecting the air around him, changing the nature of space itself, filling it with blessing and honour for a few moments here in this dry and desolate place?

He shakes his head. "Hilda Munson," he sighs.

IN THE MUNSON KITCHEN, Hilda has washed up the lunch dishes and put them away in the cupboard: cup, plate, knife, fork. She removes her apron, hangs it on a hook by the sink, and goes into the bedroom. She slips off her dress, lays it on the chair by the bureau, takes off her shoes and places them neatly beside the bed. She lies down on top of the white chenille bedspread. At the foot of the bed is a patchwork quilt, folded in half and pulled in at the centre, making it look like the wings of a giant butterfly. She pulls the quilt up to her neck, the blue and pink and lavender wings unfolding over her shoulders.

Sam did not come home for lunch. He usually doesn't. And when he does, he's distant, dark, critical, snaps at her for the least little thing. What went wrong?

Thank God she at least has her music. Not Bach or Handel, of course, but there are more pebbles on the beach than those two. And it looks as if St. John's has come to their senses this year and she'll get the choir back. Sing something pretty for a change. Imagine, Eli out there with Nettie Johnson in that old trailer. How can they live like that, him drinking and her half out of her wits? And how do they get along with each other? For a moment she sees them lying together on their bed. Nettie's head rests on the crook of Eli's arm, her toe rubs his ankle. Hilda turns onto her side. Sam used to like crawling under the quilt with her, she remembers, even in the middle of the day.

JONATHAN is still in the cellar with Eli, the children have eaten, and Christine lies down on the sofa in the living room and covers herself with the yellow afghan crocheted by her mother. She strokes the soft woolen stitches and thinks of her mother in Wisconsin, of the big house on Segoe Road, of the green yard with huge umbrella trees, of gentle air. It's not that she hates Saskatchewan. But really, who loves it? Land bare and rocky, the air dry, sharp, and unfriendly. She sees the big lake in Madison and all the green, wherever you look, so much green. She's glad her mother writes to her and sends her things: needlepoint pictures, pillow tops, candles, recently a book on the life of Eleanor Roosevelt.

How do other wives in Stone Creek have it? It would be nice if the women in town could get together more. Talk about things. Not just church things. How is it for Ingrid Sorenson, for instance, living with Eric? What do they talk about? People say he's a Communist. But is he good to Ingrid? Gentle and loving in their bed? It's hard to imagine sleeping next to a Communist. But a lot of women must be doing it. Not in Saskatchewan, of course, but in the world.

IN THE TRAILER, Nettie Johnson finds a slice of bread in the cupboard, sprinkles it with sugar, and takes it into the small bedroom. She sits on the edge of the bed, holding the slice in her two hands, horizontally so the sugar won't spill on the blanket. She eats the bread slowly, crumbling the soft pieces between her teeth, crunching down on the gritty sugar. Then she takes her shoes off and crawls under the blanket. She's tired. Looking at words, trying to see them from all angles like that, is a very tiring thing to do.

She reaches her hand to the pillow that Eli lay on just this morning, strokes the cloth with her fingers, smells the faint sour sweetness of his skin and the rum he likes to drink. It would be nice if he did come back. But if he's at the Golden West, forget it. And if he goes to visit Grace Olson, forget it. And if he's at St. John's Church, forget it. Forget it, forget it, forget it. So long, Eli Nelson.

ELI SUCKS HIS BREATH IN. Well, Reverend, he thinks, we'll see about this, won't we. It isn't over yet. He stands up and looks down at Jonathan, still sitting on the bench. "Do you remember what it was like?" he says. "All those farmers belting out the Hallelujah Chorus? Even Sigurd Anderson. He has his problem too, you know, with the booze. But when it's time for *Messiah,* Sigurd doesn't touch the stuff."

"True," Jonathan says.

"Same with Doc Long. Puts his bottle on the back shelf when the *Messiah* comes." Eli moves toward the stairs, pauses. "Remember his solo? How he'd roar out the words?" Eli sings the line in a deep, clear voice. *Darkness shall cover the earth....* He glances slyly at Jonathan. "Doc's United Church, isn't he?"

Jonathan sighs.

"And you. You came so close last year," Eli says. "Just so close."

"What do you mean close?" Jonathan asks.

"The refiner's fire, remember? The third refiner's fire?"

"What about it?"

"It should go *a refi-i-i-i-i-i-i-i-i-i-i-i-i-i-i-i-i-i-i-i-i-iner's fire.*"

"That's how I sang it."

"No. You left out the last *i.*"

"What do you mean?" He sings the line. *A refi-i-i-i-i-i-i-i-i-i-i-i-i-i-i-i-i-i-i-i-i-i-i-i-i-iner's fire.* "There. That's how I did it."

"Wrong. It's *Refi-i-i-i-i-i-i-i-i-i-i-i-i-i-i-i-i-i-i-i-i-i-i-i-iner's fire.* Don't forget that last *i* in there."

Jonathan tries again. *Re-fi-i-i-i-i-i-i-i-i-i-i-i-i-i-i-i-i-i-i-i-i-i-i-i-iner's fire.*

"Well, that's better," Eli says. "Maybe this year you'd finally get it."

He walks halfway up the stairs, then stops and turns around. "Oh, well, it doesn't matter now since your mind's made up anyway. Besides, there are too many problems. Parking for sure. Shovelling all that snow from the vacant lot for extra space. Remember that? All those cars?"

"Eli. I'll bring it up to the music committee. They'll make the final decision. Soon."

OUTSIDE, Peter is bored. He's thirteen years old and his father's a preacher. The big event of each week is church, where he has to sit on a hard pew that smells like lemons and think of ways to make the time pass: counting flies that buzz on the window sills, counting people, how many men, how many women, counting letters of long words in the hymnal (Septuagesima: 12). And now it's

October. The air is dry, the sky huge, the land so flat and empty you can see almost to North Dakota. But Peter doesn't want to see North Dakota. What he likes to see are girls, their arms and necks, their ankles, their smooth round breasts; and to feel the pressure in his groin, the hard lump down there.

The three children are sitting on the front step. They've done the dishes, Andrew washing, Peter drying with a long dishtowel, using the towel as a whip, snapping it against his sister's legs. "Stop it, Peter, you're not the king of the castle." Eli has already left and is making his way down Main Street, heading back to the quarry.

"There's not a whole lot to do in this dump town," Peter says.

"Well, think of something," Andrew says.

They could go to the nuisance grounds and look for stuff – bottles, magazines, tin cans. (Gussie Skogland found a ten-dollar bill in a soup can once.) Or they could go to Grace Olson's and hide behind her hedge and pretend they're cats. Howl. Run when she comes out. Or spy on Eric Sorenson. He and old man Lippoway are Communists.

"Or we could head out to the quarry," Peter says.

"I've never been to the quarry," Elizabeth says.

"Girls can't go there," Peter says.

"Why not?"

"Bad stuff happens out there."

"Like?"

"Stuff you don't know about yet."

"Such as?"

"She casts spells," Andrew says.

"Oh, sure," Elizabeth says.

"She's a witch," her brother says. "She eats people."

Andrew and Peter run out the front gate. Elizabeth scrambles after them.

"I'm coming," she yells.

"No, you're not," Peter says.

"Then I'll tell."

"Tell what?"

"Everything you ever said or did that I know about."

THE THREE CHILDREN race down Main Street, down the creamery hill, and across the pasture. At the foot of the quarry hill they stop. "We'll have to go around," Peter whispers. They skid across the pebbles in the creek bed and scramble to the far side of the hill. Then they begin to climb, careful to avoid thistles and loose rocks. At the top, they sneak around the quarry to the trailer. Creep behind the trailer and around to the front corner of it. See Nettie ahead of them. She's in the chair, facing the pit. They can see only the back of her head. For some reason, Eli is not there.

Nettie closes her eyes and rests her hand on the blue speller lying on her lap. She hears a rustle from the edge of the quarry and stops rocking, her back stiff. She opens her eyes and leans against the sound, a wary bird, watching.

"Get out of there you gopher. Scat, little coyote. Beat it, rabbit. I ain't in the mood for company." The rustling continues. "Hey, Mr. Badger, what are you up to?"

Then she hears a thin whistle, a long wire of sound, pierce the air.

"Oh, ho, so it's you. You did come back."

The whistling lifts, gets louder, circles the air in rings of melody.

"What way did you come? I didn't hear your footsteps in the creek bed." The whistling stops. "I didn't hear you singing your old tune by the willow tree." She peers toward the big rock just this side of quarry. "Enough tricks. I know you're out there. O-u-t." She resumes her rocking. The chair's rungs crunch the gravel.

"I was always very good at spelling," she says.

Eli rises from behind the rock. "You're number one," he says. He holds a paper bag in his hands and lifts it high above his head.

Nettie strains her neck to see, but she doesn't move from the chair.

"I have something for you," Eli says.

"I'm getting a little tired of pickled herring," she says.

"It's not pickled herring."

"What then?"

He sets the bag on the ground.

"Come and see," he says, reaching out his arms to her. "Ho, everyone who thirsts, come to the waters. Come. Buy wine and milk, without money and without price."

"You come." She sits back in the chair.

Eli waves his arms in the air. His voice when he sings is bold and lusty.

> *O, come to the church in the wildwood,*
> *O, come to the church in the vale.*

No spot is so dear to my childhood
As the little brown church in the dale.

Nettie scowls.

O, come, come, come, come...

"I'm not coming!" she shouts.

And suddenly Eli is on his hands and knees, crawling among the rocks and stones and dry strands of quack grass, squatting and lifting his face to the sky and crying out, "Ooowooooo," his coyote voice full of longing. And Nettie slides from her chair onto the ground. She crawls on stones toward the quarry. And she wails the same coyote's cry, "Ooowooooo."

Then a new sound comes to her, a snake hissing.

"S-s-s-s-s-s-s-s-s-s," it says, long and sleek.

"S-s-s-s-s-s-s-s-s-s," she answers.

And the sound changes, and she hears the warbling of a meadowlark, a trill so sweet she has to laugh. And out from the rock Eli emerges. He crawls toward her, and when she sees him crawling, she flattens her body on the ground and slithers out to meet him. They come together, tangled in each other, rocking and laughing on the stones.

The children are up and on their feet, peering forward.

"So you won't tell me what you brought, won't open the bag, won't show me what's in it. Then there's only one thing I can do. I will eat you. I will bite your tongue off. I'll chew your ears. I'll gobble up your fingers."

Eli laughs louder. "Oh, I'd like that."

Elizabeth grabs Andrew by the arm. "Let's go home now," she whispers.

"No," Andrew says.

"Shut up," Peter hisses.

"I'll tell. I really will." She runs around the back of the trailer and down the hill. Halfway across the pasture, her brothers catch up to her.

Eli, on hands and knees, opens the brown bag and lifts out its contents with exaggerated care: seven tins of soup. As he puts each can on the ground he intones its name: "Heinz vegetable, Heinz cream of mushroom, Heinz tomato, Heinz celery, another Heinz tomato because it's your favourite."

"Oh you," Nettie sighs.

"Heinz cream of chicken," he continues. Then he holds the last can high in the air and swirls it in circles above their heads.

"And finally...another tomato!"

Nettie gazes at the row of cans on the ground. "One for every day of the week! You are something wonderful."

THE SUN IS LOW in the sky. Dry grass in the warehouse yard rustles softly, brown stems swaying this way and that.

Peter is sitting on the hard ground, his back resting against the warehouse wall, his face turned upward, catching as much of a fading sun as he can. Andrew and Elizabeth sit under a leafless maple. They've run most of the way from the quarry and they're tired. Rusty wheels lean against the grey fence.

"Let's play Eli and Nettie," Peter says. He jerks his head toward Elizabeth. "I'll be Eli, you be Nettie."

"And who will I be?" Andrew says. "A rock?"

"No. A wolf howling at the moon."

Peter slides down onto his stomach. "I'll slither like a snake and hiss at you. Then you hiss back and we'll crawl around and then I'll bump into you."

"Then what?" Elizabeth asks.

"Then you climb on top of me like Nettie did, and Andrew will howl like a wolf and we'll roll on the grass."

Andrew crouches beside a rock, raises his head to the sky. "Wooooo woooo," he wails.

Peter slides his lanky body toward Elizabeth. Makes serpentine curves of his movements.

"S-s-s-s-s-s-s-s-s," he hisses.

Elizabeth sits up. "That's not what they did."

"Well, what then?"

"They slid around more and went up and down and they hissed louder and they bumped and spit and she rolled right on top of him."

She crawls to Peter, hissing and snarling, and leaps on his back, straddles him with her legs, her face close to his neck, her tongue darting in and out of her mouth. She bites his ear and Peter yelps.

"Pretend, Elizabeth. I said pretend,"

"It's more fun if you really do it," Elizabeth says.

Peter knocks her off.

Andrew wails at the fading sun.

HILDA MUNSON is standing on the sidewalk in front of the warehouse, staring up at the tin door and wondering which way to turn. Right to the preacher's house? Left to her own house? Forward into the warehouse yard? She'll have to tell somebody about this. But who? The preacher? His wife? The committee? Who will she tell? Who will she tell first?

She did not mean to hear what she heard, to see what she saw. She'd meant only to walk north from her house to the Lund house, passing the warehouse on her way, not intending to stop at all. Not intending to creep around the side of the building, staying as close to the wall as possible, or to come upon this scene.

At home, she'd changed from her house dress to her best dress, the blue polka dot with the white collar, had combed her hair with the pale green comb, examined her face in the pale green mirror that matched, gifts from Sam years ago when he was young and loved her shyly. She'd put on a white sweater, then gathered up the sheets of music from the piano and walked out the front door. She was on the sidewalk heading toward the parsonage when she heard strange sounds, animal noises, coming from behind the warehouse, and then the voices of children. She stopped, listened, walked into the warehouse yard, stopped again, yes, children's voices, and hissing sounds. She crept around to the backyard. There she saw a tangle in the weeds, a struggling, and a boy, angry, jumping up from the ground. Her skin tingled, her heart beat faster. What was this? She sensed something dark and moist and pungent, something from deep in the earth, smelling of evil. Then they saw her, and they stood, stiff and straight in front of her.

Peter said, "Oh, Mrs. Munson," and brushed dry leaves from his shirt and pants.

Hilda said nothing, just stared at the boy.

"There's no school," said Andrew. "Mr. Ross went to Swift Current."

"We were playing Eli and Nettie," Elizabeth said.

"What?" Hilda said.

"What they did at the gravel pit."

"You were at the gravel pit?" Hilda's shoulders felt weak, her skin tingled, her heart beat faster. "What did you see?"

"Nothing," Peter growled.

"They rolled in the dirt," Elizabeth said.

"Mr. Ross has gone to Swift Current," Andrew said.

Hilda grunted. "Go home right now and wash your hands." She turned and walked out of the yard, her music and her blue purse pressed tightly under her arm.

Now, in front of the warehouse, she turns abruptly toward the preacher's house. He must know about this, she thinks. But then she turns in the opposite direction. No. She'll tell the others first.

IN THE GOLDEN WEST HOTEL, Doctor Long raises his head from the small table in front of him and stretches his white loose-skinned neck over his half-empty glass toward Sigurd Anderson, sitting across from him. He squints into Sigurd's face.

"So, my good friend, is this all there is? This thin liquid?" He taps the rim of his glass with his finger. "This pale thin liquid, here in the Golden West?"

"Golden liquid," Sigurd murmurs.

"Golden yes, that's true. And you and I, two lost birds in a golden sky."

"It's not so bad," Sigurd says.

The doctor lays his head on the table, his cheek resting beside the glass.

"It is beautiful," he says.

ELI AND NETTIE are sitting in the kitchen, eating tomato soup from white bowls decorated with blue flowers, dishes donated to Nettie years ago by the Sunshine Circle at Saint John's. Eli is animated, flushed, excited about the *Messiah*. He will direct it. They can't keep him from doing that.

"Handel was German," Eli says. "Like Bach. And Beethoven."

"German!" Nettie snorts. German means the enemy. It means the time when the war took all the good men away. And the only men who came to her were ragamuffins, rejects, and sick men, like Eli.

"What excitement," Eli exclaims. "What a flurry of writing. Imagine. The whole *Messiah* written in twenty-four days. Pages and pages of manuscripts. Thousands and thousands of notes to draw. And he drew them all, every dot, every little stick."

Nettie sighs. "Those poor tired fingers."

"Imagine. Opening night. Crowds of people. Men in black suits, women in furs. Standing ovations and rave reviews. And now it's here. From London, England, to

Stone Creek, Saskatchewan. Some distance, eh? And it hasn't been easy."

Nettie is quiet, scowling into her empty bowl. She looks up at him.

"Don't do that," she says. She draws a small triangle in the air with her finger, conducting. "Stay here with me. I'll be good to you." She cocks her head and smiles up at him. "Do you know what I'll do for you? I'll pick up your socks. That's number one. Number two, I'll pass you the salt. Three. I'll scratch your back. Four. I'll cover you with a blanket when you're cold."

She leaves her chair and goes to him. She stands behind him and puts her arms around his neck. He lays his spoon on the table, reaches back, and pulls her onto his lap.

"My sweet lady," he says. She lays her head on his shoulder.

"Spell something," he says.

"What do you want to hear?"

"Anything. Your favourite word."

"S-t-o-n-e," she murmurs into his shoulder.

"Fine," he says.

"Do you want to hear rock?"

"That would be good," he says.

"R-o-c-k!"

"Wonderful. Now tree."

"T-r-e-e!"

"Grand," he says.

"G-r-a-n-d," she says.

"Lovely," he says. "You fill the air with your spelling. And it's very nice."

"Oh it's not that great."

He strokes her neck, nuzzles into her ear.

"Try bird."

"I never could spell that one," she says.

"Yes you can. Bird."

She scowls.

"Go ahead, take a chance."

"I'm too old for that now."

"Bird!" he shouts.

"Oh be quiet," she says.

THEY MEET in St. John's basement, cold and smelling of cement, four members of the music committee: Hilda Munson, Grace Olson, Olga Jacobson, and Leif Stenson. They sit at a wooden table in the centre of the room, surrounded by grey walls decorated with children's crayon drawings: green trees, pink and yellow butterflies, red birds flying under many-coloured rainbows.

When Jonathan arrives, he stalls for a moment in the narrow hallway in front of the closed door and listens to the muffled sounds from within. Then he pushes the door open and enters the room. The talking stops.

He walks to the table, looks first at Hilda, who's staring at the butterflies on the wall opposite her. Then he looks around at the others. Leif is gazing down at some papers in front of him on the table, Olga is rubbing her chin with her thumb, playing with a tuft of coarse hair growing there. Grace Olson sits with her eyes closed.

"So here we are," Jonathan booms, too loudly. "Who

would like to begin?"

Hilda looks at Leif. He's the only man on the committee, the preacher will listen to him. Olga and Grace would never speak up, especially Grace, scared of her own shadow. Why she gets the best solo every year with that tinny voice of hers no one knows.

"Well, then," Jonathan says, "maybe I could share some of my own thoughts."

Hilda leans forward in her chair. "I think Leif might have something to say."

But Leif says, "Let the preacher begin. I'll add my two cents' worth later."

Hilda sits back in her chair. Jonathan speaks.

"All of us are aware of the problem we've had with the *Messiah*. With Eli in particular. We've known of his weaknesses when it comes to drink. Now we know of his other weakness." He pauses, clears his throat, looks at the wall across from him. "I'm referring, of course, to his...new life out at the quarry."

Hilda glowers at Leif, Leif looks at Grace, Grace stares at the door, Olga examines her cheekbone with one finger.

"But I think we need to consider something else here," Jonathan continues. "We've been at this thing for five years now. We've struggled through all those notes, and now we're close to getting the whole thing together for the first time, and doing a good job of it. Maybe it's not such a good idea to quit right now."

He coughs, feels a tickling sensation in his neck.

"Let's think about Eli as well," he says, his voice higher now and tighter. "None of us approves of the situation out at the quarry, but let's try, just for now, to look at it from another angle. If Eli does continue directing the *Messiah*, the message of the music itself could work a change in his life, a repentance if you will. And who among us would want to deny him that?"

Again, Hilda waits for Leif to speak, but he doesn't. No one does. They're sheep, Hilda thinks. All of them. So it's up to her then. She's no sheep.

"Pastor. Of course we believe that the *Messiah* is good. I don't think any of us have a problem with that. Or with repentance either, for that matter. But what we're concerned with here is something else. We're thinking about the community, about..." She stutters, stumbles for words. Finally Leif comes to the rescue.

"What I think Hilda is trying to say is we're worried about the influence Eli has on young people. On children...."

"Yes," Hilda continues. And she tells Jonathan how the children of the town sneak out to the quarry to watch the goings-on out there, even those from good families, and then try to copy what they see. She doesn't mention the Lund children by name, but Jonathan suspects she's including them. Later, when he questions the children at the supper table, he knows for sure. And he knows what he must do.

JONATHAN drives his maroon-coloured Plymouth down the creamery road and past Jacobson's pasture. When he reaches the quarry hill, he parks, gets out, and slams the door shut. He stumbles across the ditch to the foot of the hill. Anger is surging up inside him: anger at Hilda, at Peter, at Eli, and especially at Christine. "Peter needs more guidance," his wife said, "but you're never here to give it, he runs wild. Imagine, taking Elizabeth out to the quarry to spy." And Christine didn't stop there. "And what about Eli? First he's on as music director, then he's off, then he's on again, then off. I wish you'd stop being so wishy-washy. You're always so wishy-washy."

Those were her words. *Wishy-washy.* So he changed his mind about Eli. What was wrong with that? Was it better to be rigid? That's what he should have said to her. Better to be wishy-washy than so rigid.

When he started out on this journey, the sun was bright, the air still. Now a grey-white cloud hovers above him and the wind is sharper. He pulls his sweater up against his neck and steps forward. His feet unsettle small pebbles that tumble down the slope to be stopped finally by rocks and cactus.

Well, Christine couldn't complain about his being wishy-washy now. He'd been firm with the children. From now on you'll stay home, he told them. Nothing to do, you say? Then clean the garage, rake the yard. When you're done, you can count the sparrows.

At the top of the hill he stops, looks over at the trailer. And suddenly he feels a weight in his stomach, a pulling in his chest. How will he tell Eli this news? True, he didn't promise him the *Messiah;* nevertheless, he's well aware of Eli's commitment and his longing. His own longing as well, if the truth be told. Standing there quietly, he hears the singing, feels the excitement. Sees his church packed, a community come together.

He edges his way around the quarry, past the empty chair, and up the short path to the trailer. He stands on the step and knocks.

Inside, Nettie hears the knock and jerks up from the chair. Her chin juts out in the direction of the door.

"They've come," she says.

"Who?" Eli says.

"The men. They've come to get you."

Eli stands up. "Don't be silly. Nobody's coming to get me."

"Don't," she says, unclenching her hand and reaching out to him.

But Eli has already gone to the door and opened it. He sees Jonathan and welcomes him.

"Come in," he says. "Have a chair. The hill's a steep climb."

"It is that," Jonathan says, and sits down at the table.

Eli turns to Nettie. "Why don't you get something for the preacher? Is the coffee still hot?"

"That's the new preacher?" Nettie asks, suspicious.

"He'd like some coffee," Eli explains.

"None for me," Jonathan says. "I wouldn't mind some water though."

Nettie doesn't move.

"The old Swede knew my name," she says.

"Never mind," Eli says, and goes to the cupboard for a clean cup.

Nettie slides around the table and heads for the barrel standing near the door, the water hauled in once a week by the men who drive the town truck.

"I guess I know how to get someone a glass of water," she says. She lifts the tin ladle from its hook on the wall and dips it into the barrel.

Eli brings the cup to her and she fills it. Then he carries the glass to Jonathan.

After Jonathan has drunk the entire glassful, he lays the cup down and wipes his lips with the back of his hand. Eli watches him, waiting.

"Well," Jonathan says. "I'm afraid..." He clears his throat, three small grunts, and tries again. "I'm afraid..."

"I see," Eli says.

NETTIE watches the two men step outside. Then she sits down at the table and waits for Eli's return. Her lips are pursed shut. Her fingers drum the tabletop.

When he doesn't come back she goes outside to look for him. But he is nowhere to be seen. She walks the short path to the quarry and gazes across it to the pasture beyond. He's not there. She calls out, her voice wheeling into the sky. Silence. She runs around the quarry to the rim of the hill, stops, and calls again. Her voice echoes across the prairie.

"Eli."

"Eli."

"Eli."

"Eli."

"Eli."

"Eli Eli Eli Eli..."

There is no sign of him.

He's not far away, however. Below the hill, on the

east side, he is kneeling on the ground, digging with both hands into a pile of rocks. There is an urgency about him.

He lifts a rock from the pile and heaves it aside, then another, and another. He stops to breathe, to rest his heart, to think. Above him, the clouds have dissipated and the sky is clear blue, as if it were spring, as if the robins were returning, as if this were a new day, a fresh beginning. He digs again. It can't be that deep in the pile. Where has he hidden it? He did hide it, didn't he? He threw out four or five empties and a couple of nearly empties, but the full one, the one unopened, he wouldn't have thrown that one out. He'd wrapped it in a scrap of old blanket and hidden it. But where? Wasn't it here, among these stones?

He pulls at the rocks, dislodging one, then another, digging deeper into the pile. And then he sees the fragment of grey blanket snuggled in a small opening in the rocks, a dark and private cave among the stones. He pushes his hand into the opening, touches the blanket, feels the bottle underneath, curls his fingers around it, and tugs at it gently. "Hey, don't break on me," he says. And he slides the bottle and the blanket out of their hiding place and heads back to the trailer.

When Nettie sees him appear on the crest of the hill, when she sees first his head, then his chest and arms, then his legs emerge from the earth, she yells out.

"So the prairie chicken's come home to roost. It's about time."

She watches him approach, sees the lump of grey under his arm.

"What have you got there?" she asks.

Eli slowly unwraps the bottle.

"I thought so," Nettie says, and goes to the edge of the pit.

Eli sits down in the rocker. He lays the bottle on his lap, the blanket on top of it, and caresses the grey mound with his fingers.

Nettie lies on her stomach at the edge of the quarry and gazes down on the rocks and stones twenty feet below.

"Watch out," Eli says, "you could have a tumble."

"I'm looking for my old pals," Nettie says. She hollers into the pit, "Hey, you bugs, come on out and play."

"Forget your pals," Eli says. "Come here. Bring me some comfort."

She sits up and faces Eli.

"So you didn't get your da da da da." She sings, directs herself with one finger, small triangles in the air. "They're mean over there. It's a mean place."

And as if it were yesterday, Nettie sees them standing on the church steps. Alice, Grace, and someone in a skirt with blue flowers. They huddle close to each other, giggling, whispering. Leaving her out. She sees the wooden church door behind them, thick and heavy, with huge iron handles, and beside the steps the single caragana bush. And then Alice says, "That's a very fine skirt you're wearing, Nettie. I wonder where your mother found a skirt like that. I guess not in Stone Creek." And Grace says, "She must have got it in Regina. At Eatons. Did it come from Eatons?" And the other girl says, "Maybe she sent to New York for it. It looks to me like it came from New York." And Nettie sees herself in the grey skirt that's too big for her and has to be folded at the waist and pinned so it won't fall down. "Or did you go to Paris, France?" Alice says.

"Come here," Eli says. "Tell me about that Swede."

Nettie shakes her head.

"Tell me," he says.

"It's not a made-up story, you know."

"I know. Tell me anyway."

She sits cross-legged, rests her elbows on her knees, her face in her hands. The air is still. The October sunlight seeps through the cold and warms the ground around her and the dry gravel and the dry and rusty grasses that grow in thin clumps here and there.

She begins slowly. "Long long ago a little girl had a beautiful mother, and the mother was alive and lived in a trailer beside a big hole in the ground."

"Little girl?" Eli asks.

"That would be me," Nettie says.

"And this beautiful mother wanted her girl to be strong and good when she grew up, so every Saturday she sent her to church to learn from the brown book. Each page had questions, and the answers were underneath. Everything was in a straight line. And on Saturday morning the mother would say, 'Nettie, get going. The preacher always starts on time.' He was real old, skinny like you, and his eyes watered, old watery eyes, and he smelled sour."

Nettie stretches her legs out in front of her.

"It was cold in that church," she says, "even when the

stove was going. The ceiling was high, and the benches were hard, and we all sat on a bench except for the preacher. He stood in front and looked at everybody."

"Who's everybody?" Eli asks.

"Oh, Martin and Grace – your Grace."

"She's not my Grace. She just sings a solo in the *Messiah*. 'He Shall Feed His Flock.'"

Nettie pushes herself up. "Well, isn't that just dandy. She gets to sing the important song."

"Tell the story," Eli says.

Nettie pouts for a moment, then continues. "Well, that old Swede would stand in front of the bench and put his head down like this." She moves closer to Eli, stretches her neck out, and stares into his face. "He'd talk half in Swede and his voice would go up and down and he'd say, 'Vy did God create man?' He'd say the same thing in front of each person, 'Vy did God create man?' His breath would come out in puffs. And everyone was supposed to say the answer without looking in the book. Only I never could. So he'd ask Alice or Grace or Martin to say it over, so I could learn it real quick. Then he'd come back to me. 'Nettie?' he'd say. *'Now* do you know vy God created man?' But the right words never came to me."

She turns to the quarry and leans over its edge. "Hey you down there, vy did God create man?"

She waits.

"No answer," she says.

She calls again. "Stones and bugs and snakes and toads, wake up!" She looks out across the pit. "Magpies and ugly buzzards, do you know the answer?" She stretches her neck back and looks straight up. "Hey, wind and clouds, and all you angels on top of the sky. Doesn't anybody know the answer?"

"The Swede knew," Eli says.

"He made it up," she says.

"So what was his answer?"

She raises her right hand in front of her, and with her finger, slices through the air in one long horizontal line. "Question! Vy did God create man?"

She waits, then cuts the air again with her finger. "Answer! God created man to be..." She stops.

"This is so scary," she says.

"Try again," Eli says.

She draws the line once more, faster. "Answer! God created man to be..." She drops her hand.

"Try *blessed*," Eli says.

"How did you know that?"

"I must have read it someplace."

"What does it mean?"

"Good. Happy. Something you'd say thank you for."

"You're lying," Nettie says.

"No," Eli says.

"Then it's true," she says, and runs to the pit and yells down into it.

"Good! Happy! Thank you! There's your answer."

Her face darkens. "And that's where he did it. That's where my daddy always did it to me after Mama died. Down there on the stones. And one day the men came. They saw my daddy and me, and they crawled down into the hole and got a hold of him, and pulled him off of me and dragged him into a car and they drove away.

And my daddy never came back."

Eli gets up, holding the blanket in his hand. The bottle drops to the ground and lodges in a clump of weeds at the edge of the pit. He goes to Nettie, puts his hand on her shoulder, and leads her back to the chair. He sits down, pulls her onto his lap, and covers her knees with the grey cloth.

PETER, ANDREW, AND ELIZABETH are in the front yard. They've cleaned the garage, straightened the pile of newspapers on the back porch, and walked the perimeter of the yard in single file, seeing who could come closest to the fence without touching it. Now they're sitting on the porch steps watching a flock of sparrows perched in a straight line on the telephone wire across the street.

Suddenly the birds swoop down into the branches of the maple tree beside the gate. With thin claws they rustle the dry twigs; then off they go as quickly as they came.

"Where do sparrows live anyway?" Elizabeth asks.

"Nowhere," Peter says.

"But where do they sleep at night?"

"Anywhere. They're wild."

"But they'd want to come back to the same place to sleep. They'd want to come home."

"Why? What's so great about that?" Peter says.

"Everything wants to come back to their own place. They may fly around a lot, but they always want to come home."

"Not sparrows," Peter says.

"You don't know that for sure," Elizabeth says. "It's not a proven fact."

THE LATE AFTERNOON sunlight spreads over the prairie in curious slants of light, glowing copper on the burnished stems of thistles, yellow white on the dying grass, a deep grey purple in rocky crevices in fields and ditches. At the quarry it spreads over house and pit and chair, leans against the rocks, forms small shadows among the stones.

Eli and Nettie are still sitting in the chair. They're watching a flock of waxwings play with the sky and with the top branches of the willow tree. The birds dip, turn, swoop up, then down again into the branches of the tree.

"Look at them," Nettie says. "They don't know if they're coming or going."

"Going," Eli says. "Getting out of here. Flying south. To Montana."

Nettie's heart thumps faster. "That's no place to go."

"This place isn't so hot," Eli says.

Nettie points to the town. "Well, if you stayed away from there," she says. "They're mean over there. Over there they do not have a heart." She taps Eli's chest with the tips of her fingers. "Do you know what they've got right there where the heart's supposed to go?" Eli shakes his head. "Well, they don't have a heart there, I can tell you that." She knocks against him with her knuckles. "Do you know what they've got there?"

"No," he says.

"A hole," she says.

"Well, so what?" Eli says. "Everybody's got a hole somewhere inside of them. And everybody fills it up the best way they know how."

And from somewhere deep in the recesses of his memory, a picture surfaces, faded at first, but gradually becoming clearer, more focused. He's nineteen years old. His father has died. He and his mother are poor. But his dad's friend has given him money so he can go to the university in Saskatoon, to study music.

One day in October, a long van drives up to the campus. Students are told to line up outside the vehicle and wait their turn to go inside. Finally, it's Eli's turn. He goes in, removes his shirt, and stands facing the wall, his chest pressed against a cold slab. A nurse snaps a switch. And it's all over. They put him on a train and send him to Fort Qu'Appelle to the TB sanitarium.

"So I was sitting on this train feeling low," he tells Nettie. "My bones ached, my skin felt clammy. I wanted to lie down, but I couldn't. There was this old man sitting beside me, really old, and he kept looking at me. He asked me what was the matter and I told him. He listened to me in a kindly way and seemed to sense just how I felt."

"Do you know why he did that?" Nettie asks. "Because right here...," she hits her head against Eli's chest, "he had a heart and not a hole."

"I tell him everything," Eli continues. "About my dad who'd been a farmer, and my dad's friend who paid my way to university. I tell him about my studies – about Haydn, Franz Joseph Haydn, a farmer's son like me. And about Mozart. Then I tell him about 1685. God's lucky year. The year Johann Sebastian Bach was born, and Domenico Scarlatti, and George Fredrick Handel. And then I say I'm on my way to Fort Qu'Appelle to the sanitarium because I have tuberculosis."

Nettie shakes her head, sadly. "A capital T and a capital B," she says.

"And after I tell him all this, the old man strokes his beard and is quiet for awhile. Then he says, 'I have no words. Your pain is very great.'

"I didn't answer him. I just turned to the window and looked out. The sky was grey, and the wind and rain beat against the skinny trees beyond the track, bent them right over so their tops nearly touched the ground. The fields and pastures looked desolate. Wet and cold. And then the old man said, 'Some day, not now of course, you may find value in this. Some worth. You might even be able to say thanks.' That made me mad, and I said, 'What value? Like zero? Like a goose egg? Like a hole?' And he said, 'So what can you do with a hole?' After that I slept. All the way to Fort San."

Suddenly, Eli nudges Nettie off his lap and stands up. The blanket falls to the ground. "I have to go in now," he says, "I need to get ready, study my music." He puts his hand on Nettie's shoulder and leads her into the trailer.

It's a warm Indian summer day. The sun is bright and the ground is grey and rusty brown, settling into rest. Jonathan is working in his study when Christine appears in the doorway. "Eli's back," she says. "He's in the yard talking to the children."

Jonathan considers whether to go down and talk to Eli in the yard or to wait up here and see what happens. He was not expecting another visit from Eli, not for another year at least.

In the backyard Peter is directing his choir. Andrew, Elizabeth, Ivan, and Vera are lined up against the garage wall, mouthing words. Peter stops swinging his arms to say, "They're dropping out like flies. We'll have to take over."

"Who's dropping out?" Elizabeth says.

"A whole bunch of them. They can't stand old Hilda."

"She's a croaker," Ivan says.

Eli speaks up from behind the hedge, where he has stopped a moment for breath. "You want to direct the choir, Peter? Let me show you how." He breaks a twig from a caragana bush, walks around the hedge.

"Try using this," he says. "Some conductors use their hands, but I've always found a stick more precise. It makes clear signals. You strike the air with it and out come the sounds." He thrusts the twig into the boy's hand and curls his own fingers over Peter's. He raises their two hands together, poised in front of the choir. "First you pause and wait for everyone's attention. Then pull down." He lowers Peter's hand and sings, *And the glory, the glory of the Lord...* He swings their joined hands up to the left and down and up again. *And the glory, the glory of the Lord...* He drops Peter's hand. "That's how you do it. It takes training and a lot of practice. It's not easy." He turns and heads for the house. Christine directs him to the study.

When Jonathan finishes reading from the sheet of paper Eli has placed on his desk, he looks up in astonishment.

"We both agree," Eli says.

Jonathan examines the paper once more. Everything's in order. Eli and Nettie are licensed for lawful marriage in the province of Saskatchewan. A red seal stamps the corner of the page.

Why should he be feeling resistance? Had he not advocated this very thing at one time? But what was he thinking of? Eli, aging, sick, homeless, and Nettie, outcast, damaged in mind and spirit, joined in holy matrimony. And then he understands. Eli is doing this for one reason: so that he can direct the choir.

"I know this is short notice," Eli says, "so if you can't do the honours, I'm sure Reverend McFarlane will."

"This won't do the trick, you know," Jonathan says. "Rehearsals have already started."

"You don't think I'm getting married just for that, do you?" Eli says.

On Saturday morning, under a yellow sun, Eli and Nettie stand in front of the trailer, facing the quarry. Beside Nettie is Christine Lund. Next to Eli is Peter. Halfway between the trailer and the pit, Jonathan in a dark suit stands facing them. He holds a black altar book in his hand. A small wind ruffles his sandy hair. The rocking chair has been moved to face the trailer, and Andrew and Elizabeth sit in the chair together.

"When is she going to put on her wedding dress?" Elizabeth whispers into Andrew's ear.

Andrew leans as far away from her as he can, but her voice still reaches him.

"There aren't any streamers," she says. "How can there be a wedding without streamers?"

Andrew stretches his neck and looks up. The sky is clear blue, like lakes he's seen in pictures, like his mother's eyes.

Christine does not want to be here. She does not approve of this wedding. "How can you go along with this?" she'd demanded of Jonathan. "You know very well what his motives are." Jonathan did not answer her. "And how could you possibly agree to having it out at the gravel pit, knowing what's gone on there?" To which Jonathan replied, "Nettie won't leave the quarry."

And now, here she is, a witness, wearing a green wool dress and standing beside Nettie, who wears a skirt and faded sweater, clothing donated by the Sunshine Circle at St. John's years ago.

Jonathan begins reading, holding his book high in front of him. His voice is small and thin in the vast air.

"In the second chapter of the Book of Genesis it is written thus: 'And the Lord said, It is not good that man should be alone; I will make him an helpmeet for him....'"

Nettie glances at Eli, Eli looks at Jonathan, Peter stares down at his shoes.

There was some confusion at first as to where the wedding party would stand. The bride and groom on the step? Christine and Peter on the ground? All four on the step? All on the ground? It was Nettie who made the final decision: "We will all stand on the ground in a straight line. Nobody's foot will stick out any farther than anyone else's." Peter has found this directive to his liking and shifts his feet forward and back, testing the measurements.

"'And the Lord caused a deep sleep to fall upon Adam, and he slept. And He took one of his ribs, and closed up the flesh thereof; and of the rib which the Lord had taken from man, made He a woman, and brought her to the man. And Adam said, This is now bone of my bone and flesh of my flesh; and shall be called Woman because she was taken out of Man. Therefore shall a man leave his father and mother and shall cleave unto his wife; and they shall be one flesh.'"

"Cleave?" Nettie says. "I wonder how you'd spell that."

A gopher peeks out of its hole beside a rock; a crow lands on the top branch of the willow tree.

"Christ saith also in the nineteenth chapter according to St. Matthew: 'What God hath joined together let no man put asunder.'" Jonathan pauses.

"It's over then," Nettie says.

"Not quite," Jonathan says.

Nettie mumbles under her breath, "Is he going to read the whole book?"

Jonathan reads from Corinthians, from Genesis, from Luke. Finally, he comes to the wedding vows.

"I ask thee, therefore, Eli Olaf Nelson, in the presence of God and this Christian assembly: In thy marriage with Nettie Orpha Johnson, wilt thou live with her according to God's holy Word, love and honour her, and alike in good and evil days keep thee only unto her so long as ye both shall live?"

"I will," Eli says.

Jonathan looks at Nettie. "In like manner, I ask thee, Nettie Orpha Johnson, in the presence of God and this Christian assembly: In thy marriage with Eli Olaf Nelson, wilt thou live with him according to God's holy Word, love and honour him, and alike in good and evil days keep thee only unto him as long as ye both shall live? If so, answer I will."

"I said I would, didn't I?"

"Then I pronounce you husband and wife."

The crow flies up from the willow tree and cuts the sky with black and glossy wings.

ON THE FIRST MONDAY in November the sky darkens, the wind takes on a hollow, whistling sound, and the people of Stone Creek wait for snow. They wait in the Chinese café at oilcloth-covered tables beside steaming windows, coffee mugs cupped in their hands. They wait in the Golden West Hotel in a room, dimly lit, where one more drink will warm the winter already in their bones. They wait in the Stone Creek School. Restless in their desks, the pupils twist their bodies this way and that, stretching their necks toward the high windows, watching the sky darken, deep, deeper still, now a dense heavy grey. And the wind, sharp and mournful, slapping at the glass.

And then it comes. Icy flakes spinning in the air,

sweeping across the roads, under telephone wires, into ditches. It blows against the café and post office, the furniture store and undertaker's parlour and the schoolhouse windows. It swirls about the elevators and across the pasture and the quarry and over pebbles and stiff clumps of thistles and all around the empty chair creaking back and forth beside the frozen pit.

Inside the trailer, Nettie peers out the small window over the sink and watches the flakes do their jagged dance in her small yard. She breathes content in the knowledge that now Eli will never leave her.

She goes into the bedroom, opens the closet door, and reaches behind a pile of blankets for the package. She removes the yellowed paper, lifts out a small black autoharp, and carries it into the kitchen where Eli is sitting. She places the instrument on the table.

"Here," she says. "Play."

"Wherever did you find this?"

"Never mind. Just play."

Eli examines it, fingers the knobs to tighten the loose strings, then plucks the strings with his thumb.

"No," Nettie says. "Use this." She plunks a thick piece of worn leather into his hand. "It's what Mama used." And Eli strums a few chords.

Outside, snow drifts around the trailer, clicks and swishes against the kitchen window. And the wind, blue and hollow, seeps under the door in chilly strips.

"Sing," Nettie says. And Eli opens his mouth to an old song.

Mid pleasures and palaces, though we may roam,

Be it ever so humble, there's no place like home.

"Speed it up," Nettie says. "You're too slow."

A charm from the sky seems to hallow us there,
Which, seek through the world, is ne'er met with
elsewhere.

"Oh, well," she says.

Home, home... Eli sings.

"Home!" Nettie shouts.

Sweet sweet home... he sings.

"Sweet home!" she shouts.

There's no place like home,
oh, there's no place like home.

Nettie sighs. "That is so true," she says.

ON THE SEVENTH OF NOVEMBER Annie Levinsky dies.
Jacob and his pupils tromp through snow down the
hill to the Russian church. Inside, they cling to the wall
by the door. The church is crowded, everyone stands,
there are no pews. Elizabeth Lund stays close to Mary
Sorenson. She has never been in this church before and
she stares at everything. In front of her, men in shiny

black suits and white shirts, women in black skirts and lace shawls, and children, too, hover around a wooden box that Elizabeth can barely see. And all around them are candles. Purple candles in tall stands that rise above their heads; pink candles in little glass cups set in cubbyholes in the church wall; candles in thick silver candlesticks on the table of the altar. Hundreds of orange flames. And she sees the pictures too, painted on the walls and on velvet banners with red tassels – pictures of old men with beards and of Mary and the baby Jesus. And the ceiling! She gazes up at the blue dome high above, where saints and angels fly in and out among the stars.

Mary takes Elizabeth's hand. The two girls press closer to the varnished box. And there she is. Annie Levinsky, lying on creamy slippery cloth and wearing a long white dress. Annie with a veil fluffed around her face and holding a red rose in her hand. Her hand is stiff, her eyes are closed, she has rouge on her cheeks, she's wearing lipstick. Mrs. Levinsky is leaning over her, crying, fussing with the veil so it lies in curves around her daughter's face. And the bearded priest is swinging a purple cord with a silver cup on the end of it and chanting in a dark strange language. Smoke rises from the cup, and Elizabeth can smell spices – cloves or cinnamon. It's too much all at one time and she closes her eyes.

And now the men in black suits are carrying the box outside. They carry it to the open grave in the churchyard. And Mary and Elizabeth are standing together by a mound of frozen dirt. Again the priest chants and

swings the smoking cup, and smoke rises in thin streamers into the cold grey air. With thick ropes, the men
lower the box into the hole, and the people throw
chunks of frozen dirt down on it, each clod landing
with a thud. Then, for the first time in the entire service, the priest speaks in English, "Let us go forth as light
bearers to meet the Christ who cometh forth from the
grave as a Bridegroom."

Elizabeth whispers into Mary's ear, quietly but with
authority, for she's the daughter of the preacher, "She
marries Jesus." Then the two girls take each other by the
hand and begin to cry, softly at first, only a few light
sniffles, then louder until they are sobbing, their bodies
shaking. Weeping for Annie Levinsky whom they didn't
know really, never played with, hardly spoke to, for
Annie was a shy girl, sick and smelling sour. But now,
oh wonder, she's the bride of Christ. And one day she'll
be pulled right out of the dirt to meet her husband in
the air.

Annie Levinsky, lying at the bottom of a frozen hole,
wearing lipstick and a long white dress, and smelling
like cinnamon.

ON THE TENTH OF NOVEMBER the choir, under the
direction of Hilda Munson, folds. At their last gather-
ing, Jonathan, the only tenor left, makes a short but
glowing speech on the contribution Hilda has made to
St. John's congregation with her faithful service.

"When we were in need, you were there, Hilda, gen-
erous with your time and talents." He stands in the

church kitchen around the oilcloth-covered table where five other loyal singers are seated, drinking coffee and eating chocolate cake. Hilda sits at the head of the table, daubing her eyes with a white handkerchief. "And rest assured, Hilda," he continues, "we haven't seen the last of you. Your skills will always be needed."

On November 12, Eli is reappointed conductor.

Again, Jonathan Lund drives his Plymouth down the road past the creamery, past Jacobson's pasture, and this time farther still so he can take the back road, the long way around, to the trailer.

"We're on," he says to Eli in the trailer's kitchen. "The *Messiah's* back."

"Hallelujah!" Eli shouts.

In the bedroom, Nettie flops down on the blanket.

"Oh piss," she says.

At supper tables throughout the parish the talk is of the coming *Messiah*.

"So Doc's put the plug in the jug again."

"But how can they get this thing together in four weeks?"

"I hear Eli's getting some musicians from Moose Jaw to help out."

"Hilda must really be burning over this."

However, in the Munson house Hilda seems strangely calm. She is standing in front of the living-room window, gazing out at the snow-packed street beyond her yard. "Do I have something to tell you, Sam Munson. A real surprise." She pulls the curtain to the side, bends her head closer to the glass. "You'll have to wait to find out though." She backs away from the window. "Grace Olson will be furious, of course, but that's her problem."

In the small house behind the frozen hollyhocks, Grace is sitting at her piano, peering at the music in front of her, her thin fingers poised above the keys. In slow, regal movements of her hands, she begins to play "The Holy City." And she's at peace.

There is no peace in the trailer, however. Eli promised Nettie he'd never leave her, and now he leaves her nearly every day, trudging into town to practise with basses, tenors, altos, and twice-weekly rehearsals with the whole choir, lasting late into the night. Nettie gets even with him in her own way: Forgets to put salt on the table, loses his socks, sleeps on the edge of the bed with her back to him. She shuts her ears to his singing, makes fun of his directing. And she refuses to spell for him even when he asks for her favourite words.

ONE AFTERNOON, after a rehearsal of soloists, Doctor Long invites Eli to his place. He has something for him. Under an amber sky the two men walk slowly down Main Street to the United Church, then west toward the doctor's house. Their thin bodies cast narrow shadows on the snow-packed road behind them.

Inside the house, the doctor directs Eli into a room that was once a waiting room for patients but now is a place empty and uncared for. The chairs are still there, and a small table holding old magazines. After all, in his dreams the doctor sees himself back in business, his at-home clinic bustling with patients.

Eli sits down in the green Naugahyde chair, and the old man leaves the room. He returns with a long cardboard box which he opens slowly, his hands shaking a little. He lifts out the black trousers, black coat with tails, the stiff white shirt.

"You might as well look the part," he says.

Eli removes his pants and shirt, lays them over the back of a chair, and puts on the black trousers and white shirt. When he has the coat on as well, he struts about the office, singing and directing with one hand, *And the glory, the glory of the Lord....* With the other hand, he holds up the pants which are too big in the waist. The doctor stops Eli's movement and kneels down beside him, an open safety pin held between his teeth. He clutches at the trousers, pinches the cloth together at the waistband, and jabs the pin into the fabric. When the cloth is secure, Eli continues directing the song, using both arms.

When the singing and cavorting end, the doctor tells Eli that Nora has something for Nettie, a dress she bought for herself at Cutler's Dry Goods, that never did fit right and now it's too late to return it. It's new, never been worn, he says. Maybe Nettie would accept it as a wedding present, wear it to the concert.

He brings Eli the dress box. Eli removes the cover, lifts up a sheet of tissue paper, and sees the dress underneath. "Well," Eli says. "Well, well."

Nettie is standing in front of the kitchen window, peering out. He said he'd be back early, but already the sun has gone down, and on the horizon jagged slabs of red and orange pile up and spread out. Her heart quickens its beat. Surely he'll be coming soon.

When she finally sees him appear over the crest of the hill, first his head, then his shoulders, she leaves the window, disappears into the bedroom, and sinks down on their small bed, covering her head with the blanket. She does not hear the song he sings as he approaches the trailer, holding the cardboard box against his chest and clumping through the snow. *Here I raise my ebenezer, hither by thy help I'm come...*

When he reaches the step, he opens the door and sends the music booming into their house. *And I hope by thy good pleasure safely to arrive at home.* He closes the door and glances about the room. She's not here. He sings louder still, *And I hope by thy good pleasure safely to arrive at home.* He sets the package on the table and stomps into the bedroom. Sees the familiar lump under the grey blanket. Her hiding place, her comfort in time of trouble.

"I was singing for you," he says. "Don't you want to hear the song?"

There's a twisting movement under the quilts and a muffled sound. He goes to the bed and leans over the grey mound.

And I hope by thy good pleasure, safely to arrive at home, he sings, more quietly now, his face close to the quilt. "And besides, I have something for you. Don't you want to see what I have?"

Nettie peaks out from beneath the quilt.

"Come and see," Eli says. "The robe of righteousness. The garment of salvation."

He sings again. *Oh come, come, come, come...*

"Oh, be quiet," she says. And seeing the black tails hanging from below his coat, she sits up in bed and stares down at them.

"What is that hanging down there?" she asks.

He turns away from her, bends over, reaches behind him with his arms, and flaps the coattails with both hands. *Lift up your heads, o ye gates. And be ye lifted up, everlasting doors.* Then he wriggles out of his winter coat, lets it fall to the floor, and stands up, facing her in his new clothes. *And the king of glory shall come in!*

Nettie stares at him, curious. Now what? What is this man up to now? She gets out of bed, goes to him, and looks more closely at the suit. She examines the shirt, touches the cloth with her fingers. She slides her hand down his pant leg, turns him around and stares at the coattails.

"Where did you ever get a hold of this?" she asks.

"Do you like it?" Eli asks. "Do you think I'm gorgeous? Yes? Then dance with me."

He presses his arm against her back, his hand in the small softness of her armpit; his other hand holds her own. He swings her in small circles around the narrow room, her body stiff and awkward. They bump against the closet door, just miss the dresser, then whirl about in the centre of the room. He stops, pulls her close to him and breathes into her hair, and her body softens, becomes light again.

Oh come, come, come, come..., he whispers in her ear. And they move slowly now in the space beside the bed.

When they are finally still, he tells her he has something for her.

"Stay where you are," he says. "Close your eyes."

"Shall I count?" she says.

"No, no. Just keep your eyes closed."

Nettie closes her left eye, squeezes it tight, and squints at Eli with the other.

"You're cheating," he says. "Close them both." He goes into the kitchen and lifts the dress out of its box. His right hand holds one sleeve, his left the other. He carries the dress into the bedroom, swinging it gently by his side as a matador swings his cape.

Nettie opens her eyes and sees the dress. She sees it moving gracefully under Eli's right arm, like a person, a friend. Like a pretty lady. A woman loved. Her breathing stops, then moves ever so lightly inside her, soft as dandelion fluff. And she feels sunlight all around her.

"It's yours," Eli says. "It's brand new. Nobody's ever worn it."

She steps closer to the garment, reaches out her hand, touches the tiny white dots embossed on the blue voile, strokes the delicate lace of the collar.

"Put it on," he says.

But she doesn't hear him for gazing at the dress.

He thrusts it toward her. "You can wear it to the concert. You can go to the *Messiah*. Sit in the front row."

And the sunlight begins to fade, to shrivel up, harden into a ball, clamp against her ribs. She backs away from the dress.

"What's wrong?" Eli says. "Try it on."

She sits on the bed, her eyes on the floor.

"Put it away," she says.

"I'll hang it in the closet then," Eli says. "Until you're ready."

"No. Hide it. Under the bed."

Eli sighs, "Oh, Nettie. Why can't you just see how you'd look in it?"

Nettie doesn't answer him.

Eli brings the box in from the kitchen and lays it on the bed. He folds the dress into the box, carefully, so the lace collar and the tiny dots fit smoothly between its thin cardboard walls. He shoves the box under the bed.

EARLY IN DECEMBER, Stone Creek prepares for Christmas. Strings of green and red lights stretch across Main Street. Silver tinselled ropes loop the store windows. In the Red and White, golden cardboard bells sway in easy motion above the cabbages and turnips. And at Gilman's Drug Store, night-blue bottles of Evening in Paris and silver-foiled boxes of chocolates line the shelves.

In the parsonage, Christine Lund thinks of her mother in her home on Segoe Road, and she washes the windows, washes and starches the curtains, cleans the furniture with lemon oil. She bakes spritz and kringla, sugar cookies and date bars, sews a new dress for Elizabeth, pale green with a white collar, practises her solo for the Messiah.

One day she sends the children downstairs to clean

the basement. She has set a large box by the stairs to hold junk. "Throw those old cartons and empty cans into this box, wash the shelves in the fruit cellar, wipe the cobwebs off the pipes, sweep up the dust and grit."

"Basements are supposed to be dirty," Peter complains.

"Just do it," Christine says.

When she disappears upstairs and the basement door is closed, Peter lowers his voice and says, confidentially, "I have a solo in the *Messiah*. I guess you didn't know that."

"Why do you always say dumb things?" Elizabeth says.

"I'll prove it. I'll sing it."

He stands on the bottom step, turns his back to them, and swings his hips from side to side. *Hallelujah, I'm a bum. Hallelujah, bum again...* He bends over, slaps his rear end. *Hallelujah, give us a handout. Revive us again.*

"You better watch out," Elizabeth says. "Mama will hear you."

Peter grabs a piece of cardboard from the floor and hurls it into the box. Andrew picks up the long pole with a rag tied to the end of it, and aims the rag at a pipe over the furnace. The pole sways to the left and to the right before it finally reaches its mark. Elizabeth starts sweeping the floor.

"A whole lot of people are coming," Andrew says. "Even a busload from Moose Jaw."

"They'll come from Swift Current, you can pretty well count on that," Peter says.

"And Shaunavon, don't forget," says Elizabeth. She

swishes the broom, too tall for her, over the crumbling concrete.

"They're coming from the United Church," Andrew says.

"Pentecostals too?" Elizabeth asks.

"I wouldn't count on it," Peter says.

"How about Catholics? Will they come?"

"Not unless they want to go to Purgatory."

"Would any Communists come?"

"Old Man Lippoway? Forget it."

"How about Abie Gilman?"

"Jews have their own Messiah."

"You don't know that for sure, Peter."

"Who do you think Hezekiah was?" Peter sneers.

Elizabeth wants to argue with him, but he seems so certain.

"Will the Chinaman be there?" she asks.

"Will Crazy Nettie come?"

AT THE QUARRY, Nettie waits for Eli to leave for choir practice. When she sees him disappear over the hill, she steps away from the kitchen window and goes into the bedroom. As she's done every day since he brought the dress home, she kneels beside the bed, reaches under it with both arms and pulls out the cardboard box. Cautiously, she removes the lid and lifts up the sheet of tissue paper. The dress is still there.

She examines it again, touches the collar, the Swiss dots, the hem. She could put it on, see how it looks, it wouldn't hurt. But go to the concert? Leave the quarry?

She thinks of the pit. Deep. It can pull you down to the bottom just like that. And it's always watching you, waiting for you to take one wrong step, spell one word wrong. She folds the tissue paper over the dress, replaces the lid, and shoves the box back under the bed. You have to be so careful.

IN TOWN, the choir is in its last rehearsal, this time with four musicians from Moose Jaw. For weeks his singers have listened to Eli plead, scold, beg, praise. "Take it from the top...once more...and don't forget to count...there are four beats in that measure, not three, not three and a half...try again...soloists, stand tall...lift up those notes, don't let them slide...think up...up... that's better...now crescendo, give it all you've got... punch it! Blessing...honour...glory...and power...excellent...not bad...not bad at all.

AND THEN THE DAY ARRIVES.

IN ST. JOHN'S CHURCH, boughs of evergreen arch the windows, frame the pulpit, bank the table of the altar. Large red bows are tacked to the ends of pews. In the corner a tall spruce tree glitters with many coloured lights, gold balls, long strands of silver tinsel. Wooden risers have been installed in front of the altar to hold the singers. And facing the risers, the podium where Eli will stand.

At the trailer, Eli is dressing. He has put on the black

trousers, pinned the waistband so the pants won't slip down, tucked in the white shirt, straightened the bow tie. Now he's examining himself in the mirror above the kitchen sink, trying to smooth the unruly strands of hair with his two hands, sprinkling the hair with water, patting it down again.

From the bedroom doorway, Nettie watches him. Eli with smooth face, slick hair, shiny pants. She sees him squat in front of the sink, reach under it, and remove a rag from an old pail. He wets the rag in the wash basin, bends down and wipes his shoes, the same brown shoes, worn and cracked, but now clean, even shiny in a few spots. He puts the rag back and goes into the bedroom. When he returns he's wearing the black coat with tails. He struts in front of Nettie, bobbing his head from side to side.

Now what? she thinks. What's all this about? He's going to town to direct his choir. So what? Why would a man rub his shoes with a rag and slap down his hair with water for that?

Eli looks at her slyly. Maybe he'll try one more time. "Put your dress on," he says. "I have to go early to set things up." Nettie doesn't move from the doorway. "Come on," Eli says. "Put it on. See what a pair we'll make."

And Eli, in four long strides, is in the bedroom, pulling out the box from under the bed. When he comes back, he's again holding the dress under his arm, waving it at Nettie.

What does he think he's doing? Tricks and more tricks. She hurries to the sink, grabs the dish towel from the rack, and flaps it at him.

"Forget it," she says. "I'm not moving."

And for the first time, Eli is angry with her. He throws the dress over a chair, grabs his coat from its hook by the door, and digs his arms into the sleeves. He's buttoning up the coat when the words come out, words he hasn't even thought of before. They tumble out of his mouth, one after another.

"That old Swede was right, you know, about the blessing. A blessing as big as a boulder...as big as this hill...as big as the whole damn prairie...and it comes to you...over and over...but you just don't see it, Nettie... your eyes are stuck shut, and you miss it."

Nettie marches closer to Eli. She holds the towel in both hands and shakes it up and down in front of him. Her face is red, her breathing heavy.

Eli pushes past her into the bedroom where he picks up his music. When he returns to the kitchen, he flaps the *Messiah* at her, its pages ragged.

"So hide, Nettie. Or the blessing might find you. And it's big. It will knock you off your feet if you don't watch out." He moves to the door, turns, and looks at her. "Open your eyes, Nettie. Wake up." He pushes the door open and walks out into the night.

Nettie shoves her feet into her overshoes, grabs her coat and pulls it on. She rushes out after him. Sees him trudging past the rocking chair.

"Open your own eyes!" she shouts.

She scrapes at the snow with her foot until she can see the dirt beneath the snow, and the stones, and dead and frozen thistles. She bends down and tears at the stones with her hands, but they're frozen into the earth.

She stands up, kicks at them with her foot, and some dislodge from their icy niche. She picks one up and throws it at Eli. Then another, and hurls it at him. And another.

"And get out of my yard!" she yells.

Eli calls back to her from the other side of the quarry. "Nettie, go inside. It's cold out here." But she doesn't move.

She watches him finally disappear over the hill. Then she kicks more stones loose, picks them up, and shoves them into her pocket. She makes her way to the edge of the quarry, to the wide white hole of the pit. And she pulls a stone out of her pocket and hurls it into the hole.

"This is for you, Daddy!"

She throws another and another until there is only one stone left.

"And I'm not saying thank you!"

When she returns to the house she sees the dress.

"Oh my," she says. She picks it up and folds it over her outstretched hands as if it were an offering, and repeats, "Oh. Oh."

She lays the dress back in the box and covers it with the tissue paper. Then she digs her hand into her pocket and pulls out the last stone. She holds it close to her face, turns it this way and that, examining its shape, each sharp edge, each small indentation.

"I nearly did a very bad thing to you." She presses it against her chest and pats it with her hand. "Hey, don't cry, I'll take you home."

A light snow is falling, sifting over the place where the stone had been. But Nettie finds a place, a hollow

bowl in a small drift, and rising out of it, a frozen thistle, its stem broken. She brushes the snow aside and lays
the stone down beside the thistle. "This is your house,"
she says, "and this is your yard. When summer comes,
the little beetles can stop here and sit with you for
awhile, and rest."

She moves through the snow to the edge of the quarry and looks down into the pit. "I remember now how
it was. I forgot but now I remember. You said I was your
new bride, that's what you said. And there were marks
on my legs, little cuts from the rock, some of them you
could hardly see they were so small."

She plods back to the house, muttering to herself.

"I guess what happened is your heart turned to dust
one day and spilled out and blew away. Past Winnipeg.
And then there was a hole there."

ON MAIN STREET, cars are slowly driving north, from
farms south of town and some from farther away,
Shaunavon and Swift Current. A Plymouth, a
Chevrolet, two Fords, a Dodge truck. They're turning
right at the corner of Wong's Café to find parking on
the street and in the vacant lot beside the church. From
the north they come as well, from Robson and
Chumsland's Coulee, driving past Donnellys' and into
town, turning left at the café. Town people are walking.
Past the hotel and post office and up the street to the
town hall, then across the street and onto the sidewalk
leading to the church. It's not such a cold evening. A
pleasant walk, really. A small wind, light snow.

Inside the church, the pews are beginning to fill. The middle section is already full, the back pews saved for latecomers. And the front? Well, who sits there if there are seats anywhere else? The preacher's kids of course. And old Mrs. Heggestad, who can't hear.

In the church basement the choir members are gathered, checking their robes, making sure they're fastened properly and hanging straight. They're reading over their scores, humming phrases, making light-hearted comments, "Well, Eli, don't faint on us up there, or Sigurd will have to take over." There is discreet whispering among the women, "I guess we better use the ladies' room now; it's going to be a long evening. I hope Jenny will be able to hold back her coughing."

IN THE TRAILER Nettie is lying on the bed, next to the box with the dress inside it. Throwing stones has made her very tired. But now she thinks about Eli. She remembers the dress under his arm and how he swung it back and forth. Remembers his song, "Oh come, come, come, come..." and his hide-and-seek games. Remembers the bags of food he carries up the hill to the quarry. And his thin body – his neck and wrists, his bony knees. And she stands up and says to the empty space in front of her, "I will go into town. I will go to the *Messiah* after all. I'll put this brand new dress on and go."

MORE PEOPLE have arrived at St. John's. In the front row, Peter, Andrew, and Elizabeth are sitting next to the centre aisle; Jonas Grunland is at the far end of the same pew by the window. Immediately behind Jonas are Mr. and Mrs. Ross and Beverly, and behind them, next to Mrs. Hagen and Norma, are Rev. and Mrs. McFarlane from the United Church. Behind the Lunds are Mrs. Sorenson and Mary. There is still some space in the front pew and also beside Mrs. Sorenson. Even so, Carl Jacobson and Bud Evenson are carrying chairs up from the basement. As they place them in position, one at the end of each pew, they smile and shake their heads apologetically, as though they'd never expected such a crowd, and what were they to do?

Then, appearing from the back of the church, Grace Olson walks down the centre aisle, turns left in front of the risers to the piano at the side. She sits down on the piano bench, adjusts the sheet music in front of her, lifts her hands to the keys and strikes the first chord of "The Holy City." There's a rustle in the audience. Since when did Grace play the piano for this affair, they wonder.

Grace is entranced by the music. Imagine, she thinks, Eli asking her to render this beautiful piece. But why not? She's sung a solo every year. Now she gets to play "The Holy City." And while more people enter the church, filling the pews and chairs, she leans forward, stiff and proud, her fingers moving precisely over the keyboard.

NETTIE STANDS beside the bed and wonders what to do first: Take the dress out of the box? Take off her skirt and sweater? Wash her face? Comb her hair? She walks into the kitchen, stands in front of the sink, and sees in the mirror above it her uncombed hair, her sharp blue eyes, and the skin of her face, wind-swept and hard. Not great, she thinks. But so what. She returns to the bedroom, takes the lid off the box, and removes the tissue paper. She lifts up the dress by its sleeves, raises it above the box, then lays it down on the bed, smoothing the cloth with her fingers. Yes, she'll take off her sweater and skirt and put on the dress. That's exactly what she'll do. Then she'll put on her coat, and walk to town, to St. John's Church.

JERUSALEM, JERUSALEM, lift up your voice and sing.... After the last note, Grace bows her head over the keyboard. This piece always moves her deeply. Then she picks up her music and walks down the aisle to join the rest of the choir in the basement. Now the pianist from Moose Jaw comes forward, sits down on the bench and places the Handel score in front of her. The three other musicians follow. Two violinists and a trumpet player. They sit on chairs beside the piano and arrange their music on the stands in front of them. Whispering stops; eyes focus on the musicians. Then suddenly the door to the vestibule swings open, and the choir enters. Members of the audience turn their heads, strain their necks, trying to see who enters first, who next, how many there are. The choir walks single file down the narrow aisle.

NETTIE RAISES the hem of her old skirt above her head. She tugs at it, pulling the waistband up to her chin.

Then she lets go and the skirt drops back to where it was. She looks over at the dress lying flat and empty on the bed. She can feel her heart beating faster now, and her breathing heavier. "What was I thinking anyway?" She leans over and touches the hem with her finger. "I can't wear this. How would a dress like this look on someone like me?" She hears a whispering in her ear, like the sighing of wind scraping over pebbles at the bottom of the quarry. "Stay where you are," it says. "Stay put."

FROM THE FAR END of the third riser, Jonathan appears to be listening to the long piano overture, but he's really watching the crowd, his eyes skimming over the pews, discreetly, marking who's there, who isn't. He knew of course that McFarlane would come and Ross and others not of his own denomination, including Mrs. Long, the doctor's wife, who's United. But he was not prepared to see Mrs. Donnelly, a Catholic, and five Mennonites from north of town. He feels a small ripple of excitement up his back and on his arms. How extraordinary. Even Mrs. Donnelly. And the Mennonites.

His focus quickly changes to Eli on the podium, Eli in smooth black pants, white shirt, and tails. Eli with gold cufflinks and clean shoes. His right hand is lifted, baton poised. It's time for the first number, Jonathan's first solo. Eli's two hands come together slowly in front of his face, then curve upward in a graceful half-circle above his head. And Jonathan begins.

Comfort ye, com–fort ye–My people...

Speak ye com-fort-a-bly to Je-ru-salem
And cry un-to her, that her war–fare is ac–complish-ed,

He pauses, breathes deeply, he wants to be sure to sing the next line in one breath.

That her in-I–qui–ty is par–don-ed.

NETTIE PUTS the dress back in the box, folding it carefully to fit neatly into the space. She straightens the collar, tucks in the sleeves, covers the garment with tissue paper, and replaces the lid. Later, when Eli's here, she'll put it on. She'll put it on just for him. That will make him happy. She goes into the kitchen and sits down at the table. She'll just have to wait here until he comes home.

THE SINGERS are gazing at Eli. They've warmed to the song and are sending out the words, loud and triumphant, over the pews. The piano, the two violins, and the trumpet lead them.

And the glo–ry, the glo–ry of the Lord
Shall be re–veal–ed, re–veal–ed.
Shall be re–veal–ed, re–veal–ed.

BUT THIS ISN'T WHAT SHE WAS GOING TO DO. She was going to go into town to St. John's Church, where Eli is, and listen to the music. That's what she just said she was going to do. So what's she sitting here for? Get up now and go. Just go. G-o.

IT'S JONATHAN'S turn again, his second solo. It's written for alto, but none of the altos can handle it, he's the only one, just him. He stretches his body tall and waits for Eli's signal.

> *But who may a-bide the day of His com-ing?*
> *And who shall stand when He ap-pear-eth?*
> *And who shall stand when He ap-pear-eth?*
> *When he ap—pear—eth?*
> *When he ap—pear—eth?*

Eli pierces him with his eyes, reminding him: Now's the tricky part, so do your stuff. Concentrate. Focus. It's a mental thing, too, you know. Wear your thinking cap. Jonathan feels the energy. He'll not mess up this year.

> *For He is like a refi-i-i-i-i-i-ner's fire.*
> *For he is like a re-fi-i-i-i-i-i-i-i-i-i-i-i-i-i-ner's fire.*
> *Who shall stand when He ap-pear-eth?*
> *For He is like a re-fi-i-i-i-i-i-i-i-i-i-i-i-i-i-i-i-i-i-i-*
> *i-i-i-i-i-i-ner's fire.*

Mary Sorenson leans over the pew in front of her and whispers to Elizabeth. "It's very good, isn't it." Elizabeth nods but doesn't look back. Very good? Of course it's very good. Her father, his church, this music, this night. It's wonderful.

IT'S SETTLED THEN. She'll do what she said she'd do. Nettie reaches for her coat. She pulls it on and buttons it, covers her head with a woolen scarf, knots the ends under her chin. She shoves her feet into her overshoes and buckles them up, puts her mittens on, and opens the door. Suddenly she turns back. She forgot the dress. She can't go without the dress. What was she thinking anyway? She runs into the bedroom, picks up the box and tucks it under her arm. She walks out the door into a light falling snow.

JEAN WILSON has never sung a solo before. She's nervous and feels dizzy. She leans toward Eli, but he doesn't seem to be there. Her neck is red. She can hardly breathe. The pianist is trilling the notes of the introduction, smooth, perfect. So many notes. Then, as if through fog, she sees the flick of the baton, and she opens her mouth and sings.

O thou that tell—est good ti—dings to Zion...
Get thee up in-to a high moun—tain...
Lift up thy voice with strength; lift it up, be not a—fraid.

Her voice wavers, cracks, she wants to stop, this is terrible. Eli is smiling, nodding, keep going he's telling her, bring it to the finish line. She takes a deep breath and pushes the words out.

Say un—to the cit—ies of Ju—dah, be-hold—be-hold...

Good. You're nearly there, now run with it, carry it over the line, bring it home.

The glo—ry of the Lord is ris—en up—on thee.

There. She did it. She looks down at Ralph in the fourth row. His head is going up and down and he's smiling. It's too warm in here, her neck is hot, her cheeks are burning.

NETTIE IS WEDGING sideways down the slippery hill, trying to follow Eli's steps, clutching the box against her chest. She slips, falls once, and is up again. She doesn't let go of the box. She wades through thick snow in the creek bed, then stumbles into the pasture. She lifts each foot high, but she can't make headway. Cut over to the road or you'll never get there.

DOCTOR LONG, on the third riser, holds his head high and looks down at Eli. His voice when he sings is black and rolling.

For be-hold, dark—ness shall co—ver the earth
And gross dark—ness the people
And gross dark—ness the people

NETTIE PLODS EAST. In the ditch by the road snow reaches almost to her knees. She holds the box above her head, the cover slips off, the tissue paper slides out, the sleeves of the dress hang over the edge of the box. She can't walk and keep the dress in the box at the same time. This is not working. Go back. Let the dress be safe and warm beneath the bed. The wind picks up the cover and blows it across the drifted snow. She grabs the dress. Let the box go too. It tumbles into the ditch and bumps and turns and flips over and slides away. She is on the road and is heading toward the creamery.

ELI'S ARM is getting tired, his legs sore, his fingers stiff around the smooth baton. The choir strains toward him, watches his eyes, his mouth, his hands, for clues. They lap up his energy, take it into themselves.

> *For un-to us a Child is born, un-to us a Son is giv-en*
> *And the gov-ernment shall be up-on his should—er;*
> *And His Name shall be call-ed*
> *Won—der—ful, Coun—sell—or...*

The sound of their voices soaks into the air and into the walls and windows, pews and floors, and there's no space anywhere without the song.

There's a small rustling in the audience. The concert is longer than people are used to. Bud Olson slips out the door to check on the furnace downstairs. Mrs. Peterson follows with her small son who needs to use the toilet. Eva Skretting from the Red and White Store fans her cheeks with the edge of her hand.

NETTIE has reached the creamery. She stops at the foot of the hill, lifts her face to the lights of town. And she remembers – the creamery, the hill, the crossroads at the top. And then what? What else will she find up there? Her chest tightens. She's come this far. Oh, Mama, look at me now.

HILDA MUNSON, on the middle riser, is looking down at Eli, waiting for his cue. She's counting to herself, doing her breathing as Eli has taught her. Lift the voice, Hilda. Put both hands beneath your voice and lift it up. And keep the sound clean. I know it's beautiful and so touching, but try not to waver, keep it straight and simple, let the purity shine through. He nods his head and flicks the baton, and when the words come out of Hilda's mouth they are just that: clear and smooth and delicate.

> *He shall feed His flock like a shep–herd,*
> *And He–shall ga–ther the lambs with His arm, with*
> *His arm,*
> *And car–ry–them–in His bo–som.*

So Hilda got Grace's solo. How did that come about? the people wonder. Christine looks down at the front pew to check on Peter. But Peter isn't moving. He's quiet, listening to Hilda's song. Jonathan scans the audience. Hilda's husband isn't there. You could have come, Sam, he thinks. It wouldn't have killed you.

NETTIE IS HALFWAY up the hill. She's walking on the edge of the road where it's not slippery. She walks carefully, sinking her feet into small ridges of snow. The dress hangs on her arm, and she holds her arm against her chest, and the dress moves slightly from side to side as she climbs.

NOW THE CHOIR HAS SPEEDED UP. The lines are coming fast. "Jerky," Peter whispers. "They're getting too jerky." Eli's stick is alive. It looks threatening, angry.

> *All we like sheep have gone a–stray*
> *We have turn——ed ev-'ry one to his own way,*
> *We have turn——ed ev-'ry one to his own way*

Why do they sing the same line over and over, Elizabeth wonders. We have turned, we have turned, we have turned, we have turned....

NETTIE HAS REACHED the top of the hill. She's standing in front of the Golden West Hotel. So this is where he soused himself with Sigurd Anderson. She passes the post office, the United Church, Gilman's, the town hall. She turns right, crosses the street and keeps going. She could find the way with her eyes closed. Vy did God create man? Watery-eyed Swede, freckled hands, old breath. Then she sees the cars. Cars on the street and in the vacant lot, even some in the field north of the church. She doesn't remember this. So many cars. She pulls her coat collar closer to her face and walks head down on the shovelled sidewalk to St. John's.

ELI'S BACK ACHES. His face is red and wet. The white shirt under the black coat is soaked. Can he finish this? His arm is lead. He punches the air. Give it more. More.

> *Lift up your heads, O ye gates,*
> *And be ye lift up, ye ev-er-last-ing doors*
> *And the King of Glo-ry shall come in.*

AND NOW SHE'S STANDING on the bottom step of the church. The caragana bush is over there, the iron railing is here, the wooden door is up there, the big handles are on the door. She hears the music from inside the church. And under the music, old voices. Maybe they go to Regina, to Hudson's Bay or Eatons, maybe to New York. Or Paris, France. She untangles the dress that has been scrunched in her hand, lifts it up so she can see it. The dots are there, the collar's there, the lace is there. She holds the dress in her left hand and grabs the iron railing with her right, fingers curled tightly around it. She better get inside right now. They don't like it when you're late.

SIGURD ANDERSON'S ADAM'S APPLE rises and falls with the words. He sees from Eli's face that it's going fine, and he lifts his voice louder still.

Un-to which of the an-gels said He at a-ny time
Thou art My Son, this day have I be-got-ten Thee?

AND NETTIE SAYS, "Just go. One more step. Put your hand on that handle, there's a space underneath it for your fingers, they've made it easy for you. So go on up there and pull."

CHRISTINE LUND lifts her head, tilts her score slightly so she can see the notes and Eli at the same time. Peter pokes Andrew with his elbow and whispers, "It's her turn now, wake up," and Andrew raises his head from his chest for a moment. Then Peter reaches across his brother and shakes his sister's arm. Elizabeth opens her eyes ever so slightly, a thin line that won't let in the harsh light.

How beau-ti-ful are the feet of them
That preach the gos-pel of peace,
How beau-ti-ful are the feet,
How beau-ti-ful are the feet...

NO. IT'S TOO MUCH. What would she do in a place like this? Nettie turns and hurries down the steps, clutching the dress. When she reaches the bottom she walks around the caragana bush to the yard at the side. She stands away from the building and looks up at the lit windows. Sees shadows of heads but can't tell who they are. Moves farther. Wades through mounds of snow, then stops again. There in the window, that little window right there above the lilac bush, she sees it moving, the small thin stick, a narrow shadow against the frosted glass. Up and down and straight across it goes. And she laughs. Isn't he having fun tonight. Well, let him. And she won't have to go inside after all. She can hear enough thumping from where she is. She pushes through the snow to the spruce tree in the middle of the yard.

LET US BREAK *their bonds a–sunder,*
Let us break their bonds a–sunder
Let us break their bonds a–sunder...

The choir is shouting. To Bud Olson and Carl Jacobson and Eva Skretting from the Red and White and Mrs. Donnelly and the Mennonites and Beverly Ross and Peter Lund and Mrs. Sorenson...

Let us break their bonds a–sunder,
Let us break their bonds a–sunder...

NETTIE STANDS beside the tree and wonders. It comes so slow. It comes from far away in the dark, in wide circles in the night. It's never in a hurry, and that's how it is. It takes a long time to get the picture. She watches the stick in the window, whizzing this way and that. And she calls out.

"I'm here, Eli. I came. A thousand miles. And it wasn't

easy." She steps away from the tree. "*Oh, come, come, come, come.* That's what I did, all right."

She looks at the church window to where the thin stick moves dimly against the glass.

"I know something too," she says. "It's a new thing." She spreads her feet apart, lifts up her head, stretches her neck, and opens her mouth wide.

"B-i-r-d. Bird! Did you hear that?"

She waves the dress in the air, back and forth and up and down, flapping.

"Sparrow, robin, magpie, owl..."

The stick in the window dips, rises, swings out wide, crashes down, then up again, and higher, cutting the air, carving through.

Hal–le-lu-jah, hal-le-lu-jah, hal-le-lu-jah, hal-le-lu-jah
Ha——le——lu——jah!

And Nettie shouts, "Crow. C-r-o-w. Duck. D-u-c-k. Loon. L-o-o-n." And the sound of her voice speeds through night, past clouds and stars, to where the white birds hover. And others gather. Blackbird, hawk, thrush, and meadowlark. Singing around the golden chair where her angel mother in her pale blue dress plucks the strings of her silver harp.

THE AIR IS MILDER NOW, the snow thicker. Nettie stands by the spruce tree and watches the flakes. She sees them whirling crazy against the steeple, bouncing on the slanted roof, falling on the lilac bush, tangling the branches. She watches them high above the evergreen, spinning dizzy in the purple blackness. And there, over there on the church windows, look, thin beaded streamers, glittering.

SHE SHAKES THE SNOWFLAKES from her dress and arranges the dress carefully over her arm. "I'll stand right here and wait until it's over. Then I'll look for him. The snow will be deep at the foot of the hill. The hill will be icy. And the sky so dark. We might as well walk together. There's nothing wrong with that."

Mother's Day

MOTHER'S DAY WAS ON MAY 9 THAT YEAR. On May 6 we had the blizzard and school was closed. On May 7 I was sick. I was sick until May 8, so I missed two days of school: May 6, the day of the blizzard, and May 7, the day I was sick. (May 8 was a Saturday, so there was no school that day anyway.) On Mother's Day I found the cat. And on Monday, May 10, everything was back to normal.

I will begin with May 6, because that is the first day of all the days. I suppose I could even start with the night before, since I heard later that the blizzard commenced in all its fury around 11 p.m. I, of course, was sleeping at that time and knew nothing of it. But people talked about it for days and weeks and months afterward, so naturally I have quite a clear picture of how it all began.

It began with the wind. Even before I went to bed

that night it was blowing. The snow had melted early that year, before the end of March, and although fields in the country were still wet and patched with dirty snow, the streets in town were dry and dusty. Every day we walked to school in whorls of dust and rolling thistles. Saskatchewan, as you know, is one of the three prairie provinces, and spring on the prairie is a dry and dusty scene indeed.

It is unlike spring in areas further south, such as the Southern States in the United States. I've read about spring in these places and seen pictures of it. In Kentucky, for instance, spring is calm and colourful and it lasts longer. In Kentucky there's more foliage: japonica, forsythia, dogwood. All these plants have lovely blooms and the blooms don't develop at the same rate. Thus the colours spread out over a longer period of time. My father subscribes to the *National Geographic*.

In Saskatchewan, however, spring is bare. And if I may speak candidly, it is quite lonesome. The lonesome period is between the time the snow melts and the time the grass turns green. (Weeds, I should say, since we don't have much grass.) The lonesome period is the dry time when the ground is grey, trees (what few there are) are bare, and rubbish, buried for months under snow, is fully exposed. The lonesome period is usually filled with wind that picks up the dust, dead thistles, mouldy scraps of paper, and whirls them across the alleys and down the streets, with no thought whatsoever to what pleases us.

I was lying in bed when I heard the wind. It rattled the windows, whistled in the chimney. It grew stronger, howling about the house like a great enemy who hated us personally and our home too, down to its very foundation. That's the feeling I got, that it really was an enemy and wanted to rip us right off the ground we'd settled on.

I got out of bed and went downstairs to see how my mother and father were taking it. But they were sitting in the living room, reading, and didn't seem at all disturbed. My mother looked at me, her face shining under the rosy lampshade, and said it was all right, nothing to worry about. "Crawl back to bed, Norma," she said in a voice that was kinder than usual. So I did, and went to sleep finally, wondering why there was such a thing as wind. Nobody likes it that I know of. No prairie people anyway. And why had God created it?

I do not question the existence of God, as my friend Mary Sorenson does, whose father runs the Co-Op Creamery here in town and who is an atheist. I can't deny what's right there in front of my eyes in black and white. But at the same time I don't condemn unbelievers. "Judge not, lest ye be judged," the Scripture says. Nor do I try to convince them. Arguments lead to nowhere. If you tell a blind man the sun is yellow and he doesn't believe you, what can you do about it? Nothing. Nevertheless, although my faith is firm, I wonder sometimes why certain things happen. Like the wind.

In the morning the sky was a whirl of grey and white. The snow was thicker than I'd ever seen it, and the wind still blowing, whining through the snow. I couldn't see the fence or garage from my bedroom window. Every inch of air was disrupted, uprooted, the snowflakes swirling about. Like refugees, I thought as I knelt in front of the window in amazement. Like lonely refugees without homes, wandering in the cold, looking for a place to settle, a quiet place where they could put their babies to bed and have some hot tea and visit one another for awhile. But they couldn't find such a place, so they wandered all in a frenzy, cold and lonesome.

I went downstairs in my pyjamas. There'd be no school, that I knew. My father was sitting in the dining room at his desk. He was playing chess, like he does on Sunday mornings and stormy days when he can't work. He plays chess by correspondence since he has no partners here in town. You may have heard of chess played like this. A huge map of the world is tacked on the wall in front of his desk. On the desk itself is a wooden chessboard, and on a table next to it, little recipe boxes filled with postcards. These cards have been sent to him from his playing partners all over the world. He even plays with one man in South Africa, and he has several games going on at the same time. Every time a player makes a move, he sends the move by postcard to my father. Then my father makes his move and sends a card back to the player. Sometimes it takes nearly a month for a card to reach another country, so you can imagine how long one game might last. But my father seems to enjoy this, keeping track of all his partners with little coloured pins on his map of the world.

My father is a very intelligent man, I must say, but he is not a man of faith. He does not attend church with me and my mother, not even on special occasions. Even my mother doesn't attend regularly. Most of the time it's left up to me to uphold the family in spiritual matters.

My mother was in the kitchen, sitting at the table, drinking coffee and gazing out the window at the blizzard. She was leaning over the table, resting her elbows on the white tablecloth, holding the cup in both hands. Steam curled upward from the cup's brim. The whole room smelled of coffee.

She didn't even notice me come in, or stand there watching. On very snowy days or rainy days my mother abandons all her housewifely responsibilities and sits in front of the window all day, just looking out. We may as well forget about good dinners or a clean and tidy house on such days. She's completely engrossed by storms. In some respects my mother is a bit lazy. Nevertheless, I find her an interesting person. In this day and age it's important to observe nature and meditate on all its wonders.

"That's some storm," I said.

"There'll be no school today," she said.

"I guess not," I said.

I went to the breadbox and sliced two pieces from a loaf. I brought out the butter and jam. I knew she was not about to make any breakfast, so I'd do it myself.

I sat down at the table to eat my bread and watch the storm with my mother. I have a very good feeling about that day, nothing at all like the days that followed. The blizzard was howling outside. The snow was so high no one even tried to get out, and the air so thick we couldn't see beyond the porch. But the house was warm, and my mother was enjoying her coffee and my father his chess. Every so often he would leave his game and come into the kitchen to drink coffee with my mother. I knew they were both having a good day. As the Catechism says: "Let husbands and wives love and respect each other."

Later, in the afternoon, the storm ended. The wind ceased, the sky cleared, the sun shone. And everyone in town shovelled themselves out of their houses. I put on my boots and my new blue parka and walked downtown between the drifts, clean and sparkling in the sun. I went to see my friend, Esther. She was helping her father in the store, straightening tin cans of soup and dusting jars of pickles. We talked about the storm and what we should do for our mothers on Mother's Day. She thought she'd buy her mother a box of chocolates. I said I'd have to wait till Saturday to decide, when I'd have some money. Then I went home. And that night I got sick.

I woke up in the middle of the night. My head was hot, my chest ached, and my throat was sore. I felt damp all over and weak. I crouched under the blanket, shivering with cold and sweating. Then I got up. I turned on the hall light and walked down the corridor to my mother and father's bedroom. I opened the door and saw them in the light from the hall. They were both sound asleep. My father was lying on his right side with his knees up. My mother was lying on her right side too, with her knees up. She was lying right next to my father, her stomach against his back and her legs fitting into his, fitting right into them like a piece of a jigsaw puzzle. I walked over to the bed and stood there. I touched her on her hair, but she didn't move. I touched her on the cheek and she twitched a little. Then she opened her eyes and looked at me.

"I'm sick," I said and walked out of the room and back to bed. In a minute she was in my room, leaning over me in the dimness.

"Norma? Did you say you were sick?"

"Yes."

"Where?"

"All over."

"Here?" She touched my forehead.

"Yes."

"Here?" She touched my neck.

"Yes."

She turned on the lights. She looked at my face and neck. She felt the sheets and pillow. They were damp.

"You are sick," she said.

"I know."

She walked down the hall to the bathroom and came back with a glass of water, a washcoth, and a bottle of aspirins. She gave me an aspirin and the water. Then she washed my face with a cold wet cloth, and my neck too. She covered me up and brought in an extra blanket.

"You'll be all right," she said. "Try to get some rest."

I didn't say anything. I just turned over on my side and went back to sleep.

In the morning I was still sick. My chest was sore and my head ached. My arms and legs felt damp and heavy. My mother came in again and looked at me.

"I'll make a mustard plaster," she said.

My mother is not an ignorant woman by any means, but she is not a woman of science. She does not read up on the latest developments in medicine as my father does, even though he's only a telephone man. She prefers remedies handed down by her mother and grandmother and even great-grandmother for all I know. Mustard plaster is a case in point. If you're unfamiliar with that remedy, this is how it works: You make a paste of water, flour, and powdered mustard. I'm not sure of the proportions, but don't use too much mustard – it burns. You spread this yellow paste on a piece of cloth cut out to fit the chest it's going on. Then you lay another cloth over it and pin the edges together. You put this on the chest right next to the skin, and it's supposed to do some good – I'm not sure what, except warm your chest considerably and make you sweat.

She came upstairs carrying the mustard plaster, holding it in her two hands like a rolled-out sheet of dough. When I saw it I began feeling embarrassed and wished like everything I hadn't gotten sick. I was eleven years old at the time, nearly twelve, and I was beginning to develop. I was the only one in my class beginning to show. Ever so slightly I know, but even so I wasn't fond of the idea that someone would see me, even my mother.

"I think I'm feeling better, better than last night," I said. "I don't believe I'll be needing the mustard plaster."

"You'll be up and on your feet in no time with a good strong mustard plaster," she said. She laid the bulging cloth on a chair and lifted the quilt from under my chin, and the sheet too. She unbuttoned my pyjama top slowly and gently, and I felt myself getting more and more embarrassed. She spread out the fronts of my pyjama top; then she lifted the mustard plaster from the chair and laid it on my chest, tucking it under my neck and partway into my armpits and down to my stomach. She pressed her fingers on it ever so gently and I felt the pressing on the soft places on my chest where I'd begun to develop. I stared at the ceiling and didn't say anything. Neither did she. It seemed as if she didn't even notice, but she must have. I don't see how she could have missed. She buttoned my pyjamas again and covered me with the sheet and quilt.

"Have a nice time in bed today," she said. "I'll bring you some magazines to read and some juice."

Maybe it doesn't make much sense to you how I felt about such things at the time. I certainly don't feel embarrassed now. But now I'm thirteen and in grade seven and I'm fully developed. My mother has explained everything to me, about my body and sexual things. So now I understand all that. I have no problems in that line. However, when I was eleven and just starting to develop, I felt quite peculiar about it. I didn't want anyone to know. When I was alone I'd sometimes look at myself in the mirror, without my clothes on. Then I'd put on a T-shirt or a sweater to see if I showed. I never wore T-shirts to school though. I certainly didn't want everyone gawking. I'd leave the T-shirts to the grade nine girls, Rosie Boychuck and her group. They seemed to enjoy letting the whole world know they were developing.

Anyway, I had a fairly pleasant morning after that,

looking at *National Geographic*s and at the icicles melting outside my window, falling asleep and waking up and drinking juice. If you're not in pain it can be quite enjoyable sometimes being sick.

Then, in the afternoon, it happened. I can't understand to this day how my mother could have done that to me. But she did. She came upstairs in the afternoon, when the sun was warm on my bed, and said she would change my mustard plaster. She'd make a fresh batch and after that I'd be finished. She pulled down the quilt and sheet, unbuttoned my pyjamas, and lifted the cloth from my chest. My chest felt icy cold, and bare. I pulled my pyjama top together quickly without buttoning it and snuggled under the covers. My mother left the room carrying the used mustard plaster, folded like a book, in her hand. I heard her walk down the stairs into the kitchen. I heard the cupboard door opening and some pots banging. I heard her chatting away to my father about nothing in particular. And I thought no more about it until I opened my eyes and saw him standing in the doorway. My father. My father holding the fresh mustard plaster. My father coming to put the new mustard plaster on my chest. I looked at him and felt my face getting hot and my heart beating faster. Was he actually going to do it? Open my pyjama top and see me? And press that bulging cloth against my chest? Had my mother sent him up for that? I felt my eyes sting and I knew I was going to cry. I felt the wetness press against my eyeballs and drip over the edges of my eyes down the side of my head, into my hair. I couldn't say anything. I just lay there and cried.

"You're not feeling well at all, are you," he said "It's no treat being sick. But maybe this will do the trick."

He lifted up the quilt and sheet. He spread open my pyjama top. He looked down on my chest. I looked up at his face and saw his eyes open a little wider, and I knew he saw my development. It was pretty clear to me that he saw.

He laid the cloth on me, smoothly and firmly, and his hands were heavy on the roundness there. Then he buttoned my pyjamas and covered me with the sheet. He wiped my eyes with the edge of the sheet and told me I'd be better soon and not to cry and mother was cooking vegetable soup with dumplings for supper.

In the evening I felt better, and on Saturday I was fine except that I had to stay inside all day and couldn't go downtown to buy a Mother's Day present. My mother told me not to feel bad; if I stayed inside and got completely well by Sunday we could go to church together, to the special service.

On Mother's Day I got up early. I washed my face and combed my hair. I put on my green dress with the long sleeves and white cuffs and went downstairs to make breakfast for my mother and father. I set the table with the blue placemats Aunt Hanna had sent from Sweden. I boiled eggs and made cinnamon toast because that's what I'm best at. My parents were pleased with the breakfast.

After breakfast my father went to his desk to play chess with someone in India or Yugoslavia. And my mother and I went to church.

I do worry sometimes about my father. His indifference to spiritual matters suggests a certain arrogance. And you must have heard what the Bible has to say about that: "Pride goeth before a fall." Of course, my father is not the only person who feels this way. Many people, at least in our part of the province, have no religious faith whatsoever. Men especially. Men seem to feel that religion is for women and children. And not even for all women. Some women they prefer without any religious faith at all. So they can have fun, if you know what I mean. But if a woman has children and has to take care of things, if a woman is responsible, if she has men and children to take care of, then she should have faith. That's what they think. Well, this kind of argument holds no water whatsoever, as far as I'm concerned.

We walked through melting snow to church, our rubber boots black and shining in the slush. When we got inside, Mrs. Franklin and Mrs. Johnson met us at the door and gave us each a carnation, a pink one for me because my mother was alive, and a white one for my mother because her mother was dead. She died five years ago. She had sugar diabetes, but it was a heart attack she died from. We pinned the carnations to our coats and walked down the aisle to the middle pew, right behind Mr. and Mrs. Carlson and Leonard, who's one year older than I am, and not very bright.

The text that Sunday was from the Book of Proverbs, written by King Solomon, the wisest man who ever lived, although he had a lot of wives. Mother's Day is the only time we ever hear it: "Who can find a virtuous woman, for her price is far above rubies."

After the sermon we sang a hymn we sing every Mother's Day. My mother says she could do without that song, but I myself feel it has a lot of meaning. We all stood up. Mrs. Carlson sang in her usual voice. Mr. Carlson didn't sing at all, just looked at the words. Leonard turned around and stared at me a couple of times.

Mid pleasures and palaces, though we may roam,
Be it ever so humble, there's no place like home.
A charm from the sky seems to hallow us there,
Which, seek thro' the world, is ne'er met with elsewhere.
Home, home, sweet, sweet home,
There's no place like home,
O, there's no place like home.

THAT AFTERNOON, I found the cat.

I had just come from Mary's house to see what she had done for her mother on Mother's Day. I knew it would be something clever because that's how she is.

The cat was in a ditch when I first saw it. A kitten actually, scratching at a little drift and meowing. It was grey and skinny, its voice thin and unpleasant. I leaned over the ditch, picked it up by the fur of its neck as I'd been taught to do, and set it down on the concrete walk. But it didn't go anywhere. It didn't move. It just stood there by my ankle. I walked away and it followed me, meowing after me in its ugly voice. I didn't know what to do, so I scooped it up with my two hands, laid it on the crook of my arm and took it with me back to Mary's house. I stood in their porch and showed the cat to Mrs. Sorenson. She leaned against the porch wall, against a giant-sized pile of newspapers and magazines, and told me I should take it back where I found it.

"In the ditch?" I asked.

"Wherever you found it," she said. "Its owner will be looking for it."

"In the ditch?" I asked. "Will the owner look in the ditch?"

"It may be diseased," she said. "It's best not to bring it in the house." She spoke kindly but firmly. Mrs. Sorenson is not a cruel person, but she's no lover of cats.

I left Mary's house and went back to ask my mother if we could keep it. She said the same thing as Mrs. Sorenson. "Take it back where you found it."

"I found it in a ditch," I said.

"By whose house?" she asked. "It no doubt belongs to the people who live near the ditch."

"To Sorensons?" I asked. "Mrs. Sorenson can't stand cats."

"Maybe another house," my mother said. "Ask at the other houses. I understand Mrs. Gilbertson has cats. But come home soon," she added. "It's nearly suppertime."

I walked down the street, carrying the shivering kitten in my arms. I began knocking on doors. Everyone said the same thing: "Take it back where you found it." And I said the same thing too. "I found it in a ditch." Then they said maybe Mrs. So and So would like to have it. And I'd knock on a few more doors.

The last door I knocked on was Mrs. McDonald's.

Mrs. McDonald had always seemed like a very friendly person to me. Whenever she saw me she'd ask about my parents. "How are the Hagens?" she'd say. She always called them the Hagens. "You Hagens are good people." So I thought this might be my lucky chance. Maybe Mrs. McDonald would take the kitten.

"Me?" she said, standing under the light in her front hall, rubbing her thin hands on the pockets of her apron. "Oh, no, honey, I couldn't possibly, as much as I'd like to, not with my allergy. But aren't you a precious one for caring so. Aren't you just the sweetest little girl, looking out for that poor animal. You are the kindest little thing," she said. I thought she'd said enough, but she went on and on. I stood in the doorway and listened to every word. "You're going to make a very good little mother," she said. "Just the best mother ever. Look at you with that poor thing. What a sweet little mother you are." I believe she finished right then because she started closing the door, quite firmly, easing me out on the step, still holding the limp and whining cat.

What happened next is what I'm trying to figure out. I've spent two years now trying to figure this out, but I'm not sure I understand, even now.

I didn't know what to do with the kitten, so I headed out of town on the dirt road that leads to Goertzens'. It was getting dark and windy and much colder, so I shoved the kitten under my jacket to keep it warm, and I pulled the sleeves of the jacket over my hands to keep them warm. I felt the cat under the cloth, pressing against my chest, its claws pushing back and forth into the softness there. I bent my head against the wind and stumbled through the ruts, my boots oozing down into the half-frozen mud. I didn't know where I was going, just leaving town with that ugly kitten pushing on my chest, nibbling at me, purring and pressing against me as if I were its home, as if I were the place where it belonged.

When I passed the correction line I looked back and saw the town lit up behind me, all the houses behind me with orange light shining out of the windows. I turned and saw the blackness ahead of me, the night dark and empty as a cave. I tried walking faster through the mud, the cat still clinging to the softness on my chest. Then I realized I wasn't going anywhere. There was no place to go. Only Goertzens', and that was too far – five miles at least.

I stopped. I stood in the middle of the road and pulled the cat out from under my jacket. I held it up by the fur of its neck, looked at it by the light of the stars and the snow that shone in the ditch. I saw its eyes glimmering, its small kitten eyes looking at me.

"You ugly cat," I said. "You stupid cat." Its eyes gleamed. "You don't know anything, do you. Not your father or your mother or even where you come from. You are so stupid." And I hated the cat. I hated its thin voice and its loose sickly body. I hated its sticky fur and thin bones under the fur. But most of all, I hated it dangling there alone, under the stars, watching me, waiting.

That's when I did it. I grabbed its tail and lifted the cat above my head. I swung it in circles high above my head. I swung it faster in big circles. Then I let go, and I saw its body, tangled and crooked, flip through the air and land in the ditch. I stepped in closer and looked at it – a small stain on the snow. I bent down and scraped at some stones on the road. I scraped with both hands until I found a big stone. And I lifted it up and hurled it down on the cat. Then I lifted up another and smashed it down. And the cat sank a little in the drift. And there was blood on the snow. When I'd thrown all the stones, I turned around and headed back to town.

I saw the lights of town in the distance, the orange lights from all the houses. I used to like going home after dark and seeing those lights. In winter, when it was dark at four o'clock, I'd walk home from school and look at the houses with light shining out of the windows. I'd think of children and fathers going home in the dark. And when they got there, the house would be warm, the supper cooking, and the mother setting the table and humming. But that night, walking into town, it wasn't like that.

When I got home my parents had already eaten supper and were sitting at the kitchen table drinking coffee.

"You've been gone a long time," my father said. "Did you find a home for the kitten?"

"Yes," I said.

"Oh? Where?" my mother asked.

"Some Ukrainians took it," I said.

"You mean you walked all the way past the tracks?"

"Only as far as Levinskys'," I said.

"Did Mrs. Levinsky take it then?"

"No," I said. "But Mrs. Levinsky said she knew some Ukrainians who live on the other side of the Hutterites. She said they'd take it because they have a huge barn and a lot of other cats and fresh milk and hay, so the cat would be warm and comfortable and have friends. Mrs. Levinsky will take it there tomorrow."

"That was kind of Mrs. Levinsky," my father said.

"I thought so," I said and went upstairs to the bathroom to wash my hands for supper.

I didn't think about my experience that night. I was too tired. I went to bed early and fell asleep right away. But since then it's been on my mind. I've thought about it for two years now – what I did, and the orange lights. And I've wondered how I could have done that. And how there's no getting away from that. And how do you go on from there? What do you do next if you're a person of faith?

I know what the Buddhists would do. I've read about Buddhists in the encyclopedia. They think that if you know you'll do wrong by going places and doing things, then just don't go there. Stay where you are. Sit. Then you won't sin.

But I'm not a Buddhist. I think it's more like this. You go to places, knowing all along it won't be just right or true. There'll be darkness there, and some damage. But you go just the same. There'll always be some light. Pieces of it anyway. And you can notice that.

On Monday I went to school as usual. At recess I met Esther at our special place by the poplar tree and we talked about Mother's Day. I told her I made breakfast and went to church with my mother. She told me her mother liked the box of chocolates and they spent the day at Cutlers'. Her family doesn't go to church because they're Jews, not to synagogue either because there aren't enough Jews in our town to have one. They do celebrate festive occasions in their homes, however. Like the Passover. And Mother's Day. At least they do in our town. I don't know if they have a Mother's Day in Israel or not. I know in Japan there's no special day set aside for mothers. Instead they have a Boys' Day and a Girls' Day. But the Scandinavian countries celebrate much the same as we do, at least in Norway, with flowers and gifts. I'm not sure what the customs are in Africa or South America.

But one thing I do know. And no one can argue against this fact, whether they're Communists, Christians, Buddhists, or Jews. There's no nation in the whole world, not a single solitary one, without mothers.

Memorial

WHEN DOCTOR LONG DIED, WHEN HE was cleaned up and laid down on white ruffles of satin and the news was spread abroad throughout the county, Jacob Ross, fifth grade teacher, decided his students should add their tribute to the many tributes already delivered to Louie's new furniture store and undertaking parlour, where the old doctor lay in black suit, white shirt, and white bow tie.

He presented his plan in this way: "Doctor Long, as you know, was a doctor in this town long before you were born, even before some of your parents were born." Here he rose from his swivel chair, slid his thin grey-suited body around the heavy wooden desk, and sat on the desk's front edge, leaning forward in the manner of one sharing intimately with a precious and chosen group.

It was Monday morning. A yellow glow from the

June sun had, in a most remarkable way, penetrated the glass of the school's tall windows, had come right through the glass and was now spreading itself inside the room, surrounding the objects there: the pencil sharpener attached by silver screws to the window ledge, the ledge itself, grey and slivered, the round globe hanging in the corner, a small blue world suspended from the ceiling by a frayed and faded rope.

And the light surrounded the wooden desks and the people in the desks: Label Cutler, fat, restless, smelling of garlic, ginger, tobacco, smells of his father's house; Norma Hagen, clean and tidy in a blue skirt and starched white blouse; Annie Pilcher in a stained and faded green dress, smelling of stained rooms, old and acrid; Freddie Wong, thin, solemn, smelling of Saturday morning in his father's café. The light encircled them all as they sat quietly listening to Mr. Ross.

"You know in his last years Doc Long had his problems. We all know what those problems were, what *the* problem was..." Here they looked away slightly, changing their focus from Mr. Ross's eyes to his grey jacket, his tie, or the blackboard just behind his head. They had heard their parents some mornings talking at the kitchen table, or sometimes in the living room after the day's work was done, talking about Doc Long and his wife Nora as well.

"I don't understand it," a mother would say. "Here's an educated man, not like us, been to university, medical school, a brilliant man...."

"Brains don't always have much to do with it," her husband would say.

Another would say, "I don't know how Nora puts up with it and least of all why, him staggering around the way he does and his skin that awful yellow. Especially when she herself is so...just so..." The woman could have finished with any number of easy words: respectable, dignified, loyal, and certainly a wonderful gardener. But none of these words, by themselves at least, was exactly right. And none would impress her husband who, in all likelihood, would answer without looking up from his paper, "Maybe a man needs something more than that."

And they themselves, sitting in their tidy rows, had witnessed the problem. All of them at one time or another had seen Doc Long, stooped and thin, shuffle down the hill to Sigurd Anderson's small house next to the old livery barn, or walk the long road to the Golden West Hotel to drink whisky with Sigurd or Aleck or others of his drinking pals and later, under cold and distant stars, stumble back the way he'd come, home to Nora.

They had seen him. But they'd never heard him speak, although they knew he used to sing. Only Norma Hagen and Freddie Wong of all the fifth graders could actually remember ever hearing Doctor Long talk. Freddie would never mention it. Norma would only to Mary, her best friend, and much later to Label Cutler, when they both came back to Stone Creek from university and were sitting in Wong's café having coffee. Label, whom she never did marry because of the differences in their religion.

Ross continued. "Drink is a sickness that affects

many – not only the down and out, not only the transients and derelicts we see outside the Golden West Hotel, not only the Sigurd Andersons of the world...." They could sense their teacher warming up to his subject with a rhythm and passion he displayed when he read them his favourite poem, "Abou Ben Adhem, may his tribe increase!"

"It is," he continued, "a disease that can cripple people with the best education and training. However," here he rose from the desk and stood in front of it, his arms folded on his chest, "we cannot let his misfortune blind us to all those acts of mercy that have benefited so many of us in our town."

They wondered what sort of mercy Doc Long had shown to Jacob Ross in particular, since to their knowledge Ross had never been sick a day in his life. But perhaps it was to his daughter Beverley that he alluded. Beverley with the bad stomach. Pale, sad Beverley Ross, who had to turn somersaults on the living-room floor before she could pass gas. Poor thin Beverley, who stayed home most of the time, lying on the davenport under an orange afghan, cutting out pictures from magazines, getting up regularly to roll on the floor and, on her good days, passing gas.

Or maybe he was thinking of someone else. Lars Homstol, perhaps, who sawed his leg to the bone while trimming a poplar tree in his front yard, and the doctor had to sew the leg back together, right in Homstol's kitchen, with blood everywhere. Or when Vera Campbell got Scarlet Fever and no one else would go anywhere near Campbell's house. Or the time the hockey team all got drunk and had the big fight behind Wong's Café, and the doctor had to stitch them up.

The students sat back in their desks. Sunlight fell on their heads and shoulders and on their arms resting on the desktops. Warm and persistent, as tenacious as grace, it followed each particle of dust in its agitated journey throughout the room.

"So," continued Mr. Ross, "shall we too, all of us in this room, express our own gratitude in some way?" Here he sat again on the desktop, raised his right knee and held it between clasped hands, letting a neatly shod foot dangle there in front of the class. "What do you think? A memorial of some kind? A gift? An expression of sympathy?"

No one answered.

"After all, most of you in this room came into the world with the help of Doctor Long. You know that, don't you?"

Mike Donnelly in the back row turned his head ever so slightly toward Douglas Foster, raised his eyebrows, and leered.

Mr. Ross unclasped his hands, letting his knee drop. He leaned toward the class, more intent now.

"How many of you knew that?"

Elizabeth raised her hand. "Mr. Ross?"

"Yes, Elizabeth?"

"I moved to Stone Creek when I was one. I was born in United States."

"Yes, Elizabeth, that's true. For you and maybe for some others too. But even so..." He stood up and walked toward the window side of the room. He stared at the blue world hanging in the corner. "But even so," he repeated, "haven't your families at some time or another received some medical aid, some healing, if not your own immediate family, then the families of relatives or friends?"

No one could deny that. Nearly everyone in Stone Creek was either a relative or a friend.

Mary Sorenson raised her hand.

"Yes, Mary?"

"I think it would be a good idea to express our gratitude to Doctor Long with a memorial gift."

She was sorry she had to say it. If any of the others would ever speak up she wouldn't always have to. But they were so backward sometimes, and thoughtless. Didn't they see his predicament? Couldn't they sense his feelings? Why did they just sit there? She knew what they'd say about her later, Mike and the rest: "Oh, look at Mary. Wants to give a memorial for Doc Long. Thinks it would be such a nice thing to do. She always does such *nice* things. Going to Ross's every Saturday to stay with Beverley. Playing Chinese Checkers with Beverley Ross and waiting for her to fart." So let them say it. Let Mike and Label and Douglas say what they wanted. She could care less.

"Well, then, we've heard one opinion. What do the rest of you think? Do you agree? Shall we vote on it? How many of you think it would be a good idea to give a memorial gift?"

Vera's hand went up. And Elizabeth's, and Label Cutler's. Then the other hands rose in the air.

It was decided.

THE WOMEN of the United Church held their June meeting the day before Doctor Long's funeral. The funeral was to be held from that church since Mrs. Long was a regular worshipper there. The grade five memorial was discussed at this meeting by the fourteen women who sat on wooden folding chairs in the church basement, waiting for tea and cake. Mrs. Long, of course, did not attend that day.

"Dandelions?" Mrs. Foster said. She glanced at Jane McFarlane, then turned to Mrs. Campbell again. "Is that really what Mr. Ross plans to do?"

"That's what Vera told me," Mrs. Campbell said. "She said the plan was to cut a gunny sack down one side and across the bottom, spread it out, and then poke a dandelion stem into each of the little holes in the sack."

"Every hole?" Mrs. Foster asked.

"Maybe not in every hole. Maybe every three or four holes, just so the heads of the dandelions lie flat on top of the burlap," Mrs. Campbell explained.

"That is going to be the fifth grade memorial?" asked Mrs. Foster again.

"I'm not finished yet," Mrs. Campbell said. "When the sack is covered with dandelions so it looks like a soft yellow carpet," – here she leaned forward in her chair, cheeks flushed, neck pink, "that's how Vera described it, a soft yellow carpet, you know how smooth those petals are, like velvet really – then they plan to use irises, purple irises to form the letters D-O-C in the centre. For Doc of course."

There was a moment of silence. Then Abby

McIntyre asked, "Where would this memorial go?"

"Where? Well up there, at the funeral of course," Mrs. Campbell said, flicking her right hand toward the ceiling.

"I mean where would it be located at the funeral?" Mrs.McIntyre continued.

"That's what I was wondering too," Mrs. Foster said. "Exactly where would it be situated?"

"Well, I suppose with the other flowers," Mrs. Campbell said a bit snappishly.

"It couldn't go on the casket," Mrs. McIntyre said. "Orville's bringing a bouquet from Regina. Those will have to go on the casket."

"I suppose the varnished table in the hall could be brought in." This from Jane McFarlane.

Mrs. Foster stood up. "I think we've forgotten one very important fact."

"What is that, Ellen?"

"Nora Long hates dandelions." She sat down abruptly, then stood right up again. "And yellow is not her favourite colour besides." No one contradicted her.

It was not unusual in late spring in Stone Creek to see Nora Long, even at her age, in denim coveralls with a blue kerchief tied under chin, kneeling in one spot or another of her large yard, digging around clumps of dandelions. Pushing and prying with a small trowel, pulling the long roots out of their deep holes, careful not to break them, and laying the plants, roots and all in heaps about the yard, to be gathered up later in a wheel barrow and dumped into the garbage bin behind the garage.

Nora's yard, everyone agreed, was the finest in Stone Creek. Clumps of lilacs here, a honeysuckle there, maple trees by the front gate; and in wide strips of cultivated, watered, and cleanly weeded earth edging the fence and sidewalk there were flowers. In spring, tulips, hyacinths, irises; and later, pansies, marigolds, petunias, sometimes even gladioli. In a good summer, one with less wind and more rain, it seemed to the people of Stone Creek that there were not as many flowers in the rest of Saskatchewan as there were in Nora Long's garden.

Abbie McIntyre broke the silence. "Ellen's right, of course. Dandelions just won't do."

Mrs. Campbell's neck turned from pink to bright red. "But it's half finished and they've worked so hard."

"Somebody will have to tell them" Abbie said.

Mrs. McFarlane stood up. "I think it's time for tea," she said and disappeared into the kitchen.

AT 4 O'CLOCK, while the women tidied up after their meeting, while thick white cups were arranged in orderly rows on the oilcloth-covered shelves in the church kitchen, the pupils gathered in Ross's backyard to finish the memorial for Doctor Long.

Afternoon sunlight poured down on the fence and woodpile, on wood chips and stones and the new leaves of the lilac bush and lilac buds still closed. It made flickering patterns in the quack grass. Fell recklessly on the six people sitting on the back step of Ross's small white house resting among weeds at the edge of town.

Mary Sorenson and Vera Campbell sat together on the top step, the half-finished carpet of burlap and dandelions spread out on their laps, covering like a warm blanket their bare knees, the tight skin of their knees, the small round bones under the skin.

They leaned over the brown burlap, smoothing the thin yellow petals with their fingers. With one hand, they'd push the stem of a fresh dandelion through a hole in the sack, and with the other under the burlap, pull the stem tight so the flower settled into the mass of other flowers.

When a stem broke before it was secured and the milky juice inside spilled out on their stained fingers, and the air around them smelled green and musky, they would cry, "Oh, no," and Label, sitting next to Freddie Wong on the middle step, would knock his head with his fist and groan, "Not again," and call down to Elizabeth and to Annie Pilcher, sitting on the edge of the little group, to these Label would cry, "Another stem crushed. Pass up the flowers."

And Annie and Elizabeth would reach into one of the pails sitting on the grass to search for blossoms that weren't too crumpled or wilted or brown at the edges, and they'd pass the plants to Label, who'd peel off the leaves and hand the flowers up to Vera.

And all the time Freddie sat quietly beside Label and smiled and looked down on his thin fingers.

At 5:30, when shadows cast by woodpile and fence made grey and rusty patterns in the grass, Douglas Foster and Mike Donnelly scuffed their way up the alley toward Ross's backyard. First they stood in the alley, watching. Then they shuffled toward the wooden gate and stood again, digging the toes of their worn shoes into the dirt. Finally, Douglas flicked the gate open with his slim right hip, and they walked in, through the weeds to the back step. There they stood and watched and scoffed: "Some memorial." They edged closer to the pails; and Mike, glancing at the flower-covered burlap, said, "Well, I guess I can find a better one than any of those." He rummaged through the pails, and he did find a better one. He held up a blazing golden flower, and with a triumphant sneer, tossed it up to Label.

There was a shuffling behind them, a quiet scuffing of shoes on the porch floor. And when they looked up, Beverley Ross was standing just inside the screen door. Pale and thin, she was looking down on them through the mesh of screen and smiling.

No one spoke or moved. Small shadows of bodies lay motionless on the ground. Then Beverley said, in a voice so small it seemed to come from a distant shore, from some ancient land:

"I've brought you doughnuts."

Label and Freddie scrambled down to the others on the grass. Mary and Vera followed, holding the yellow-petaled burlap between them. They laid the sack down on the ground, gently as if it were a baby's blanket, and looked up at Beverley.

Frail as an old woman, she stood on the top step and held out the doughnuts, warm and sugared, heaped high on the tray.

"You can have as many as you want," she said.

She stepped down, holding the tray up but all the while watching her narrow feet in their stiff brown shoes move cautiously over the wood. Shivering, she stood in front of them and held out the tray.

One by one they reached out. Then they sat together on the grass and ate the doughnuts.

"YES, I WOULD LIKE SOME MORE. It's fine tea. Thank you," Mrs. Campbell said.

Mrs. Ross rubbed her left hand against her hip, long fingers sliding over the blue flowers of her dress. She held the teapot in her right. "How nice of you and Abbie to drop by. I'll get more," she said and disappeared into the kitchen.

The two women had come at eight, walking together on the narrow dirt road that led from the centre of town to Ross's house on the west end. They had hesitated before knocking, huddled there on the front step like two chilly birds. Mrs. Campbell had said, "But you'd handle it so well, Abbie," and Abbie McIntyre had replied, "It's you that has a way with words," then lifted her small clenched fist to the flaked and peeling door.

Now the two women sat on the davenport where Beverley had lain before going to bed in her own small room off the kitchen. They sat and looked down on the rose pattern of the linoleum, examining stems and blossoms, gazing at them fondly it seemed, with a certain longing – bright shiny roses in the space behind the radiator, flowers more worn and faded in front of the davenport and rocking chair.

Jacob Ross leaned back in the rocker and crossed his legs. He looked at the two women staring at the roses, and he said, "You've come about the memorial, haven't you?"

Mrs. Campbell's neck turned from light pink to bright red. "The ladies just don't see how it will do," she said, "knowing how Nora feels about gardens and flowers."

Jacob sat forward in the rocker and clasped his fingers over his bony knee.

"I understand," he said.

ON THE MORNING of the funeral Nora Long's brother from Regina drove up to the Stone Creek school, the tires of his Chevrolet crunching gravel. He leaned for a moment against the steering wheel, then turned off the motor, leaving the key in the ignition. He opened the car door, squeezing his heavy, dark-suited body through the opening, then closed the door carefully and walked across the yard to the front steps.

Inside the hallway, he stopped Douglas Foster, who had just come up from the boys' toilet in the basement, where he'd unwrapped his last stick of Juicy Fruit gum, licked off the fresh sugar with his tongue, bitten down on the limp stick with his teeth and chewed as he peed, loud and free in the musty room beneath the stairs.

Nora's brother stopped Douglas and said, "I want to see Mr. Ross."

Douglas gazed for a moment at the strange man, then ran up the stairs to the second floor to get Mr. Ross, who was right then teaching arithmetic.

"Orville," Jacob said, halfway down the stairs.

"Jacob."

"Sorry to hear about Doc."

"Thanks, Jacob. That's what I've come about. I've heard about the plan."

"The memorial."

"Yes, the ladies in the church have talked to me."

"Tell them we've taken care of that. It's all right. We won't be bringing it."

"I really appreciate your thoughtfulness, but those particular plants," (he couldn't say the exact word, it seemed) "she's been at war with those buggers forever.... I've tried to tell her not to be so fussy."

"Please. Don't worry. We won't be going through with that plan."

"Do you have a minute?" Orville asked, a hand on the knob. "Could we talk a minute about this? Maybe there's some way..."

Orville opened the door and the two men moved outside. They sat down on the top step. They sat together under the warm June sun and talked.

THE FUNERAL was to begin at 2 o'clock, but people started to arrive as early as 12:30. By 1:30 the sanctuary was full, and the wooden folding chairs in the basement were being set up.

Jacob Ross had instructed his students to sit in the back pew on the right-hand side of the church so they could all leave together immediately after the Lord's Prayer, to get ready. Jacob himself sat with Mrs. Ross in the pew opposite. Beverley had not come.

The pupils stretched and stared. They wanted a closer look at the casket resting on wooden trestles at the front of the church. The casket was open, but from the back pew they couldn't see anything in it, only a small patch of black. "Probably his sleeve," Douglas whispered. Even when he stood up to get a better view, he could not see Doctor Long himself, his face a yellow grey, sunk in white ruffles at the bottom of the box.

But they also wanted to see who was there. To see if their parents had arrived, if there were strangers, relatives perhaps. To see if Sigurd Anderson had come, or Aleck Majesky, or other of Doc Long's drinking buddies.

But Sigurd wasn't there, or Aleck either. At that moment, in fact, they were raising their glasses inside Sigurd's small house beside the old livery barn.

"To his memory," Sigurd said. "A wonderful man."

"A *very* wonderful man," Aleck said, and emptied his glass.

"A peculiar thing," Sigurd said. He swirled his glass in small circles in front of his face and watched the amber liquid slide around inside. "And sad."

"*Very* sad," Aleck said.

"One minute you're standing in the light of day, your heart just ticking away, tick tick tick..." He rocked the glass from side to side, slowly, like a pendulum.

"Tick tock," Aleck said.

"Then without any warning whatsoever, poof, you're in the bottom of the pit."

"*Very sad,*" Aleck said. "*Very, very peculiar.*"

But everyone else was there, nearly everyone. The Cutlers sat five pews from the front on the left side of the aisle. Mr. Cutler large and prosperous in his pin-striped suit; and beside him, Mrs. Cutler in a purple dress with a strand of pearls resting on her bosom. They had closed their store for the occasion.

Behind them sat Mr. Wong in black pants and white shirt, the first time people had seen him dressed up, the first time in church. He looked neither to left nor right but kept his eyes on the back side of the pew in front of him. He had closed the café for the afternoon. Mrs. Wong, of course, was not there.

One pew held several Ukrainian women in full skirts and scarves. Perhaps they were women who'd had difficulty in childbirth, a baby coming out the wrong way, foot or arm first. And the midwife had sent for Doctor Long, and he'd come.

Even Eric Sorenson was there with his wife, and he never went to any church, not even when his own daughter Mary had a recitation in the Lutheran Sunday School program, or a part in a play.

Of course, all the members of the United Church were there: Campbells, Fosters, and the rest. The Lutheran minister and his wife were also there. And the old musician from south of town.

Annie Pilcher peered over the congregation to see if she could find her own mother, but she couldn't see her. Maybe she was late and had to sit in the basement, Annie thought. But Millie Pilcher was not there.

She had meant to come. After all, it was Doctor Long who, unlike most of the men in town, was not afraid to touch her: to press his hands on her tight belly, stretch her legs apart, look directly into that gaping hole, and pull the weak and sickly thing out of her. And when it was over and the tiny body was put in the shoe-box for burial, the only comfort she'd received, the only consolation had come from him. That was before Annie was born.

"I'll see you at the funeral; I'll be there early," she'd said that morning to Annie, pleased with herself. She'd examined her face in the mirror, combed her hair, then sat down at the kitchen table thinking of how she was going to the United Church to attend the funeral of Doctor Long, and wasn't that a fine thing to do.

But by noon Millie Pilcher was beginning to feel a certain uneasiness inside, a fear of something she knew not what. At 12 o'clock she opened the cupboard door, reached behind the pots and pans, and lifted it out, tall and familiar. She unscrewed the top carefully, laying the cap in the sink, rinsed out a milk-clouded glass, and filled it half full. A little encouragement was all she needed.

When she finished drinking it, she thought again how good it would be to attend the funeral of the old doctor and she poured herself another glass. The room lightened. Golden rays of sun shone through the window. In the sink, dishes caked with old food looked clean and new. Walls were not stained and greasy. Fluffs of dust caught on sticky plaster shone quiet and silver in the light. And she was still young and pretty, really she was, and she would wear the black skirt and white blouse because that would be the most appropriate thing to wear, and Annie would see her and be proud. But first she would have one more glass.

And when Annie would return from the funeral and find her mother sleeping on the floor in front of their bedroom door, she would fix herself a slice of sugar bread, eat it, then step over the snoring woman to enter the small room they shared. Fully dressed, she'd crawl into bed, pull a sour blanket up to her chin, and turn to face the wall papered with faded daisies.

SUDDENLY everyone was standing; the whole congregation was on its feet. Through the church's swinging doors the mourners entered: Nora Long, thin and tall on the arm of her brother, then Nora's daughter from Victoria with her husband, followed by three grandchildren who looked nearly as old as their mother. While they walked down the aisle to the front pew reserved for them, the minister read the Twenty-third Psalm.

And Mary Sorenson thought: It's right for everyone to stand like this when mourners enter. It shows respect and thoughtfulness. She was pleased. That's how it should be, everyone showing respect for one another, especially in time of sorrow.

Louie closed the lid of the casket. He rearranged the spray of gladioli that Orville had brought from Regina, moving it from the foot to the centre of the velvet-covered box, then sat down. On plant stands at either end of the coffin were Boston ferns, one from Mrs. Long's own dining room, one from Mrs. Foster's front porch. The grade five memorial was not there.

Then everyone turned in the hymnal to number 692 and the service began. *Abide with me, fast falls the eventide.*

IN THE NIGHT they would hear her crying, muffled hiccups against her pillow. They would go to her, rub her back, stroke her hair. Beverley would tell them she was sorry, she tried not to cry, but it hurt. And Mrs. Ross would sit with her so Jacob could get some rest; he would have to teach in the morning.

They had taken her first to Shaunavon. "Give her Milk of Magnesia," the doctor there had said. And they did that.

In Swift Current they were told. "It may be a tumour. She should see a specialist."

In Regina the specialist informed them cheerfully that there was no tumour.

"What is it then?" Jacob asked.

"We can't tell for sure. Something she'll probably grow out of."

"But the pain," Ross persisted.

"Try bland food, warm milk, mild exercise. There may be an intermittent blockage somewhere. Is she anxious? Nervous?"

"She's quiet, doesn't like going out, can't take a whole day at school."

"Does she have friends?"

"Occasionally a student comes to visit."

"She should mix more. It would relax her. And try the diet and exercise. Keep the passages clear."

Back in Stone Creek they had followed the specialist's directions. But she was weak and always tired. Raising her arms and bending down to touch her toes wore her out. After two or three efforts she'd fall on the davenport, exhausted.

So early one evening Jacob Ross walked the narrow road to Long's house at the west end of town.

In the front yard Nora was on her hands and knees beside a flower bed, digging out the baby weeds with her trowel: quack grass, thistle, dandelion. He told the woman in coveralls that he wanted to see the doctor, an illness in the family. Nora explained, as she'd done so often, that the doctor no longer practised – he'd stopped five years ago. Jacob told her that he knew that, but this was an emergency, his daughter Beverley, only thirteen years old. Even for emergencies, Nora said, people drove to Shaunavon now, only thirty minutes away. She stood up, holding the trowel.

"Just this once," Jacob said.

"He has no license."

"She's in pain."

"Well, go inside then, Jacob," the woman said. Her voice was gentle.

The living room was dim. Thick vines of ivy covered the windows outside. Only small flecks of sunlight crept in, patterning the walls and ceiling with pieces of amber light. The doctor was sitting in a leather armchair, his head resting against the chair's tall back. The thickness of the chair, the size of its back and arms made the man appear even thinner than he was, a wraith of a man with white hair and beard, white shirt, tweed pants. Nora kept him tidy as much as she could. When he saw Ross he leaned forward to get up, but Jacob stopped him and sat down in the chair opposite. Then he told the doctor everything he could about his daughter.

That evening Mr. Ross and Doctor Long walked

together on the road to Ross's house, the shadows of their bodies stretching out behind them like tall trees.

The doctor looked at her face, her skin. He examined her mouth, touched her hard tight stomach with his fingers. She cried out. He agreed with the specialist – she needed exercise. But she's sick, she can hardly bend, Jacob explained. Then you'll have to help her, the doctor said. He asked for a blanket or quilt, something soft to put on the floor. Mrs. Ross laid a yellow comforter on the linoleum, covering the roses.

He told Beverley to lie on her back and raise her legs in the air. He helped her, holding her thin legs in his hands and pushing them over her head to touch the floor on the other side. Then he told her to turn a somersault. She didn't know how. She couldn't. "Like this," he said and knelt on the quilt beside her. He put his head down, ready to turn over. His legs creaked. "Well? Give me a hand," he said to Ross. And Jacob held the doctor's feet and rolled him over.

"See?" the doctor said, rubbing his neck. "It's not so bad. I'll help you."

Beverley tucked her pyjama top inside the bottoms so no part of her would show and kneeled on the quilt with her head down. Then Doctor Long lifted her legs with one hand, supported her back with the other, and turned her over. He did this again and again until she cried, exhausted.

Then it came. Streams of sour air from her body. Puffs of stagnant gas, coming and coming, filling the room with pungent vapours. Beverley sat up. She stopped crying, touched her stomach, and smiled.

"Good girl," the doctor said. "You did just fine."

THE CONGREGATION SANG, holding firmly to the small black books in their hands. *When other helpers fail and comforts flee...*

FREDDIE WONG awakens to glass shattering, a woman screaming. It's the middle of the night; the café is closed. Robbers, he thinks, and sits up in bed.

Then silence.

Then his mother's long, shrill wailing. And his father, pleading.

Then his name cutting through the darkness, his father's call to come.

He stumbles through the room, across the hallway, down the back stairs to the café. His father is holding her in his arms. She's twisting and crying. The mirror beside the freezer is shattered. An iron pot lies on the floor among shards of glass. He has seen his mother dark and sad before, but not like this.

"The doctor," his father says in Chinese. "Get him."

Freddie runs to the door, then remembering, rushes back upstairs, pulls on his pants and shirt, then down the stairs again, through the café, and out the front door.

Across the road to the town hall, down the sidewalk past the drug store, turn at the United Church, up the narrow road to the doctor's house. His purpose and his fear are one: a ball of steel in the centre of his stomach.

He opens Longs' gate, runs across the yard to the

front step. He rings the bell. Again. Once again, until Mrs. Long appears. When she sees the Chinese boy on the step at midnight, she turns swiftly and goes inside to get the doctor.

Now the boy must walk slowly. Old man and young boy walking together on Main Street, narrow shadows under the street light.

Inside the café his mother is leaning over the table. It looks as if she's vomiting, bent over and jerking her head. Her nightdress is ripped below the waist, a thin leg shows through the tear. His father stands beside her, his face shiny with sweat, his eyes wet and shiny. Neither son nor father speak. They turn to the doctor and look at him.

The doctor moves slowly toward the table where the mother stands. He pulls out a chair, sits down, rests his creased hands on the pink oilcloth. He looks up at the woman, at her eyes filled with some nameless horror. He looks long and carefully. He lifts an empty glass from the table and holds it out to her. Perhaps she will take it, fill it with water, and serve him. Perhaps some sane and homely task will reach her. She takes the glass. She holds it in her hand, examines it, then turns toward the kitchen. Before she reaches the doorway, she sees herself in the cracked and shattered mirror beside the freezer. She sees herself in broken pieces moving toward the kitchen. She lifts the glass in the air and hurls it against the face in the mirror, screaming.

The doctor is up and at her side. He locks her in his arms. He holds her tight, doesn't let go. Screams turn to cries, to sobs, to whimpers. He tells the boy to bring him a glass of water.

Now she calls out words in jerky, muffled Chinese. The strange words sink into the doctor's chest. The father speaks to the doctor for the first time.

"She is saying names of people still in China: mother, father, brother. She is saying names of people who are dead: grandmother, sister, friend."

When Freddie comes with the water, the doctor frees one hand and digs into his pocket. He pulls out a small vial. "Give her one of these with water." The boy coaxes his mother to swallow the pill.

"She wakes in the night," the father says. "Sees wild dogs with tails of dragons, worms as big as snakes with small black eyes. Every night she cries, but tonight she goes crazy."

The doctor covers her head with his hand, feels the coarse black hair, the round bone under the hair. So small a room inside, such little space to hold the terror. He tries to explain to the father: the medicine will not make her well. It will dilute the fear for a time, soften the sharp edge of her despair.

The woman becomes quiet. Dogs stop yelping. The worms close their beady eyes and go to sleep.

THE CONGREGATION has finished the hymn. They've closed their hymnals and sat down. *Help of the helpless, oh, abide with me.*

LAST YEAR the Explorers held their Halloween party in the United Church basement. Members could bring friends, so everyone in school was there: Pentecostals, Jews, Lutherans, Ukrainians, even Ivan Lippoway, whose grandfather was a Communist. They'd decorated the basement after school: covered light bulbs with orange and black crepe paper, pasted black cats and white skulls to the walls, hung apples from the ceiling with a string. The church kitchen was transformed into a haunted house. Blindfolded, the visitors were led through mazes, made to touch the bones and hair, the flesh and blood of the dead – soup bones from the Red and White, brushed twine, tapioca, ketchup. At the refreshment table a witch served poison brew from an iron pot, ladling the purple liquid into thick white cups. The party was a big success.

Vera Campbell was on the cleanup committee and had to stay to the very end. She would take a shortcut home: past the hotel, down the road to the Russian church, and through the churchyard to her own house south of town. She'd avoid the little cemetery on the other side of the church.

It was dark, but just beyond the churchyard was a street light. And above her, a rim of moon hung below the clouds. And it was cold. The frozen ground formed hard ruts and unexpected mounds beneath her. Dead weeds cracked and whined in the wind.

In the centre of the yard she looked up toward the light ahead. And she saw him, walking through the tall grass in her direction. If they both kept walking, their paths would soon meet. She stopped, turned back, stepped into the ditch beside the yard, and crouched down among the frozen weeds, watching.

He was walking slowly, taking tiny steps, swaying

out to one side, then the other, lifting one foot and setting it down, and slowly lifting the other. His arm
would rise, then fall at his side, then rise again, balancing him through the ruts. Would he keep on coming?
Would he see her in the ditch? Or would he walk
straight on, not looking left nor right? He must be on
his way home from Sigurd Anderson's shack. He must
be drunk. She crouched closer to the ground, felt stones
and frozen dirt against her hands. She'd heard what
drunk men did to girls in ditches.

When she looked up again, he'd stopped. He was
standing still under the narrow moon. Then she saw a
shiny arc in front of him, a glowing liquid rim shimmering in the moonlight. It came and came, splashing
down on stiff weeds and frozen earth. Doctor Long peeing in the churchyard. Old Doctor Long holding his
small flesh in his hand and peeing. Vera could smell the
sharp earth wetness.

"Thatta girl, Lindy Lou," he said.

He aimed the stream in a straight line, then in a
small circle, then a bigger one, and bigger still, and the
golden yellow hoops coiled out in front of him. And he
began to sing in a thin, wavering voice.

Will the cir-cle be un-brok-en
By and by-y...by and by-y?
Will the cir-cle be un-brok-en
In the sky-y-y...in the sky.

And then the circle did break. All the shining circles.
And the night was still again. The old man wiggled his

pants shut, leaned into the night, and moved on.

Vera took a deep breath, stood up and rubbed the grass and dirt from her hands. She looked down the road to see if she could still see him. But he'd disappeared. And she turned and walked home.

THE SERVICE WAS OVER: songs, readings, obituary, sermon. And everyone was standing up. "Thy kingdom come," they said, and Jacob Ross and his pupils slipped out quietly through the swinging doors.

The funeral procession, with Louie's new hearse in the lead, began in front of the church. It moved slowly down the road, past Kvemshagens', past Olsons', past Longs' own house, to the school. And in front of the school, the people in their cars looked out at the school steps. And they saw the memorial for Doctor Long. The grade five pupils were holding it up like a banner.

Vera and Mary, in Explorer uniforms, red kerchiefs at their necks, stood on the top step and held the two top ends of the burlap. Label and Freddie, three steps down, held the bottom ends. Beside Vera stood Elizabeth. Beside Mary stood Annie. Beside Label stood Mike. Beside Freddie stood Douglas. Mr. Ross had picked up Beverley after the funeral and she stood beside Annie. Students who hadn't helped at all were allowed in, but only on the edges.

And the people in their cars saw the memorial. From the road it looked like a small faded rug, but with something purple shining in the centre, a design they couldn't quite make out.

Then the procession moved on – past the school, past Majeski's field, past the small clump of poplars a mile down the road, to the town cemetery. And Doctor Long was buried.

EACH SPRING the cemetery in Stone Creek is cleaned up. The hedges are clipped, the grass cut. After that it's left alone for the most part. Weeds grow tall beside the graves.

Haircut

THE LAMP BY HER BED IS TURNED OFF. A yellow blind covers the top half of the room's only window. From somewhere outside, a shaft of light has entered through the uncovered portion of glass, crossed the room in a long beam, and met the wall opposite, in a precise rectangle over some violets.

Ingrid lies on her side in the narrow bed and looks at that piece of light. She can see nothing else in the darkened room, not even Jesus in a wooden frame, hanging just beyond the light. Then she closes her eyes and opens them again slightly, lashes thin over her eyeballs. And the violets begin to move, to sway gently in a pale breeze.

She lifts her hands from the blanket, curls her fingers into fists, and presses the fists against her closed eyes, knuckles hard against the skin. And from the shapeless dark a single black ball emerges. The ball splits into lines of dark and light, thin rods that flash under her eyelids. She presses harder and the rods bend into curves and circles, into tiny purple stars shooting out from the eye's centre, to where she wonders, who knows where?

She uncurls her fists and rests her hands on top of the blanket. She's only eight years old, and her mother has told her to stop doing this, she could harm her eyes, but she's curious about the changing shapes of light.

She remembers tomorrow, moves one hand to her head, and rubs her fingers against her hair. Ragged hair that won't stay in place, yellow tufts that grow in clumps this way and that, hair her mother brushes every day, wets down, combs, puts in place, sometimes with bobby pins, sometimes with gobs of thick gel waved into stiff ridges.

"What can we do about this hair?" her mother says. "There must be something we can do."

"Norwegian hair," her father says. "Skrukerud hair."

Her mother says, "But look at Freda Jacobson's, very soft. And Anna Peterson's, so pretty the way her mother fixes it, always smooth and even."

"Let it be," her father says.

"Like that?" says her mother.

Ingrid turns in her bed, lies on her back. "But tomorrow things will be different," she murmurs to the empty air above her. "Something's not going to be the same again," she whispers to the ceiling.

Tonight the ceiling is still. Not like some nights when, lying there silent and waiting, fists released from their pressure, she would look up and see it begin to move slightly, to turn and sway above her like a narrow path curving around a low hill in a dusky evening. And sometimes, when she was very patient in her waiting and so still she couldn't feel her breathing, a little tree would grow beside the path, and flowers. Once, when she had waited a long, long time, a child appeared and sat down in a patch of yellow buttercups beside the tree. A rosy light swirled above her in gentle circles, in soft waves around her head, lifting and turning delicately. But that child didn't come back.

IN THE MORNING she dresses quickly. She had laid her clothes out the evening before on a wooden chair beside the bed – the new blue skirt and white sweater she got for Christmas, blue leggings that matched the skirt, clean underwear folded neatly beside the leggings. Then she hurries down the hall to the bathroom, to wash her face and to comb out the snarls in her Norwegian hair.

In the kitchen, her mother is standing at the counter buttering toast. Her father is sitting at the table, sipping coffee from a thick mug. When he sees Ingrid, he puts the mug down and smiles.

"Well," he says. "Well, well. Don't we look like a million dollars."

His wife carries the plate of toast to the table and sits opposite him. "Come," she says to her daughter, lingering near the table. "We'll have a good breakfast before we go."

"So, Ingrid, are you working for Mr. Rockefeller today?" Her father's voice is loud, jovial.

"No," she says and sits down.

"Mr. Rockefeller's private secretary, is that it?"

"I'm not going to work."

"That's something, to work for Mr.Rockefeller."

"I'm only eight, how could I be going to work?"

"You're so spiffed up, I thought you must be working for Mr. Rockefeller."

"We're going to Travises'," her mother says. "You shouldn't tease like that."

"Travises'," her father says.

"Ed says if we take it all off, it will come out even, more healthy."

"Ed says? Ed fixes machines."

"And Ellen agrees. She and Ed agree. Both of them. This will do the trick, they say. Clara Peterson thinks so too."

Her father is quiet. Then he says, "Well, have more toast then." He passes the plate to Ingrid, who picks up a slice, and eats.

"But not all of it," she says.

After breakfast she stands in the back porch and waits for her mother. The porch is cold, the linoleum gritty under her shoes. The rug in front of the door is matted, caked with hard dirt. It hasn't been shaken today.

Her mother comes out of the kitchen into the porch. She's wearing a dress with pink and mauve flowers, and over the dress her husband's thick grey curling sweater. Two green ducks have been knitted into the front of the sweater. They face each other, one on either side of the zipper. At the bottom of each sleeve, little ducks swim, all in the same direction.

"Button up your coat," she says, "the wind is nasty. And don't forget your cap, it's on the hook."

She follows her mother out the door, down the front steps to the gate. She stops and fumbles at the top button of her coat. The wind blows through the caraganas, branches click and rattle, dry leaves flutter on thin twigs. It's the first day of Lent.

Her mother lifts the latch, pushes the gate open, and they pass through. The gate bangs shut, the latch snaps, and they're on the dirt road that leads to Travises'.

The road is hard, the ground frozen. Clods of ice stick to the earth, raising small barriers against their walking. She holds tightly to her mother's hand.

"After the Lenten service tonight we'll ask Jacobsons to come over," her mother says.

"Freda too?" Freda is the same age as Ingrid.

"Of course."

They step carefully over the hills of ice. "Will Travises be at the Lenten service?"

"No," her mother says, "they don't come."

In Lent the roads are like this: deep-rutted, sharp, and rigid. Large stones are frozen into the ground. Even if you kick them they don't move. Even if you kick them so hard your toes hurt, the stones don't budge. They're hard as marble. They stay right where they are.

When they reach Travises' house, they can see Ellen Travis at the window of her front porch. She's holding back a curtain and peering out. Before they get to the door, she has already opened it and squeezed herself onto the front step. She's tall and thin and wears a brown jacket. She talks fast.

"Ed has set up a space in the shop," she says. "It's handy for him there." She holds the collar of her jacket close to her neck. "And it doesn't track up the house with people coming and going. He's already had a few customers. People don't like driving all the way to Swift Current."

They follow her around the house to the backyard, cross over a frozen garden past a clump of bushes, careful to push aside the thorny branches that swing out against them. Mrs. Travis shoves open the gate, and they're in the back alley. Ahead of them in a large lot is Mr. Travis's machine shop, a huge garage covered with ragged tin siding and set amidst piles of old tires, engines, metal rims and discs, all rusty and leaning into frozen weeds.

They step into the yard, avoid ice patches under their feet. There is no sidewalk. The wind blows hard against them. When they reach the shop, they stand for a moment in front of the big door. A thin light from the distant sun warms their backs

With a chapped hand, Mrs. Travis clutches at the knob and pushes the thick door open. "We're here," she calls into the dimness. They step inside. The door creaks shut.

From where she stands behind her mother, Ingrid cannot see Mr. Travis or the workbench, but she can smell – grease, metal, wood, everything dark and old, kept inside, locked tight.

"So, we're all here, are we?" the man's voice calls out.

Her mother takes her hand and they move to the bench. They step around boxes of nails and screws, heaps of rusty chain, to where Mr. Travis stands. He's short, his stomach round under a blue apron. Except for a rim of hair just above his neck, he's bald. Light from a bulb hanging from the ceiling shines down on the top of his head; his skin glows.

"Yes," Mrs. Travis says. "We've all come together."

He smiles. His teeth are white, his face a rusty colour, his eyes friendly. He looks at the girl, and his teeth are smooth and even under his thin lips.

She looks away from him to the bench where the tools lie – hammers, pliers, wrenches, small boxes of nails and bolts. The bench itself is rough and splotched with oil. Beneath it, a few skinny weeds, white-stemmed and almost leafless, have pushed up through cracks in the floor. Outside, the wind rattles the tin walls.

"So you've all come together, and we're going to have a haircut, are we?" He smiles at Ingrid, then steps toward her. She clutches at the sleeve of her mother's sweater. He leans over her and examines her hair more closely, "We'll get this cleared out, cleaned up." He twists a strand between his thumb and forefinger.

"His room's in the back," Mrs. Travis says. "He has a nice space there, clean and neat, not like here."

"Not like here, ha ha," Mr. Travis says. "Not like here." In single file they curve around oil drums, engines, bunches of thick rope, to the back of the shop. Mr. Travis leads the way.

The room they enter is swept and tidy. On the back wall a window looks out to a frozen yard. Under the window is a low bench, and on the bench a closed box. In the centre of the room, a metal chair sits on a low wooden platform. Ingrid and her mother hover near the door. Mr. Travis moves to the platform and waves his arm at it.

"Here's the throne," he says. "What do you think of my throne? Here's where the princess sits." He laughs. The women say nothing. Ingrid, too, is silent. "It's a throne, you see."

Mrs. Travis smiles and steps forward. She walks in a wide circle around the platform. "Isn't this nice?" she says. "Isn't this a fine barber shop?" She tips her hand to the chair, then moves to the door. "I'll just go on home then," she says. "Ed can take over from here, can't you Ed." She steps out of the room.

"You bet," Mr. Travis says. "I'll take over from here." He motions to Ingrid's mother. "You go on too," he says. "We'll do just fine, won't we, princess."

"No, I'll stay," her mother says. "I'll just stand here by the door. I won't get in your way."

"Suit yourself," he says.

He turns to Ingrid still clinging to her mother, holding tightly to the sleeve of the curling sweater, grabbing onto the little ducks swimming in a row on the edge of the sleeve.

"Now, little princess, if you'll take your place on the throne, we can begin."

She doesn't move.

"It's all right," her mother says. She leads Ingrid to the platform, helps take off her coat. "I'll hold it for you," she says, and returns to her place beside the door.

Mr. Travis bends over Ingrid, places his hands under her arms, and lifts her up, onto the chair.

"So, we're going to fix this," he says, stroking her hair, "get it right this time." He moves his hand to her shoulder and holds it there for a moment, pressing lightly. Then he steps down from the platform to the bench under the window and lifts up the metal box. He places it on the floor by her feet, and opens it. She sees inside – brushes, combs, scissors, a pair of clippers wound in cord, a white cloth rolled up. Mr. Travis picks up the cloth, shakes it loose, and lays it over her shoulders. It covers her body, reaching almost to the floor.

"Isn't she an angel now?" he says, "A real little angel." He laughs, then puts his mouth to her ear and whispers, "It's to keep all the little hairs off." His thick hand curls around her upper arm.

Then he stoops down to the box and lifts out the clippers. He unwinds the cord and plugs it into an outlet on the floor of the platform. She looks out the window. A small poplar in the middle of the yard is bending in the wind, its thin branches twisting this way and that. She turns her head to look at her mother, but her mother is examining a calendar on the wall. Her back is to Ingrid. The wind makes hollow sounds against the building.

Suddenly she feels the metal on her neck, the steel hard against her skin. She hears a click, then a buzz; and the steel comes to life, vibrates, twists, pushes forward a little.

His left hand is on her head, spread fingers capping her skull. His right hand moves the clipper, a flick from the centre of the neck to the base of the skull, then back and up again and farther up, and out and back. He moves the clipper a little to the left and up and up. Then to the right, up up up, and her hair falls in yellow tufts onto the platform floor.

With his fingers he combs through the hair on top of her head. He holds up a section in his left hand, pulling it tightly.

"Well, maybe the scissors here, eh?"

He lays the clipper on her lap. It slips into the fold of the white cloth. The muscles of her legs clench. He picks up the scissors and cuts through the clump of hair, then returns the scissors to the box. His hand moves to her lap, and his fingers slide under the clipper and lift it up. "We'll have an easy go of it now," he says.

The clipper comes to life, sliding against her skin, moving above her ears, and over the top of her head. Hair falls in little wisps onto her shoulders and down to the floor.

"Aren't we doing just fine," he says. "And aren't you a good little girl, no fussing or complaining. You're a very good little girl. I wish I had a little girl like you, not five sons, all wild and off somewheres."

Ingrid is silent. Her mother keeps looking at the calendar.

He rubs the small remaining growths with his thumb – behind her ears, above her neck, and a circle at the top of her head where the cowlick was.

"There. Nearly done. I'll use my silver-bladed razor for these little stubs that won't budge."

She stares out the window at the poplar tree. She closes her eyes, tight, and opens them again slightly, and the tree begins to sway, one moment touching the ground, the next sweeping against the clouds. She doesn't feel the thin scrape of the razor against her skin. Then she sees the tree loosen itself and lift and float up, roots and all, over the fences and hedges and hills of town. It flies far away from earth, and disappears into the sky. She sits dizzy, eyes closed, in the metal chair. When she opens them, Mr. Travis is brushing her ears and neck. He flicks her chin with the brush, laughs, then throws it into the box. He lifts up the cloth, shakes it, and folds it over the brush. He lifts her up, his sausage fingers tight beneath her arms. "Down you go." He sets her on the floor. "There's a good angel."

She turns to her mother, who's holding the coat in her hand. She's holding it away from her stiffly. Her arm is rigid, her face pale and stern. Why is she mad, Ingrid wonders. Why is she so mad? Her mother grabs her by the arm, jerks the arm into the sleeve, then the other arm. She pulls her through the doorway and back into the shop.

They move in crooked steps around the kegs and coils and heaps of chains, all the while her mother's fierce hand gripping. Why is she holding on so hard? I sat still, didn't I? I didn't cry.

Outside, they stand a moment on the step. It has begun to snow, not thick flakes but small particles whirling about. They hurry down the path into the alley. They're about to turn into Travises' yard, to take the shortcut, when her mother jerks her away from the gate. "We'll take the long way," she says, her voice sharp. They stumble down the alley over frozen ridges of earth.

Suddenly her mother stops. She stands in the middle

of the road, and her face in the wind is the colour of copper. "Where's your cap?" she says. "I told you to bring it. I said don't forget your cap, but you forgot it." She shakes her daughter's arm, back and forth roughly, and her voice is stiff and cracked. Ingrid crouches against the voice and against the wind. "You forgot it. You didn't bring it. Why didn't you bring it?" Then her mother drops her hand from Ingrid's arm and reaches to her own mouth. She covers her blue and rigid lips with her fingers, trying to stop the sound, but a cry seeps out. Long and thin, it circles the air around them. Ingrid looks up to her mother's face and is astonished to see her cry, to hear the sounds of her crying. And she too begins to whimper.

She reaches her hand to her head, feels the bare skin and the tiny growths of stubble here and there, and she catches her breath and sniffles and begins to sob. The wind has risen and the sleet has turned into thin pellets of ice that come down against her, against her face and neck and the skin that fits so snugly over her small skull. She stands on the icy road and wails. And the sound of her wailing joins the cries of her mother and the moaning wind, and fills the space around them from earth to sky.

Then the crying wears itself out, and it's quiet. Her mother unzips her curling sweater and pulls it off. She lays it over Ingrid, covering her head and shoulders, and puts her arm around her and says, "Let's go home now."

It's quiet at the supper table. A fork clicks against a plate, her mother coughs, her father asks for the salt.

Ingrid takes small bites of mashed potatoes.

She's wearing a purple tam. She wears it at a slanted angle as she's seen women in pictures wearing tams, pressed flat against the left side of her head and puffed out at the right.

"Maybe I won't ask Jacobsons over for coffee," her mother says, breaking the silence. "We can come right home after the Lenten service; it's been a long day."

"Will Freda be at the Lenten service?" Ingrid asks.

"Oh, I think so," her mother says.

"That tam looks awfully good on you," her father says. "It looks jaunty."

"I don't want to go if Freda's there."

"We won't stay long," her mother says. "We won't visit."

"Cute and jaunty," her father says. "Very jaunty."

SHE SITS BETWEEN her parents on a varnished pew in the centre of the church. Straight ahead of them is the altar, three wooden arches connected to each other, a tall wide one in the middle reaching toward the vaulted ceiling, and two shorter ones attached at either side. The altar is white, its curved edges trimmed with gold. On the face of the middle arch a painted Jesus, tall and blue and sorrowful, is standing on a rock step and knocking on a door. Vines hang down over the lintel. He holds a lamp in his left hand and knocks with the other.

On the altar's right is the organ, on the left, the pulpit. Organ, altar, and pulpit form a kind of triangle in front of them.

The church is dimly lit. Fat white globes suspended from the ceiling have been turned off, but small tulips of amber glass, attached at intervals to the side walls, glow in the dimness. One candle on the table of the altar is burning, its flame steady. It sends a thin circle of light up to the feet of Jesus standing on the stone step in front of the heavy door. From her place between her father and mother, she can see the light swirling around his feet.

Mrs. Hjortaas walks slowly up the centre aisle toward the organ. When she gets there, she smooths the back of her navy skirt with her hand and sits down on the bench in front of it, her back to the congregation. She flicks on the light above the keyboard, rustles through the pages of the hymn book. The small door behind the pulpit opens and the Pastor appears. He walks to the altar and stands in front of it, facing it, his head bowed. Then he turns to the group before him and announces the first hymn. Mrs. Hjortaas begins to play. Ingrid's mother finds the page in her little black hymnal. Her father doesn't sing. Ingrid remembers the hymn from last year's Lent.

A lamb goes uncomplaining forth
To save a world of sinners.

She pulls her tam more tightly against her own head, leans forward slightly, and gazes past her father's chest to see who's there. The preacher's family are sitting in the front pew on the far side of the church. Behind them, next to a window, sits Mrs. Skrukerud. She sits by herself, head bowed over the hymn book as though she's trying hard to see the print. Her hair is a grey tangled ball, like steel wool. She doesn't see Jacobsons, or Freda.

He bears the burden all alone,
Dies shorn of all his honours.

On her mother's left sit the Kvemshagens. They always sit in the same place, Mr. and Mrs. Kvemsagen, and their two boys Johnny and Jerome, their hair combed smooth and slick. And ahead of them, Mr. Reitlo. Even from where she sits Ingrid can smell the cigar smoke from his clothes and hair.

He goes to slaughter, weak and faint,
Is led to die without complaint,
His spotless life he offers.

Mrs. Aasen sits in the front pew, her small son beside her, restless, fidgety, his white Norwegian hair going this way and that in rowdy tufts.

For us he gladly suffers.

She checks the tam again, pressing it into place with her two hands. Has anyone noticed it? The tam is all right, it fits, but it's not as cute and jaunty as her father keeps saying, not that jaunty.

The Pastor is talking about the road to Calvary and how hard it was for Jesus to lug the cross up the hill, and how all the people were there watching, and his mother too. His mother is the Virgin Mary, she knows that for sure. But who's his dad, and where is he? He should be there too, on a day like this.

She looks at Jesus. His hair is brown and long, straight but not quite, a bit of a wave on the side. His expression is sad. He's been knocking for a long time, but no one's answered yet. Maybe they're not home. His head is bent toward the door, to listen.

She closes her eyes, lifts her hands to them, and presses down on them with her fingers. Then she drops her hands and opens her eyes narrowly. Through her lashes she sees the vines above the lintel tremble as if a small wind has come up, and Jesus' long hair move ever so gently, his eyes warm and tender toward her.

And then, suddenly, she hears rattling above her, rusty metal chains and the sound of whips. She closes her eyes tightly and opens them again, and there beyond the altar and chancel, beyond the ceiling itself, high and lifted up, she sees him on the dusty road. He's small and only partly clothed, no shirt even, just a thin pair of pants reaching below his knees, and he's barefoot. Two big soldiers are on either side of him. Swords hang from their hips, and their shields are thick and dusty. One carries a greasy rope with nails stuck in it, and he snaps it against Jesus' bare ankles. The other twists and pulls on his little arm. She looks closely at Jesus' face. He's only a boy, her age, eight or nine maybe, and he's mad and scared and trying to jerk his arm away from the soldier's hand. He's crying too. He's trying not to, but he can't help it; tears are running down his cheeks. His face is twisted, his hair bloody and tangled. Other soldiers march ahead of him, and thousands are following behind.

Then she looks at the people gathered on the side of the road as if they're watching a parade, waiting to see what's going to happen next. And the women are there in the ditch, kneeling on the hard dirt among the thistles. His mother, too, is crouching there.

Suddenly Jesus stops, so quickly the soldiers nearly trip. He stops right in the middle of the road and looks at his mother in the ditch. He yells, "They're jerks, Mother, just a bunch of jerks. Don't kneel down to them. They're stupid."

Then everyone freezes as if in a photograph: Jesus between the two soldiers, the soldiers themselves, all the people on the roadside, the women in the ditch, and Mary. No one moves a muscle. The chains stop rattling, whipping ropes are quiet, there's not a sound or movement on the road to Calvary, even the clouds of dust are motionless.

Very slowly his mother gets up off her knees, stands a moment among the thistles, then steps onto the road. She walks toward the soldier who's grabbing at Jesus' arm, stands in front of him, and looks directly into his face.

"That's my son," she says. "Be more gentle. He's only a boy. And try to show him some respect."

Now what will happen? Will the soldiers tell him he can go back home with his mother? Ingrid presses against her own mother, sitting beside her in the pew. The soldiers pay no attention to the mother, Mary. They move forward again, dragging the boy between them. And Ingrid knows that this story will end the same way as the other one: three crosses at the top of the hill.

She closes her eyes, and when she opens them the space above the altar is empty, and her dad is nudging her to stand. The congregation is praying, "Our Father who art in heaven...." It's time to go home.

SHE LIES ON HER NARROW BED and looks at the violets in their little yard of light on the wall beside her, delicate lavender flowers, still and quiet. She thinks about the Lenten service and what she saw there, and she wonders if others have ever seen the same thing, and if so why haven't they spoken up? She'd always heard he was old when this happened, over thirty. No one ever told her he was just a kid – small, thin, scared, mad.

She looks up at the quiet ceiling and wonders: People know some things, but they don't know everything. This is something she will have to think about for quite awhile.

In the meantime, however, now that the Lenten situation is a bit clearer to her, there is one thing she can do.

She reaches to the lamp beside her bed and turns on the light. Then she gets up, goes into the hall, flicks on the hall switch, and moves down the corridor to her parents' bedroom. She stops in front of the closed door, raises her hand and knocks. There's no answer. She leans her head toward the door and listens, then knocks again, louder. Now she hears a stirring, a cough, a raspy voice, her father's voice.

"What?" the voice says. "What is it?"

"It's me," she says. "I want to come in."

"Then come." The voice is stronger now.

She turns the knob, pushes the door open, and stands in the lightened doorway. Across the room her father has propped himself up in bed and is peering toward her in the dimness; her mother is a crumpled mound beside him, under the quilt.

"Is something wrong?" her father says. "What is it?"

Ingrid stands against the hall light, a narrow silhouette framed by the door's moulding.

"What?" her father says again, and her mother's body moves beneath the quilt.

"I've got something to tell you," Ingrid says. Her mother moans softly and her head emerges from beneath the covers, brown hair tousled.

"Yes?" her father says.

"I won't be going to Travises' again for a haircut."

"What was that?" her father says.

"I said I won't be having Mr. Travis cut my hair anymore."

Her mother lifts her head. "What's happening? What's she saying?"

"She's saying...she wants to say...."

"What is it? What do you want to say?" her mother asks.

"I already said it."

Her father explains, "Ed Travis won't be cutting her hair again. That's what she said."

Her mother sits straight up in the bed. "Oh...oh...so...yes...well...."

"Of course," her father says. "Of course. Ed Travis won't do that again."

Her mother's head and neck stretch forward. She tries to see Ingrid more clearly, to grasp the picture of her in the doorway, how little she is, how strange and unfamiliar, and how she just stands there, her daughter. She calls out, "Of course, of course. Come here then. Come. Let's have a look at you. Let's have a hug."

"No," Ingrid says, "I'm going back to bed now. That's all I have to say."

She stands there a moment longer, her thin body centred in the light, her bald head glowing under the lintel. Delicate pink marble. Iridescent rose.

She closes the door, walks down the corridor, flicks off the hall light, and enters her own room. She lies down on her bed, reaches to the lamp, and turns off the light. She rolls onto her side and shuts her eyes. Her body curls under the blanket. Her head rests on the pillow.

Oh Wild Flock, Oh Crimson Sky

O N THE DAY MY HAUGEAN GRANDFATHER arrived in Stone Creek for his annual winter visit, Ivan Lippoway, who was a year older than me, announced at the skating rink that he was an atheist.

It was the afternoon of New Year's Eve. My mother had told us that if we finished our chores early we could skate for a couple of hours before the train came in at 4:30, when we'd go to the station to meet Grandpa.

How the topic of atheism had even come up I don't know. We'd just been rambling on about the Christmas holidays that would be over in two more days, who was at our houses, and what we got for presents. Mike showed us his pocket knife that had three different-sized blades in it as well as a corkscrew and a pair of scissors. I told about the book my parents had given me, *Rilla of the Lighthouse,* which I read cover to cover on Christmas

Day. Vera said they'd eaten turkey until they were stuffed.

Then Ivan said, "I'm an atheist."

He said it out loud in front of everybody: me, Vera, Mike, my two brothers, everyone. We were in the warming house lacing our skates up. I was sitting between Vera and Mary on a wooden bench against the back wall. The three of us were in grade seven and stuck close together. My brothers, Andrew in grade nine and Peter in grade ten, sat across from us near the door. Ivan was in the middle of the room in front of the crackling stove, which was sending out waves of heat in every direction. He'd already done his skates up and was standing there on the wooden floor that was gouged and chipped from all the skaters who'd stood there before him.

I was about to stick the tip of the lace into the top hole of my skate when he said it, but I stopped right then and held the lace in mid-air, I was that surprised.

The word atheist had been mentioned in our history class before Christmas. Mr. Ross had asked if anyone knew what it meant, and Ivan, slouched as usual in his desk, muttered only two words, *No God*. I knew, of course, that Ivan was Russian, and I'd heard that Russia was now a godless country; but I didn't think that just because he knew the definition of the word, he necessarily was one. He'd never even been to Russia.

In fact, he was born in Stone Creek. His mother died when he was born, and he was raised by his grandparents. No one seemed to know where his father was. Then last year his grandmother died, so now it was only

Ivan and his grandfather living in the small house south of the Russian church. And it was small. I'd been in it. That's all I knew about him except that he was very clever, that he always wore the same pants to school, brown and tweed and rather shabby, and he smelled of garlic, which is their national dish.

And now I knew this: He was an atheist.

After the big announcement, he headed for the door, shoved it open with both hands, and went out. One by one the rest of us got up and stumbled after him. For whatever reason, no one commented on his statement.

Outside, the sunlight was dazzling. The snow sparkled on the huge banks outside the fence. And inside the fence, the ice shone like clear water. The sky was blue and cloudless. A perfect winter day.

But it was cold. The air stung my face and stuck inside my nostrils so it was hard to breathe. I pulled the wide collar of my jacket up against my cheeks and skated to the centre of the rink, where I stopped sharp, my skate blades scraping sideways on the ice. I looked around and saw Ivan at the far end. He was making wide swoops on the ice, his whole body curved forward and his arms swinging out in unison, first to one side, then to the other. He was smooth on skates, I'll give him that. Of course, his grandfather was a shoemaker and he also sharpened skates in winter, so he had an advantage there.

Suddenly someone shouted, "Crack the whip!" And we all skated to the far end of the rink. It didn't take us long to line up against the back fence. Ivan took an end position, saying he'd crack that whip. I took the other end, meaning I'd be the one who'd swing out the far-thest and fastest. We all grabbed hands and off we went, Ivan leading. He skated furiously, his body bent forward like a madman and his head down. Then, just after the halfway mark, he stopped short and pulled back hard on the arm of Mike next to him, and the rest of us swung out in a wide circle on the ice. I swung so fast I couldn't turn soon enough to miss the side fence, and I slammed into the boards. It nearly knocked the breath out of me, and I just stood there for awhile leaning into the fence. Andrew skated up to me to ask if I was all right, and deciding I was, muttered, "Why do you always want to be at the end? You should stay in the middle where it's safe." Only after I'd caught my breath and skated away did I feel the full effect of the collision. My right shoulder and arm felt scraped, and my hip hurt.

In the warming house I sat for a few minutes on a bench near the stove and stretched my legs out in front of me. I felt the pain of the crash gradually subside and I thought, if Ivan Lippoway was a typical atheist then I'd learned something else about atheists: they had a mean streak in them.

At quarter to four my brothers and I quit skating and walked home. As soon as we got there, we piled into the car for the drive to the station. My mother and dad sat in the front seat, my brothers and I in the back where we engaged in our usual competition, seeing who could sprawl out against the back seat and who would have to lean forward to give space to the other two.

I knew on the way home my grandfather would be

sitting in the front seat with Dad; the rest of us would be squashed in the back. But there'd be no fooling around then. Grandpa was a follower of Hans Nielson Hauge.

He was also a huge man with a thick chest and wide face. He was dark skinned, and his hair and beard, now grey, had been pitch black in his youth. This, together with his wide cheeks and squinty eyes, made him look more like a Siberian than a Norwegian.

Ivan's grandfather, who really was Russian, had light brown hair and fair skin. He was a milder man than my grandfather; the few times I'd heard him talk his voice was gentle. Grandpa roared when he spoke, especially when he got going on his favourite topics: the Word of God, the dangers of Rationalism, and his great Norwegian hero, Hans Nielson Hauge.

Halfway to the station, I saw my father put one arm around my mother and pull her close to him. He stroked her neck in a comforting way. Grandpa was Dad's father, not hers.

At the station we piled out of the car and headed up the steps to the platform. The platform was like most station platforms, wide and made of wood, stretching in front of the station house and alongside the tracks in both directions. Tonight it looked like a skating rink. Huge snowbanks were piled high on either end, and the boards beneath our feet were slick with ice. They looked glossy in the snow-speckled light shining out from the station window. Peter and Andrew slid in and out of the light on the slippery boards, Mom and Dad huddled together beside the tracks, and under the lamppost at the end of the platform, old Gibbs, with his cap pulled down on his forehead, bent over his snowy mail sacks.

Then we heard the whistle, a long and lonely sound that touches my soul, especially on winter nights when sounds are so clear and travel such a distance.

When the whistle blew, Peter and Andrew skidded over to the edge of the platform; my parents stepped back. I lifted my head to watch the drizzle of flakes above me, and I think I knew right then why Grandpa wanted to visit us in January: He missed the Norway winters of his childhood, missed his mother buried in a snowy grave in Utsira, and he was tired of rainy Vancouver, where he now lived with his daughter, my Aunt Elsa, and her shrill family.

Again the whistle blew, this time nearer and louder, and we could hear the huffing and panting of the engine.

Then we saw it, black and roaring, its huge eyeball headlight sending a thick beam of light down the tracks as it headed toward us. We watched the engine car pass by and the engineer high up at his window, waving. We heard the screech of the wheels brake against the tracks, smelled the smoke spewing forth from under the cars. And the train stopped.

And suddenly there Grandpa was, his dark body filling the passageway. He was wearing a black coat and fur cap and his face held a severe expression. Down the steps he came, one big boot after the other. My dad went to him, and Grandpa's face lit up and he threw his arms around Dad and shouted, "Takk Kjaere Gud!" in a voice as big as the night. Then he moved to my mother and bowed, and shook hands with me and Andrew. When he saw Peter he pounded him on the head and laughed, "Peder, Peder, the one much loved."

Why Grandpa got along so well with Peter I could never understand. Peter was such a fake when they were together, a real hypocrite, agreeing with everything Grandpa said about the power of the Word and the dangers of Rationalism, which Peter knew nothing about but pretended to. "Absolutely," he'd say to Grandpa. "You're absolutely right."

I doubt if even Grandpa knew as much as he let on. He'd been a fisherman all his life until he got too old. First as a boy fishing for cod in the North Sea, then in Canada, fishing in the Pacific Ocean for salmon.

Even my dad didn't agree with everything Grandpa said, and Dad was the Lutheran minister in town and a Haugean himself. He wouldn't wear a robe when he preached or a cross hanging from his neck. But he was gentler than Grandpa. He didn't pound on the pulpit when he preached.

During the ride home Dad and Grandpa talked Norwegian, which they enjoyed doing whenever they got together, even though they both spoke perfectly good English.

When we got home, we could smell the roasting chicken from the back porch, where we all crowded together, stomping the snow off our boots. Inside, the table was already set, a big wooden table in the middle of the kitchen. We didn't have a dining room, like they had at Vera's.

After we'd hung up our coats, Mom discovered she

had no milk, and how was she going to make her special gravy without it? It was New Year's Eve, the stores would be closed, and also closed the next day. Dad said he'd walk over to the café and ask Mr. Wong if he could spare a quart. Then I blurted out that I'd do it. The café was only a block away and I'd be quick. Dad dug in his pocket for a quarter. "Go ahead," he said.

I was getting my coat on when Grandpa announced that he wanted to go with me. After the long train ride the fresh air would do him good, he said. I wasn't pleased, but what could I do? I waited by the door while he took forever tugging at his coat and pulling on his boots. With Peter right beside him, pretending to be helpful.

When we got outside, I led the way and Grandpa followed. I could hear his boots crunching in the snow behind me and his heavy breathing.

"How are you doing, Grandpa?" I yelled.

"Ya, ya," he said, puffing. And I slowed my pace.

As we lumbered along, I wondered if Ivan would be at the café with his grandfather. Since Mrs. Lippoway's death, the two of them were known to eat there on special occasions. So it was possible. Not likely, though, in this cold.

Sure enough, when we got to the café, Ivan wasn't there. Freddie Wong, who was fourteen, the same age as Andrew, stood alone behind the counter. The new lady at the post office was sitting on a stool in front of him, her elbows on the counter and a thick mug in her hands. The windows of the café were steamed over and steamy cooking smells were coming from the kitchen, but there was no sign of any other customers.

Then the front door opened, letting in a draft of cold air and with it Jackson Armor, who everyone said was missing a few marbles but was harmless. He shuffled into the restaurant in a way those people often do, his body moving slightly from side to side. He was wearing a bright red cap with the flaps down over his ears, and a plaid jacket, red and black. His mother dressed him in interesting and colourful ways, but I still found him creepy. He flapped his arms against his chest to get warm, and smiled at us. He smiled all the time no matter what the occasion, even at funerals. And he never talked, even though he was way older than Peter.

Grandpa stood by the counter, eyeing Jackson. I wanted to leave before anything strange happened, so I asked Freddie about the milk and he went into the kitchen to ask his father.

The door opened again, and Sigurd Anderson and another man came in. They were drunk, which wasn't surprising since it was New Year's Eve and Sigurd was usually drunk anyway. They wavered in slow motion to a table against the wall, then took their time getting settled in their chairs. Grandpa looked stern. Being a Haugean, he had no use for liquor. Then Mr. Wong came out from the kitchen and I paid him for the milk. I tucked the bottle under my arm and went over to Grandpa to lead him out of there. But when we got as far as the door, Sigurd shouted, "Hey! What's the rush?"

Grandpa turned around and stared at the two men. He stood there like a monument. His black coat and thick boots, his fur cap and wide rusty face made him look even fiercer than before.

"It's New Year's Eve!" Sigurd shouted. "Time to celebrate!" He tried to get up from his chair, but the effort was too much for him. Jackson waddled over to the table to help him. He tugged at Sigurd's coat sleeve, and finally Sigurd stood, balancing himself with his two hands on the tabletop. He leaned forward, gazing at us with bleary eyes.

"It's an order!" he said. "So celebrate. That's what it's all about."

He laughed and immediately got into a huge coughing fit. Jackson rocked from side to side, smiling.

Grandpa slowly made his way toward Sigurd. When he got there, he stopped, leaned forward, and peered at him with his Siberian eyes.

"No, sir," he said. "That's not what it's about."

I was still by the door, holding the milk, Freddie was behind the counter, Mr. Wong stood in the kitchen doorway, looking puzzled, and the lady from the post office twirled her stool around so she could see.

"Listen to what the WORD OF GOD has to say!" Grandpa shouted.

I clutched the bottle against my chest, wishing like everything that Grandpa hadn't come with me and that he wasn't a Haugean.

He rumbled on. "If MY people who are called by My name...." He paused and breathed in the steamy restaurant air. "If they HUMBLE themselves and PRAY and SEEK my face and TURN from their wicked ways...." I was hardly breathing and my cheeks were burning. Freddie and the woman were staring at Grandpa, and the Chinaman was shaking his head. I looked at Sigurd. He appeared to be shrivelling up right in front of our eyes.

His body slumped forward, his head hung down, and he sank into his chair. Then he started to cry, whimpering and hiccupping like a baby.

Grandpa opened his mouth to continue. I have to stop him, I thought, he's out of control. I went over to him and touched his arm. "Grandpa, we have to go now." He looked at me as if he were surprised to see me there, and he turned to Sigurd and said, more quietly *"Then* I will *hear* from heaven, I will *forgive* their sins, and I will *heal* their land." But this good news seemed to have no effect on Sigurd. He sat there, sobbing like a child. Grandpa turned and walked out the door, and I followed.

When we got to the church corner, Grandpa stopped. He tilted his head back and his words rolled into the darkness. "The heavens declare the glory of God and the firmament showeth forth his handiwork!"

I looked up to see the glory. But all I saw was a black sky and a few stars, cold and far away.

Suddenly Grandpa seemed lonesome to me, like someone far from home. I remembered his stories about Utsira, how he and his father and brother would leave that rocky island in their fishing boat and head into the the North Sea, and how they were away from home for two or three days at a time, and storms would come up and howling wind. His brother had drowned in that sea and was never found. And I could see his brother sinking into the icy water, his hair streaming.

I was glad to get home and walk into our own house, and everyone was there, no one was missing.

Supper was even more delicious than I thought it would be. I ate a lot of everything, especially the stuffing and chicken gravy, my mother's specialties.

We were having a fairly good time at the table talking about our relatives in Vancouver, when Grandpa leaned back in his chair, cleared his throat, and said, "I suppose no one here knows how Hans Nielson Hauge spent New Year's Eve in Norway in 1823."

Suddenly everyone was quiet. I looked at Peter, Peter looked at Dad, Mom and Andrew stared somewhere into space. Then Dad said, "Isn't it time for dessert?"

Grandpa straightened his back and stretched his neck. "I can tell the story while we're eating dessert," he said.

"Go ahead, Papa," Mother said. She got up from the table. "I'll dish out the pudding while you begin."

Grandpa got right into the story.

"On New Year's Eve in 1823, Hans Nielson Hauge was in jail. A dungeon, cold and damp, where his hands and feet were bound in chains and his bed was a wooden plank." He lowered his voice and squinted his eyes so they were nearly closed. "And there were rats scurrying about, sniffing and scratching." He paused. "Well, I'm not entirely sure about the rats, but in all likelihood they were there. I'm almost certain of it."

"Why was he in jail?" Andrew asked.

"Why?" Grandpa roared. "Why? Because he preached the Word openly and boldly, a simple layman, wandering up and down the coast of Norway, on foot, knitting and singing as he went."

"Knitting!" Andrew said.

"Exactly. Socks and mittens and scarves to give to the poor peasants."

"Why would anyone go to jail for that?" Peter said.

"Ah. Good you should ask. The higher-ups got nervous," Grandpa said. "The pastors and bishops. They did-
n't think a simple peasant could be trusted to proclaim
the Word. And besides, what would happen to *them* if
such a thing got started? So do you know what those
windbags in their stiff collars and fancy robes did?"

"No, what?" I said.

"They reported him to the authorities. And on a
cold winter night in 1823 the police broke down the
door of a simple peasant house and grabbed Hauge and
carried him off to prison."

The story was more interesting than I'd expected.
But then Granpa went on to explain how Norway finally became independent from Denmark, thanks to
Hauge (at least this was Grandpa's version), and we all
began to fidget. Later, we played dominoes.

ON JANUARY 2, I was standing in the school hallway
getting used to the smells again, when Ivan stomped
through the front entrance, his shoulders bent forward,
his head down, and clamping a bundle of papers under
his right arm. He went straight up to Mr. Ross's room
without even taking his jacket off. I didn't know what
his hurry was. We had a few minutes before the bell,
and his friends were still hanging around in the hall,
bumping into each other and making noise.

It wasn't long before I discovered the mystery. At 10
o'clock, in World History class, Mr. Ross made the
announcement. He sat on top of his desk, dangling his
legs in front of it, and told us, "Ivan has suggested a

topic for a debate." Ivan was his favourite because of his intelligence. "He thinks that because we're studying the Russian Revolution and the rise of Communism it would be useful if we debated that subject in class and wonders if anyone else would be interested." He waited for a reply. Of course, no one spoke up. Who would be crazy enough to debate Ivan?

"He'd like to get to the heart of the matter and suggested this for the proposition: Resolved: that there is no God."

I was dumbfounded. How could Mr. Ross even consider such an idea? And why did he always make us do stuff that got him in hot water? Like having us count the needles on the spruce tree across the road, taking the whole morning to do it and getting nowhere, not even the number of needles on one branch, and the people downtown complaining, is this what we pay him for? And why would Ivan bring up such a thing?

"Any takers?" Ross asked. "Anyone interested in meeting his challenge?"

I glanced over at Esther and Mike sitting in the row to the left of me. They were completely dead-faced. Mr. Ross stood up and walked to the window. He gazed out at the grey sky and stroked his chin with his thumb and fingers. Then he turned to us and said, "Does that mean everyone agrees with Ivan?"

Of course I didn't. But I kept my mouth shut.

"WHAT?" my grandfather demanded at the supper table. "You didn't stand up to an unbeliever?" He stabbed the air with his fork.

"I'm not a scientist," I said. "I can't prove anything about God."

"You're not called on to be a scientist," Grandpa thundered. "You're called to be a witness. To stand up for the truth." And he began to sing, holding his fork upright in his fist, like a pitchfork.

Dare to be a Daniel.
Dare to stand alone.
Dare to have a purpose firm.
And dare to make it known.

Then he recited a verse from Genesis: "'And the earth was without form and void, and darkness was upon the face of the deep, and the spirit of God was moving upon the face of the waters, and God said, 'Let there be light, and there was light.' There's proof for you," he said. "It's in the Word."

Finally, Dad spoke up. "I think what she means is that if someone doesn't believe the Scriptures in the first place, you can't very well use the Scriptures to prove your point to him."

This silenced Grandpa for about ten seconds. Then he banged his fork down on the table. "The fool has said in his heart there is no God!" he roared.

"I don't think Ivan's a fool, Grandpa," I said. "He's very bright. The smartest in class."

"Fools think they're smart, but they're not, they're fools."

WALKING TO SCHOOL the next day, I saw Ivan climbing the hill from his house. His whole body leaned forward and his head was lowered. I kept on walking as if I didn't see him, but we met at the school steps.

"Scared?" he said.

"Of what?" I said.

He didn't answer, just walked past me and climbed the steps.

In front of the door he turned around and looked down at me in a strange way, and I found myself breathing differently.

He didn't have any reason to hate me, I thought. Hadn't I delivered the box of cookies to their house before Christmas, cookies my mother had made, knowing that Ivan and his grandfather wouldn't have many goodies since Mrs. Lippoway was dead? Hadn't I trudged down the road and across the tracks to their house even though the wind was freezing cold?

In summer their whole yard was one thick vegetable garden. Mr. Lippoway worked in it every morning, digging and watering and sometimes covering plants with tin cans for protection against the wind. From the schoolyard we could look down and see their garden. In the late summer, tall yellow sunflowers swayed in the wind.

But on the Saturday of my Christmas delivery the yard was packed full of snow. The long path that led from the road into the yard and to their back door had a wall of snow on either side as high as my armpits.

I knocked on the door and Ivan answered. He looked shocked to see me. He didn't even invite me in until his grandfather called out, "Who is it?" When I stepped inside I was surprised at what I saw. One room was the kitchen, living room, and workshop all combined. And maybe even someone's bedroom as well; a couch at the far end of the room was covered with a quilt. I noticed the smells right away: leather, pipe tobacco, and the cabbage cooking on the stove. Mr. Lippoway was sitting on a stool at his workbench, which was littered with shoes, hammers of various sizes, boxes of tacks, pieces of leather.

The old man rose from his bench and stepped forward to greet me. He was thin and wore a dark blue apron. I handed him the parcel and said it contained a few cookies my mother had made. He seemed pleased and thanked me in his broken English. He held up the box in both hands and examined the wrapping, blue tissue paper with small silver stars pasted on it. He turned the box this way and that, shaking his head in admiration of my mother's artistic ways. Then he placed it on the kitchen table, which was littered with Ivan's school books, and shook my hand. His hand was hard and smooth, except for some nubs of thick skin that stuck out on a couple of fingers. Ivan didn't move from the door. He just stood there, scowling.

Now, seeing him at the top of the school steps looking down at me, I thought of that box. I knew what was in it: shortbread, spritz, rosettes, fruitcake. I was quite sure he'd enjoyed eating all this, so why was he being so peculiar?

At 10 o'clock it was time for history. Again Ross challenged us to debate and no one responded. I don't know yet why I did it, but I felt my hand go up and I heard myself saying I would debate Ivan.

"So Elizabeth's decided to have her head chopped off," my brother said at the supper table.

"What's this?" Dad asked.

"What are you talking about?" Mother added.

"She's debating Ivan the Brain," Peter said.

"I've accepted the challenge to prove there's a God," I said.

"My little jente," Grandpa said. "So young but with courage like a lion."

At school the next day I began my preparations by looking up key words in the dictionary. All our library books were on a shelf at the back of the room: the dictionary, the Encyclopedia Britannica, a book on insects, and a play entitled *A Doll's House.* I lifted the dictionary from the shelf, carried it to my desk, and settled down for some serious work. The room was quiet. Everyone was at their desks, busy with something or other. The sun was shining through the tall windows onto our desks. Mr. Ross was in his swivel chair, watching over us.

I found the words I wanted and wrote down the definitions in my scribbler. "God: the one Supreme Being, creator and ruler of the universe. Atheism: disbelief in or denial of the existence of God or gods." But I already knew all this, so I moved on to the encyclopedia for more information. I was surprised at how much there was under that one word, atheism.

I found out that in ancient Greece Plato had argued against the idea of atheism. Plato was quite famous, so I decided I might use him to prove my point. Then I came across something called logical positivism. It said,

"Propositions concerning the existence or non-existence of God are nonsensical and meaningless." This was my view exactly, but I was startled to discover that this viewpoint was considered atheistic.

I brought my problem to Mr. Ross, who was still relaxing in his chair. I showed him the article in the encyclopedia and described my conflict.

"Why don't you look up gravity?" he said.

"Gravity?" I asked.

"It's the power that holds the universe together so we don't fly off in all directions."

"Is that about God?" I asked.

"It could be," he said.

I went back to my desk and looked up gravity. I found long equations in the article like $w = G. \frac{4}{3} \pi R^3 \Delta$ $M/R^2 = G. \frac{4}{3} \pi R \Delta M$.

I decided to just study the definition. "Gravity is an action between masses of matter that makes every mass tend toward every other." I looked up *tend* and saw that it meant to be disposed toward or attracted to. This tendency is so powerful, the encyclopedia went on to say, that "a mass of matter in Australia attracts a mass in London precisely as it would if the earth were not interposed between the two masses."

Every once in awhile I'd glance over at Ivan to see what he was up to, but he had no books in front of him at all. He just kept scratching away in his scribbler. I did catch a glimpse of one page, and all that was on it were numbers and mathematical signs. My heart sank when I saw this. If he was using algebra to prove his point, I didn't have a chance.

THAT NIGHT Grandpa asked me how I was getting along. We were in the living room after our family devotions. He was in the big chair; I was sitting on the piano bench. I told him not bad, but I hadn't gotten a firm hold on God yet. He started to laugh. He slapped his leg and said: "A hold on God! That's a good one. Ha ha." Then he looked at me with one of his severe expressions and shouted, "God is not tame!"

Later, I told my dad I just didn't know what to do. I wasn't good enough in math or science to prove my point. And I couldn't quote Scripture like Grandpa wanted me to. Ivan didn't accept the Bible as proof of anything.

"You'll find a way," was all he said.

"Well, that helps," I said.

But when I woke up the next morning, it came to me. Lines from a poem by William Wordsworth were moving around in my head, a poem Mr. Ross had made us memorize months before.

It is a beauteous evening, calm and free,
The holy time is quiet as a Nun
Breathless with adoration; the broad sun is
Sinking down in its tranquility....

I knew right then the path I'd take. It would be poetry. Beauty. Why was there beauty? Answer me that, Ivan Lippoway.

As SOON as I got to school I looked up the definition. "Beauty: a quality or combination of qualities that gives pleasure to the senses or to the mind and spirit. 'A thing of beauty is a joy forever.'" I copied the definition into my scribbler.

Then I borrowed the thick poetry book Mr. Ross kept on his desk and looked up Wordsworth. If he'd written one poem about beauty, he'd probably written more. And he had.

> I wandered lonely as a cloud
> That floats on high o'er vales and hills,
> When all at once I saw a crowd,
> A host of golden daffodils....

As I went through the book I realized that Mr. Ross had been reading us only the easy poems. Most of the others were beyond me. But even some of those contained a few lines that made sense, and I copied these into my scribbler. For example, Samuel Taylor Coleridge wrote:

> All thoughts, all passions, all delights,
> Whatever stirs this mortal frame,
> Are all but ministers of Love
> And feed his sacred flame.

I noticed that Love was capitalized. I knew what that meant.

Then I found this line by John Dryden: "From harmony, from Heavenly Harmony, this universal frame began." I figured out what he meant by Heavenly Harmony, since he, too, used the capital letter. And I thought that this could be a strong point in my argument. Where did harmony come from? I would ask. Did the petals of a rose, the wings of a bird, the fingers of my own hand happen accidentally? Without a design or a designer? Could "The Hallelujah Chorus" by George Fredrick Handel have just appeared out of thin air? Without a composer? But as I continued my reading, I became less sure of my direction. It seemed to me that too many of the poems tended toward confusion.

I got up from my desk and walked back to the library. Passing Ivan's desk, I saw that he was reading from a book I hadn't seen before. I glanced down at it, but when he saw me looking, he covered the whole book with his arms, and I moved on to the library shelf.

It seemed to me that arguments could be made from the world of nature, so I picked up the book on insects and paged through it. I saw a picture of the parts of a beetle: head, thorax, abdomen, wings (both front and back), legs, feet, claws, antennae, all with their own work to do. I read how important legs are in an insect's life, and how grasshoppers even sing with their legs by rubbing them together. On another page I found pictures of fireflies and read that these insects flash light signals to attract mates. Male fireflies signal as they fly in the summer night. Females flash back their light signals from the ground since they don't have wings. Some species of fireflies even have glowing eggs.

WHEN I CAME HOME from school, Mom was in the kitchen standing at the sink peeling potatoes. I sat down at the table and told her about my idea to use beauty to support my position in the debate, and about using poems to prove my point.

"Aren't you the smart one," she said. Sometimes she could be quite encouraging.

"But it's not working so well," I said.

"How so?"

"Most of the poems are confusing."

"Hm," she said and went back to her peeling.

"I suppose I'll have to write my own," I said.

Upstairs, I started making a list of things that were beautiful. My list, not Wordsworth's, although I agreed with him that daffodils were beautiful, especially when seen in such large numbers.

I began with beautiful sounds: crashing thunder and falling rain, meadow larks warbling from the fence posts, loons on the lake, Rivney's dog barking at suppertime. I moved on to beautiful scents: apples, cinnamon, lilacs, evergreens. Beauty. Beauty. It was everywhere. And without realizing it, I found myself writing my own poem.

A flock of wild geese,
A crimson western sky,
Tall pines and poplar trees
Through which the evening breezes sigh....

It looked like a cinch, but the next day everything changed.

I WAS ON MY WAY HOME from school and took a short-cut across the back alley behind the hotel, a route I'd taken many times before. The day was mild. Long icicles hanging from the hotel windows were dripping water on the snowbanks below. Icicles and snow. These, too, were beautiful, I thought. I was in the middle of the road, facing the back door of the hotel. To the left of the door was a row of garbage cans and to the right a storage shed. As I stood there, the door of the shed creaked open, and out stepped Jackson Armor. He was wearing the same red cap and black and red jacket he'd worn on New Year's Eve. The jacket was scrunched up a little in front of him and his hand was down just below the jacket. Then I saw what he was doing. He was holding his thing in his hand. When he saw me he smiled and waved it from side to side.

I froze in my tracks. I tried not to look at it, but there it was. He took his hand away and his thing dangled in front of him. It was long and white, except for the tip which was kind of pink. Even though it was big, it looked sickly to me. Suddenly, he stepped forward. I backed up cautiously so as not to startle him, which is what you're supposed to do, I'd read, when you come upon a wild animal. I headed for the sidewalk. When I glanced back I saw Jackson standing in the middle of the road, smiling and jiggling it. I walked away very slowly. I was barely breathing.

I had crossed the vacant lot and was by the church. I stopped, looked up at the steeple, then walked up the steps, opened the heavy doors, and went in.

It was cold inside. I stood shivering in the aisle. I

smelled the familiar smells: varnish, wax, old books. I touched the arm of a pew, rubbed my hand on the oily wood. A thin light came in through the arched windows. I sat down in a pew and lifted the hymn book out of the rack in front of me. I didn't open it, just held it for awhile. Then I got up and went home.

When I opened the back door I found Mother in the kitchen. I took off my boots and jacket and sat down.

"I'd like your opinion on something," I said.

She waited.

"Do you believe God created the world and everything in it?" I asked.

"Yes," she said.

"And do you think what he did was good?"

"Very good," she said. "Why?"

"I think he could have done some things better," I said.

"Do you?" she said. "Like what?"

"Just some things," I said, and went upstairs.

But after supper, when I was alone with my mother, she wormed it out of me. Before I realized it I was telling her the whole story. She was quite upset and asked if Jackson had touched me. He hadn't and I told her so, but she still seemed agitated, so I said not to worry, I'd stay clear of Jackson from now on.

We sat there for a minute or two without talking.

Then I said, "It wasn't a pretty sight."

"No, I'm sure not," she said.

"I don't know how I can go on with the debate."

"Why not?"

I was surprised she had to ask.

"Where's the beauty?" I said, and left the room.

Later in the evening I was in my room, sitting up in bed thinking about Jackson. I saw him in his red cap and black and red jacket, standing in the alley, wagging it and looking proud. And I thought of all the men who had that same thing: Mr. Ross, Gibbs, Rev. McFarlane, the boys at school, my brothers, Ivan. In fact, all the men and boys from the time of Adam to the present day. Holding it up, so pleased with themselves.

My mother came in and sat at the foot of the bed. She was quiet for some time, then said, "Maybe you could look at it this way." She put her hand on my foot. "In Scripture all the bodily parts are called members. Feet, arms, ears, eyes..." She hesitated. "Jackson's part that you saw today is also a member. It's called the male member."

"That's new," I said.

"Of course, the body has many members," she continued, "and each one has its own job, so the body can do many wonderful things because of all these parts working together so harmoniously."

I didn't know what she was getting at.

"But if a member is cut off from the body... well, like you said, 'Where's the beauty?' If you saw a finger lying by itself on the table, it would be disgusting, or an ear, or an eyeball. They're not meant to be alone." Her face was getting flushed and she was talking quite fast.

"So?" I said.

"What I'm trying to say is Jackson's member by itself looked ugly to you, just as an eye lying by itself on a table would look ugly. It needs to be connected, to be

184

part of the whole."

"Jackson's member was connected!" I said. I was beginning to get a little impatient with her.

"In a way it wasn't," she said, "because he's not connected. I don't know how to put it. He wants to be, but he doesn't know how. That's all I'm saying."

After she'd gone, I was left to ponder her words. I knew she'd meant well, but what she said only filled my mind with even more gross pictures. An eyeball, a finger, a big toe, all cut off from the body and lying on the countertop. And the body itself with gaping holes where the parts had been.

THE NEXT DAY at school there was something different in the air. I hadn't been in the classroom very long before I noticed it. I was finding it hard to keep my eyes off Ivan. I also knew, even without looking, when he had his eyes on me. A few times when he went to the front of the room he'd walk on my side of the aisle so his hip bumped against my desk as he passed. Afterwards, I'd rest my hand on the spot he'd touched and my hand would feel warm. Then I started thinking about his house across the tracks. I remembered exactly how it had looked and thought of ways it could be made to look a bit more cheerful, a pretty cloth on the table, a colourful afghan on the sofa.

I was in the middle of one of these thoughts when Mr. Ross announced that the debate would be held on Friday because we needed to move on to the next chapter in World History.

AT THE SUPPER TABLE, Peter told them the news.

"Doomsday on Friday," he finished cheerfully.

"Not for me," I said.

"Will your poem be ready?" Mom asked.

"Poem!" Peter said. "You're not reading a poem!"

"Why not?" I said.

"That's not what they do in debates."

"It's what I do. My whole debate's going to be a poem."

Grandpa frowned. "Hauge had no use for poetry. He used plain words and said them straight."

THAT NIGHT I lay in bed under my heavy quilt and thought about gravity. Holding everything together. Mountains and oceans, planets and stars. And holding me together, and everyone I knew, and all the people on earth. Holding us. If gravity ever started to crack, we'd be in trouble. Then I thought, is God bigger than gravity? And I wondered if I could say this in the debate.

I tossed and turned, unable to sleep. Finally, I sat up, switched on the light, and reached for my scribbler and pencil. I wrote furiously into the night.

ON THE DAY OF THE DEBATE I rose early to get ready. I put on the dress Mom had sewn for me before Christmas, a long-sleeved navy blue dress with a red collar, red cuffs, and red buttons down the front.

At breakfast we ate the usual, Cream of Wheat, and Grandpa told me again to stand up bravely and be counted. My stomach felt loose and jittery. I left half the cereal in the bowl and left early for school.

I was partway down the walk when I heard Grandpa calling. I turned around and saw him standing on the front step in his shirt sleeves. Frozen vines above the door arched over his head.

"If God is for us, who can be against us?" he shouted. Little steamy clouds puffed out in front of his face.

"No one!" I yelled.

"That's right!" he said. "And don't forget it."

MR. ROSS stood in front of the room, facing us. He was a tall thin man, and today, standing there in his grey suit and white shirt, he looked even taller than usual. He'd invited the older students to join our class for the debate. Peter, Joe, Abie, and others, who sat together against the side wall, nudging each other and trying to look important.

I sat at my desk with my notecards stacked neatly in front of me. On each card was a verse of my poem, and I had twenty verses all together, so I'd divided the stack into two piles and numbered each card to prevent confusion. Ivan didn't have any cards on his desk, just his scribbler. And I thought that maybe he wasn't as well prepared as I was.

Then Mr. Ross announced the judges: Freddie Wong, Mary Sorenson, and Mike Donnelly. Freddie was Chinese and as far as I knew, not religious. Mary Sorenson came from a Communist home. Mike's parents were Catholic. He'd almost have to vote for God, I thought.

Mr. Ross called on Ivan to begin. "You get fifteen

minutes," he said. "Then Elizabeth will get fifteen minutes. After that you will each have five minutes for rebuttal."

Ivan slid out of his desk and shuffled to the front of the room. In his right hand he carried his scribbler, rolled up like a scroll. Mr. Ross had moved to the window side of the room where he half sat on the window ledge. Ivan stood in front of the teacher's desk with his seat scrunched against it, trying to look like Mr. Ross. He was wearing the same brown tweed pants he always wore and a sweater that was too small for him. It stretched tight across his chest, and the sleeves didn't even reach to his wrists. He held up the scroll, like a flag.

"I am here today to ask each of you to stretch your mind, to rethink old beliefs, and to be open to new thoughts and discoveries," he began.

I started feeling nervous.

"Specifically," he continued, "I am here to challenge the outworn belief in a Supreme Being who brought into existence everything in the universe."

The room was quiet. Everyone was waiting to hear what he would say next.

"Let me describe the origins of life in the words of the scientists I've been studying, men who have spent their lifetime in the search for truth." He tried to open his scribbler, but the pages kept rolling back. When he finally got going he said, "Everything is energy. Light is energy. Heat is energy. Even matter. Matter is stored energy. It's all energy. And it has always been here."

Then he described how everything got started, how particles of energy moved about in the universe, sometimes colliding and creating more energy, and how this energy expanded in space, farther and farther out, and some parts separated from other parts. He said that particles of light separated from particles of matter. And because of gravity, the particles of matter attracted each other and united and became the sun.

"Gravity is the great force in the universe," he said. He described it as being like billions and trillions of strings attached from everywhere to everywhere.

He'd beaten me to one of my main points. I hadn't thought of that possibility. I looked around the room. Andrew was sitting with both elbows on his desk, holding his face in his fists, concentrating. Vera sat with her head leaning toward her shoulder, paying close attention.

Ivan talked about stars that had burned until they used up the hydrogen, then exploded, and heavier matter was formed. And then, because of gravity, these particles of matter came together and formed the earth. And everything went on from there.

He stood up straight, looked at me, raised his voice and said, "Every single piece of matter in the universe has evolved from one primal matter." I stared back at him, trying to look fearless.

Then he brought up names of people I'd never heard of. Thomas Dodd, the alchemists, Dmitri Mendeleev. He got excited when he talked about Dmitri, who'd worked in his dad's glass-blowing factory in Siberia, and later organized the atoms and came up with the Periodic Table, the very same one as we had over our blackboard. As he spoke, his voice got higher and his cheeks flushed and the scribbler shook in his hand. He described Dmitri shut up by himself in a little cottage by the Black Sea, and how he spread small squares of paper on the table, each square with the name of an element on it, and how hydrogen was the lightest atom and was first in the row. And I pictured Dmitri sitting at his little table by the cabin window, organizing the atoms, while the wind whistled down the chimney and the wolves howled by the sea.

Then he said a lot of other things like the universe is not perfectly symmetrical and that's why we're all here. He lost me at this point. I looked around the room. The others seemed confused as well. The speech got more and more complicated. Peter began to squirm, and Joe and Abie slouched lower in their chairs.

When Ivan had finished, Mr. Ross called on me. I went to the front, laid my notecards in two piles on his desk, and stood in front of it.

"Mr. Ross, honourable judges, worthy opponent, and fellow students." I got right into my speech, wasting no time on an introduction. I didn't need my notecards for the first verses.

A flock of wild geese,
A crimson western sky,
Tall pines and poplar trees
Through which the evening breezes sigh.
But there is no God, some people say,
Maker or Creator? No.
These things just are – like night and day,
And ever will be so.

I looked out over the class. Peter was squiriming.

Ivan was shaking his head. I realized I had to be more compelling, so I recited the next four lines louder.

> The wind howls in the night.
> The mighty oceans roar.
> "God is not tame!" the wise man says.
> "Not napping on the floor."

I glanced at Vera. She was nodding her head in agreement. I decided to recite the next verse in a lighter tone, for contrast.

> The smoothness of an egg,
> The scratching life within,
> The breaking of its brittle shell,
> And lo, our feathered kin.

The grade ten boys began to snicker. I picked up the second stack of cards, flipped through them quickly, and decided to read only my best verses.

> Roaring thunder, slashing rain,
> Tempestuous, violent weather.
> Rough winds can roar and rip and groan,
> But still we hang together.

No one was squirming now.

> The mighty force of gravity,
> Yet...
> LOVE IS EVEN STRONGER!

When all around would pull us down,
Love lifts us up and holds us there,
And we are sad no longer.

For the next verse I again lowered my voice, but I
pronounced each word slowly and distinctly.

A tiny grain of love,
So small one hardly sees it,
But still it travels through the air
(Fast as sound and quick as light!)
And lands on one who needs it.

I repeated the refrain, "But there is no God, some
people say..." I'd decided not to use it after every verse,
but to stick it in here and there.

The body's shrewd design,
Each part a purpose serves,
The neck that holds the head upright,
A narrow hip that swerves.

I felt my cheeks getting warm. I glanced down at
Ivan. He was looking at me curiously, but he wasn't
sneering. For the next verse I raised my left hand. On
the second line, I curled and uncurled my fingers.

Five fingers of a hand,
And knuckles so they swing,
Two fingers hold a yellow rose,
And one, a wedding ring.

Things were going quite well, so I decided to skip over to the end.

A million needles on a spruce,
A billion stars on high,
Ten thousand dolphins in the sea,
WHY? WHY? WHY?
Whose idea was it to GIVE and GIVE and GIVE?
Whose idea was it to LOVE and LIVE?"

I had come to the last verse. Now I looked at everyone, individually. I'd seen my dad do this, and it seemed to work quite well.

Dear friends who've gathered here,
I very strongly urge you,
Throw off the blinders from your eyes,
Scrape off the scum that lingers,
And see the LOVE that touches YOU,
Your ears and eyes and lungs and heart,
Your hands and all your fingers.

The room was quiet. Everyone was looking at me. I saw Vera wipe tears from her eyes with her clean white handkerchief. And I knew I'd won.

THAT NIGHT I went to the rink. All the lights were turned on, every string, as they were each Friday night. And music was playing over the loudspeaker. Tonight it was "The Blue Danube Waltz."

I was skating by myself in the centre of the rink. Light from the bulbs hanging above glittered over me and around me in small circles and sparkled on the blue white ice at my feet. I felt as if I were gliding on the Blue Danube itself, heading into the Black Sea.

Then, from the corner of my eye, I saw Ivan skating toward me, head bent, arms swinging. He was zooming right at me. I jerked sideways to get out of his way, and I fell on the ice, legs and arms sprawling. He circled around me, his skates pointing in opposite directions, his body leaning over me, gliding smoothly around and around. He scraped to a stop, and snowy bits of ice sprayed up from his silver blades. Then he bent down and shoved his hands into my armpits and lifted me up, and I stood wobbling beside him. He stretched his left arm around my back, his left hand still in my armpit, his fingers pressing into me. He grabbed my right hand in his and held it tight, and off we went down the ice. He swirled me around the corners, whizzed me past the other skaters, moved me swiftly and surely through the circles of light.

I looked up at the black sky and the stars. The air was cold on my face. And, oh, the beauty! I could hardly breathe.

The Ground You Stand On

ONE SATURDAY IN SPRING, WHEN THE brother was twelve and the sister was nine, they climbed the ladder in the church tower to the belfry. The tower was dim except for a yellow square of sunlight far above where the tunnel opened onto the bell deck. It was dusty, smelling of old feathers and bird droppings.

The sister was first. The brother followed below. She knew, climbing in her pink and flaring skirt, why he wanted to be second, and soft slender pleasures curled about in the centre of her stomach. But as she stepped up on the wooden rungs, clinging with stiff hands to the bars, she scraped her feet against each rung, sending bits of dust and shrivelled bird droppings down on her brother's face, his upturned nose.

When they reached the top he shoved her with one free hand through the opening into the belfry and followed close behind. They lay on their stomachs, clutching with arms and thighs at the safety of the deck. Their heads leaned over the edge, their feet rested under the great iron bell suspended above, there was no railing, the height made them dizzy.

They looked down on the churchyard: the brown wet earth, the caragana hedge sprouting bits of green, a few old graves beyond the hedge, shabby in spring mud and winter's limp weeds.

From here they saw everything: the hotel on Main Street, Louie's place, the Chinese café, the vacant lot between the church and the café. Then they saw their father in the vacant lot, walking through straggling weeds toward Main Street. He was wearing a sagging grey sweater. "Why doesn't he get rid of that old thing?" the brother said, crouching lower on the belfry floor. When he lifted his head again, his father was gone.

They crawled closer to the edge and looked out beyond Main Street. They saw the school and the onion dome of the Russian church, and south of the church, the small Ukrainian houses in yards that would soon be filled with green vegetables and tall yellow sunflowers.

"When I'm seventeen I'm going to leave this dump."

"Why?" the sister asked.

"Why! Who wants to rot in this dump?"

"It's nicer than Graveltown. I heard some people from Graveltown are moving here next month."

"They can have it," he said. "It's a dump."

They heard an airplane somewhere to the north, saw its distant curve approach, watched it roar over Main Street.

"Take me to United States!" the sister shouted, aiming her voice with her cupped hands.

"Take me to United States!" she yelled again, louder.

"United States! Who wants to go to United States?" the brother said.

"Where do you want to go?" she asked.

"Halifax," he said, "to join the navy and see the world.

> *If they ask us who we are*
> *We're the RCNVR.*
> *Roll along, wavy navy, roll along."*

His voice bounced off the iron bell, filling the tower and spilling out into the yard below.

WHEN HE WAS THIRTEEN, he got a job cleaning the church. Each Saturday he was paid fifty cents to straighten hymnals, dust pews, change numbers on the little wooden board above the pulpit that told what pages the hymns were on. The job didn't include the altar, however. He didn't wash the starched white cloth or polish the sacramental vessels. Only the women did that. A few complained. Mrs. Carlson said that just because he was the preacher's son he shouldn't get special privileges. "It doesn't look right," she told Eva Skretting in the Red and White. Eva said that Peter was a wild one and needed watching. "I wouldn't be surprised if he wasn't in on that Gussie Skogland business, and didn't Gussie get two months in Reform School?"

But he kept the job for one whole summer, every

Saturday flicking a limp cloth smelling of lemons over the dusty pews. Each time he finished, he'd stand in his father's pulpit, observing his handiwork.

The morning Louie hauled Frank Schultz to St. John's, the two children stood on the church steps and held the door for him. Louie and Zig Karetsky lugged the casket out of their truck, each hugging an end. They lifted it up the steps, Zig first, backing through the lobby, past swinging doors, down the nave's long aisle. Louie told him, bumping against the pews, to watch his step. Zig said how could he with this thing right under his nose. The two men set the grey box on metal stands in the chancel of St. John's, a few feet in front of the altar.

The news spread to the edges of town like spokes in the wheel of a bike. "They've got Frank Schultz down at St. John's." By 10 o'clock they'd gathered: Joe, Douglas, Ivan, Andy, Abie, Mary. The brother stood beside the swinging doors in the entrance, holding an offering plate.

"If you want to see him, it'll cost you a nickel," he said.

"Highway robbery," Ivan said.

"Can you go in with someone?" Andy asked.

"With someone it will cost a nickel extra. A nickel apiece plus one if you go in by twos."

The sister leaned back against the varnished wall. "I know a certain person who wouldn't think too much of this idea of yours."

"So are you going to tell?" her brother said.

"Yea, you better tell, Elizabeth," Joe said.

"Who's first?" the brother said.

"You be first."

"No, you go."

"I'll go next after you."

"Hell," Joe said. "I'll go." He threw a nickel into the brass plate and disappeared through the swinging doors. He was back almost immediately. "It's Schultz all right, and is he dead." Abie and Ivan went in together. Three nickels clanged into the plate. Their stay was only a little longer.

"Did you see his hands?" Andy asked, standing under the bell rope, his hair the colour of the rope. "They were folded, like he was praying."

The brother scoffed. "Louie just gets them to look like that. He's the one who finally gets them looking good."

"He didn't get the thumb right," Abie said. "It was sticking straight up. Louie should have tried to get the thumb right."

When the sister went in with Mary Sorenson, she saw only the face, bluish white like skim milk, shiny as mucilage.

In the afternoon during the service, they sat by the hedge, snapping beetles between rocks and making whistles out of caragana pods. The sun was shining, warm and orange. The air smelled of upturned soil, crushed pods, the cracked shells of beetles.

Ivan said, "Soon old Schultz will be galloping his way to glory. Flying through the sky to the sweet by and by." Ivan lived south of Main Street with his grandfather who spoke mostly Russian. Then he sang, "I don't care if it rains or freezes, I am safe in the arms of Jesus."

"Okay, Lippoway, you can shut your mouth right about now," the brother said. Certain irreverences he would not allow.

"Yea, Lippoway, zip your lip." Abie said.

"I understand the Communists in Russia hardly believe in anything any more," the sister said, her neck stiff against a branch.

Later, at the cemetery, the small group watched from behind a clump of honeysuckle bushes. They saw the mourners on one side of the grave, huddled together beside a pile of dirt. The preacher stood on the other side, holding a shovel. With three ropes, the six men, three on each side of the grave, lowered the box into the hole. Then the preacher spoke. His voice was thin, like a wisp of smoke. "From dust thou came, to dust thou shalt return, from dust shalt thou arise again." He shovelled clumps of earth down on the box below.

When she heard her father's words, the sister crumbled a small lump of dirt between her fingers and wondered why Frank Schultz had suddenly become a thou. Up until now he'd only been Frank, a farmer six miles south of Stone Creek. When Ivan heard them, he flapped his arms like a bird flying. Abie heard a different voice, an old voice from an ancient flame: "Take off your shoes, Moses. The ground you stand on is holy ground."

ONE AFTERNOON in fall she caught him smoking. He was sitting on the ground behind the garage, nearly hidden by Russian thistles. First she saw the wisps of grey rising from the thistles and the red spark of his cigarette. Then she saw him sitting there, leaning against a rock. She stood and watched, strong in the righteousness of her sex.

"So. Here's where you keep yourself," she finally said. He jerked the cigarette out of his mouth. "I didn't know you smoked." He held the glowing object down by his knee.

"So? Now you do."

"Well, isn't this interesting. I guess Dad would find it interesting too if he knew about it."

"Make sure you let him know then," he said, holding up the cigarette with a flourish.

"I didn't say I was going to tell him. I only said that if he knew he'd find it interesting. That's all I said."

"Well, if he'd find it so interesting I think you should tell him. I think you should go right now and tell him." He rubbed the cigarette into the dirt, snuffing it out, then covered it with stones and grass. He picked up a thin stick, placed it on the end of his nose, the tip resting on his forehead. This was a favourite trick of his. Only he could do it because of his odd-shaped nose.

"You think that's quite clever, don't you, balancing things on your nose like that. I suppose you think the girls at school consider you very smart and clever when you balance pencils on your nose like that and get them to laughing."

"Do you know anyone else who can do it?"

"I should hope not."

"It might interest you to know I've made fifty cents doing this, for people who appreciate it."

"Oh, really," the sister said and walked away.

"Hey, wait a minute," he shouted after her. "Have you ever heard this song before?"

She stopped, stood there among the swaying weeds

and listened to her brother sing in that curious new voice of his that she detested.

Hang out your washing on the Siegfried Line
If the Siegfried Line's still there.

"Certainly I've heard it. Mr. Nelson sings that when he's mowing the grass."

"Do you know what it means?"

"How should I know what it means?"

"Well, I guess you haven't heard what that song's all about, have you. That," he lowered his voice significantly, "is the dirtiest song in the English language. A very obscene song."

"What's dirty about it?"

"I'd never tell." He leaned back against the rock and slipped another Sweet Caporal out of its cellophaned package.

"What can be dirty about hanging out your wash on the Siegfried Line?"

"O. You said it."

"Said what?"

"The dirty words."

"You mean those are the dirty words?"

"That's what I said." He flicked a match against a rock, bent his head into the weeds, out of the wind, and lit the cigarette, inhaling deeply.

"What part is dirty – hanging out the wash? or the Siegfried Line?"

"O. You said it again."

"But you said it first."

"I sang it. Singing's different. It's like quoting."

"Well, tell me what it means then."

"Me? Never."

"Does it mean the same as what Gussie Skogland did to Rattray's cow?"

"I'd never say. You wouldn't get me to talk about anything like that."

She stood in a patch of dandelions and looked at him.

"So. You said the words, didn't you." He raised his head smoothly, easily, sending a delicate ribbon of smoke curling into the prairie sky.

He didn't forget. When she stood by the kitchen sink in a white apron, washing the supper dishes, he crept up behind her, nudged her with his shoulder, and whispered the song in her ear. When she climbed down the basement stairs to use the toilet behind the furnace, he followed her halfway down the steps, then stopped, and sang between closed teeth.

Hang out your washing on the Siegfried Line
If the Siegfried Line's still there.

Once in the living room, where their father was kneeling at the front door, working with a screwdriver to fasten a broken hinge, her brother sprawled on the brown sofa and hummed the song under his breath. She left the room, her heart pounding, and asked her mother in the kitchen if there was anything she could do to help.

Later he told her. "You really thought that was a dirty song, didn't you. You were scared I was going to tell. Ha."

"Oh, really. Wasn't that a smart thing to do. Weren't

you smart and clever to think of something like that." She ran, furious, down the street to Sorensons'.

WHEN HE WAS FIFTEEN, he got Zig Karetsky's old job working for Louie in the undertaking parlour.

"Do you think it looks right?" Mrs. Carlson asked Eva Skretting in the Red and White. They were standing next to the bread shelf. "The preacher's son working for Louie like that? Won't people think it's kind of fishy? It could cause talk."

"What's a mystery to me is why Louie would hire him. He's one who needs watching," Eva said, fitting a loaf snugly into the row of other loaves.

But he went to work every Saturday, leaving the house at nine, whistling down the driveway.

One morning in June he forgot his lunch. His mother picked up the brown bag from the kitchen counter and told his sister to take it to him. She combed her hair, preened in front of the hall mirror until her mother called her to stop fussing and get started. She slipped on her new blue sweater and examined herself again from different angles in the hall mirror. She was going downtown to bring her brother his lunch.

Outside, the sun was pouring down, shining on the purple blooms of lilacs, stippling the young leaves of caraganas. It flecked the wings of a meadowlark perched on a fence post and spread over weeds and grass onto the gravelled driveway. It soaked into the little crevices between the stones, warming the sleek backs of ants and beetles. There was no space anywhere without the light.

At the end of the driveway her father was kneeling beside the car, fiddling with his tool box. The sun spilled out over the car's slick top and down on his greasy tools. It shone warm on his curved shoulders and smooth grey back.

She walked past the lilacs to where her father knelt by the blue car. He looked up. "My, aren't you spiffed up this morning," he said. "Are you going to a wedding?"

She held the brown bag out in front of her. "He forgot his lunch. I have to bring him his lunch."

She opened the gate and walked down the sidewalk to Sorensons'. She stopped to watch her friend Mary do a back bend under the clothesline, her body curved against the earth, her hair streaming.

"Where are you off to?" Mary asked, upside down.

"To Louie's. I'm bringing my brother his lunch. You knew he was working for Louie, didn't you?"

"Well, I guess," Mary said, her back circling the grass.

She turned at Sorensons' corner and walked over to Main Street. She stopped in front of Cutler's Dry Goods, where Label was sweeping the sidewalk. The straw of his broom gathered dust, gravel, crushed candy wrappers, guiding them over the sun-warmed cement into the narrow ditch at the curb's edge.

"Where do you think you're going?" he asked.

"Me? Oh, nowhere special. My dumb brother forgot his lunch and I have to bring it to him. You knew he was working for Louie, didn't you?"

"Of course." He continued sweeping, tufts of yellow

straw swirling over the concrete.

At Louie's she walked across the oiled floor, past lamps and sofas, to the office at the far end. She opened the door. Her brother was sitting on a wooden chair, his feet up on the desk, staring at the ceiling.

"Is this all you have to do?" she asked.

He jerked his feet off the desk and sat up straight. "All! Don't you know Louie's away? Who'd answer the phone if I wasn't here? Who'd take care of things?" He picked up a yellow pencil, held it by his ear, ready for any important message.

"It doesn't look like much of a job to me," the sister said.

"Some jobs take muscles. Some take brains." He laid the pencil on the desk blotter and fussed about in the drawer with a box of paper clips. She looked at a closed door across the room.

"Is that where you keep them?"

"When we've got them."

"You don't have any today?"

"Not in there."

"Well, here's the lunch you forgot." She set the bag on the desk and turned to leave.

"Hey, wait a minute," he said. "You might be interested in that shoebox." He pointed to the shelf beside the desk. The shelf was littered with old magazines, an ashtray, and a white shoebox with 5.98 written in black on one end.

"Why?"

"Oh, no special reason. I just thought you might like to know what's in that box. But I guess you wouldn't be interested after all."

She walked over to the shelf and grabbed the box. She opened the lid, lifted up a gauzy sheet of tissue paper. She saw it for less than a second, smaller than her hand, tiny fingers curled tightly like the claws of a kitten, eyes shut tight. She felt a ragged lump in the centre of her stomach, and shoved the box back on the shelf.

"Why did you do that?" she shouted. "Why did you do such a stupid thing as that? What a stupid thing to do!"

"What did I do? I didn't make you open the box."

"Why is it in a shoebox?"

"Because they're going to bury it. Any smaller they'd flush it down the toilet."

"Oh, you're really something, aren't you? You really think of marvellous things, don't you? Brilliant and marvellous. It must make you very proud to think of such marvellous things. Well, have a nice time eating your lunch, that's all I have to say."

She fled from the room, past the sofas, lamps, and cane-back chairs, out the front door. She ran past Cutler's, cut across the back alley to Sorensons'. She didn't stop running until she reached her own yard and leaned against the gate, her heart pounding.

Her father was still working on the car. He was lying under it on the gravel, hammering away at something. She saw only his feet twisting under the bumper.

She ran into the house, hurried through the kitchen where her mother was chopping walnuts, into the living room.

She sat down in front of the piano and paged

through ragged song books. She looked up at the photographs sitting on top of the piano. A picture of her grandparents on their Golden Wedding Anniversary, standing in front of a poplar tree, holding a cake. One of her cousin Wesley on his Confirmation Day, standing on the church step, holding a scroll. One of her and her brother, when he was six and she was three, sitting in a chair together, holding a ball.

"KETCHENS," she said.

"Ketchens?"

"The chickens in the kitchen at Ketchens'. Don't you remember? We made up a song about them. They'd walk in through the screen door that had no screen and wander all over the house."

She was lying on a narrow bed in a Toronto hospital. The head of the bed was raised, making it look like a chaise lounge. She was wearing a green hospital gown. Her brother, in a tweed jacket, was sitting on a chrome chair beside her, holding a pair of sunglasses by one stem and swinging it in little half-circles in front of him. A huge bouquet of yellow roses rested on the windowsill behind him.

He stopped twirling the glasses. "I remember now. The place with the flies. Everywhere you looked, flies."

"Well, the door had no screen," she said. "Just a big hole where the screen was supposed to be. And it was summer."

"And hot," he said.

"And there was no screen, and the chickens just wandered in and out."

"And the buzzing flies."

"Mrs. Ketchen asked us to stay for lunch and Dad said yes, and she served canned peaches on a flat dinner plate. You couldn't manage them with your spoon and started laughing, so Dad told you to use your knife and fork."

He uncrossed his legs and leaned back in the chair. September sunlight streamed through the window onto his back, his shoulders and his greying hair.

"Why would he take us to a place like that anyway?" he asked.

"He wanted us with him sometimes, when he made his calls."

He leaned forward. "And why does he choose to stay in that God-forsaken town?"

A nurse, plump and middle-aged, her clipped hair tidy under a white cap, walked into the room, carrying a trayful of tiny paper cups.

"For your bowels," she said and set a cup on the bedside table. "I'll bring the baby in later for her snack." She turned and walked out of the room. They heard her footsteps clicking down the corridor.

"In the final analysis, it's the bowels that count. It's all they care about now," the sister said. She sat up higher against the pillows. "It was good of you to come. Toronto's a long way from San Francisco."

"It was time for a visit. How long has it been anyway?"

"Too long," she said.

"So how was it?" he asked. "The birth I mean. The baby looks healthy."

She lay back against the pillow and yawned.

"Remember the summer I worked at the new hospital? You were still working for Louie, I think. Well, one morning I was picking peas in the hospital garden. I was on my hands and knees in the dirt when I heard a woman screaming. And I remember thinking that when I grew up and had babies I wasn't going to do that. I was going to be poised the whole time, make a few jokes, ask the doctor if he'd like a cup of tea. I'd be real cute."

"And were you?"

"Are you crazy? I roared, I yelled at them to stop, stop the whole business, I'd changed my mind. But when it was over. Lord. It was lovely. The doctor held her in the palm of his hand. She was all bloody red, sleek and shiny. And I shouted hallelujah like a Holy Roller."

When her brother got up to leave, he leaned forward and kissed her on the forehead.

"Goodbye, Elizabeth," he said.

"Goodbye, Peter."

After he'd gone, she turned over on her side, closed her eyes, and sank her head into the green pillow. Everything's so green here, she thought.

SHE'S SITTING on a wooden bench in a narrow boat. The bench is pressing hard against her legs and against the dark sore between her legs. She tries to move, to lift the aching from the wood's hardness, but she can't budge. The baby is tucked under her blouse out of the wind. She hears its sucking noises. The boat glides silently over the blue green water.

She looks up and sees her brother. He's leaning over

the side of the vessel, observing the waves. He's wearing sunglasses and he's alone. Where are the others? Andy and Joe and Ivan, and the rest who gathered on summer nights under the lamppost?

Her father is kneeling at the forward end of the boat. He's fastening a loose piece of tin to the prow. He clutches the tin with one hand. With the other he rummages through his tool box, searching for the right tool to do the job. The tin rattles in the wind like the old Imperial Oil sign on Main Street, on a dusty spring night on the prairie.

Her brother lifts his head and looks out on the passing islands. He's enjoying the scenery, she thinks, but doesn't see his father kneeling there, fastening the tin. She wants to tell her brother, turn around now and look at your father, see what he's doing, observe how he fixes things. She wants to tell everyone: That's what my dad does. He mends things. Doors and carburetors, people's sorrows. But the words stick in her bowels. Her father bends over the tool box. His thin hair rises and curves like threads of smoke in the wind. Her brother gazes out to the edge of the sea.

In October it happened.

In Toronto, she stood in her large kitchen, staring at the telephone on the counter in front of her. Her right hand lay on the black receiver.

In San Francisco, in his twenty-fifth floor office, her brother looked up from a yellow legal pad on the walnut desk in front of him and gazed out a wall-sized window to the ocean. He stared at the ships in the harbour, from Rio de Janeiro, Yokohama, Hong Kong, and at the sun's brightness on the water. He was thinking of Manchuria.

When he finally picked up the phone he heard his sister's voice. "Dad just died. He was knocked down by a car in Regina. He's dead."

In Manchuria it was 8 p.m. Outside of Mukden, some old Chinese farmers were squatting in a barley field. After a long day of work they were smoking their pipes under a darkening sky, the smoke rising silently above the barley as they emptied their bowels into the field.

"No," her brother said. That's all he said. For a long while he sat in the leather chair in San Francisco, his hand on the telephone.

But he didn't see the telephone or his hand resting on it. He didn't see the wall-sized window or the ocean or the sunlight on the water. He didn't notice the light pouring in through the window. Moving over the desk and the chair and himself sitting in the chair. Over his arm, his hand.

Then he saw it.

He saw the remarkable brightness of it.

And the light rolled off the iron bell and spread out over the town. It spilled down on Main Street, on the café and the hotel and on Louie's place, where he sat in a wooden chair holding a pencil near his ear. It poured down on the vacant lot, on weeds and dead grass, and on his father walking through the grass.

Then it drifted into the street, mingled with the dust along the curbs, rose in swirls above the town, and lost itself in glimmering waves over the prairie.

Hosea's Children

WHEN HOSEA DROVE UP FROM MEDICINE Hat to look for Gordon in Edmonton, she brought her two youngest children to her sister in Rocky Mountain House. The girl, Doloros, was seven and Bittern, her son, was ten. Her oldest child had already left home and the last Hosea heard was living somewhere in British Columbia. She moved from place to place and didn't keep in touch with her mother. She'd left the Hat with a man named Joe, who worked the rigs, and who called her Ann.

Hosea had thought about Edmonton on and off all spring. She still knew a couple of people in the city from the time she and Gordon lived there – she could stay with them for awhile. She also thought that besides locating her husband, she might find work and move to the city permanently. So on April 11 she packed the children and an old suitcase of clothes and a few toys into her green

Chev and headed north. It was the day the story came out about a seven-year-old girl, with her father and flight instructor, dying in an airplane crash in the United States. The girl had wanted to be the youngest pilot ever to fly across the country, but the plane, which had taken off in California, crashed somewhere in Wyoming.

Hosea listened to all this on the car radio as she drove north on Highway 2, then west on Number 11 into Rocky Mountain House. The girl, the *pilot,* was the same age as Doloros.

On the drive west a snowy drizzle came down, wet and slushy against the windshield, and she had to lean close to the steering wheel and peer out past the clicking wipers in order to see the road ahead. She told Doloros, sitting beside her, to please be still, and Bittern, in the back seat, to stop asking questions. But the boy wouldn't quit talking about the plane crash.

"Would you let Doloros drive an airplane in a snowstorm?" he asked. "If she wanted to?"

"Think, Bittern," Hosea said. "Just be quiet and think about it." She clutched more tightly at the steering wheel.

"I am thinking," Bittern said. "I'm thinking what if she wanted to do that."

"I do want to," Doloros said, snuggling into her small frayed blanket. "I want to drive an airplane in a snowstorm."

Right, Hosea thought. As if you won't have danger and treachery enough on the small path you'll walk here on earth.

The snow stopped before they reached Rocky

Mountain House, and when they drove into town the sun was out and the western sky was a deep purplish blue. The mountain range on the far horizon shone silver.

Judith was waiting for them on her porch. She was sitting on a white plastic chair in a patch of sunlight, wearing her husband's curling sweater and drinking coffee from a yellow mug. The children saw her even before the car slowed down, and they waved and pounded the windows and shouted, "Judith. Judith. There she is. Judith."

When the car stopped at the curb, they scrambled out and ran into the yard and up the porch steps to their aunt. They threw themselves at her, the three of them a tangled bundle in the sunlight.

"Well, you," Judith said. "If it isn't you and you. Right here on my porch. Isn't that something. Isn't that just lovely."

"Me and her and you," Bittern said.

And Hosea, climbing the stairs, suitcase in hand, said, "Don't forget me."

Judith turned to her sister and reached out her arms.

Bittern said, "Do you know what Mom is going to let Doloros do? Drive an airplane in a snowstorm. Even in a raging blizzard."

"So you heard about that crash," Judith said.

"We get to skip school," Bittern said.

"I'm a very good reader," Doloros said.

"Do you still have the rabbits?" Bittern asked.

"We certainly do," Judith said.

Bittern jumped down the steps and ran around the house to the backyard; his sister followed.

Judith went into the house and returned with a fresh cup of coffee for Hosea and a refill for herself. The women sat down in the white chairs – Judith, her body softly round, brown hair curling about her face, Hosea, thin, almost gaunt, sandy hair tied at the back of her neck in a tight ponytail.

Judith had been thinking about Hosea and her children all morning. Particularly about Ann. She wondered if she should tell her sister what she knew, but Ann had asked that her mother not find out yet. So as Judith was making up the cot for Doloros in her daughter Carly's room and the sofa bed for Bittern in the small study across from it, she decided that today she would try just to listen to Hosea without offering opinions or advice. She'd *try*.

The last time the two sisters were together, Hosea had lamented again the disappearance of Gordon. And Judith's reply again was, "But he always leaves. You know that. He's a jerk. He thinks if you're a bigshot writer, which he isn't – how many books has he actually finished and published? Zero – but he thinks he is and therefore he's not required like ordinary human beings to be responsible. He can do anything he pleases. He can leave his own children...."

"Stop it, Judith, you don't know the whole story so just stop talking." And she told Judith (again) in her strained voice that Gordon had signed a certificate with a gold seal on it, on July 8, 1980, in a church lit with white candles and decorated with pink carnations, and that he'd pledged his vows before God and Rev. Hunter (you remember Norman), and before Thelma, their mother, who died six months later, and all the other rel-

atives and Gordon's folks as well. And she just wanted
to remind Gordon of these facts.

The two women sat, quiet in the sunlight, sipping
their coffee.

"You've heard from Anxiety, haven't you," Hosea said
finally.

Judith waited a moment to answer.

"Why do you keep calling her that?" she finally said.

"It's the name I gave her," Hosea said.

"She wants to be called Ann. You of all people
should know that. *Hosea.* Some old prophet married to
a hooker that he had to keep tracking down."

"You've heard from her, haven't you."

Judith sighed. "She wrote to Carly, not me." Carly
was the same age as Anxiety.

"It's funny," Hosea said. "It's her dad who left her,
but it's me she can't stand. She has no respect for me."

"She's doing all right," Judith said. "Joe seems like a
good person."

"Running off with a fifteen-year-old?"

"Sixteen now," Judith said. "You were only seventeen
the first time you took up with Gordon. Remember?"

"Are they in BC?" Hosea asked.

"Revelstoke, but they're moving, she didn't say where."
She stood up. "I've made sandwiches," she said. "Let's call
the children and have some lunch before you go."

HOSEA DROVE out of town under a dark sky. Leaving
Rocky Mountain House, she'd felt warm and safe. The
children were with Judith, who enfolded them in her

arms and cared for them with an easy confidence. But now, as she drove north toward Edmonton, the peace she'd felt began to unravel. Why was she doing this? Looking for Gordon like this? Every woman she'd talked to on this subject had said the same thing: dump him, he's a loser.

And then there was Anxiety. Where was the balm to heal the wound of a child gone?

It started to snow again. Wet flakes splashed against the glass. Hosea stared at the road ahead, kept her eyes on the yellow line.

SHE'D LAIN IN BED that night, awake and restless. Then she'd gotten up and gone into the kitchen for a glass of milk. She paced the living-room floor, turned on the TV, checked on Doloros and Bittern, safe and sleeping soundly. Then she went back to her own bed, and stared up at the darkness.

At 3 a.m. she heard the door opening and closing and footsteps creaking on the hall floor. What relief. Everyone was in; she could go back to sleep. But instead, she got out of bed and met her daughter in the hallway.

"Where were you?" she said and heard her own voice, hard, accusing.

"Who needs to know?" Anxiety muttered.

"Don't talk to me like that."

"Like what?" Her voice was slurred.

"You've been drinking again."

Anxiety walked, straight and deliberate, past her

mother toward her own room.

Hosea yelled, "Why are you so hateful?"

Anxiety swayed toward the wall.

"Why not, Mama?"

Hosea was forty.

Anxiety was thirteen.

AT THE LACOMBE TURNOFF she started to cry. Tears ran down her face and dripped off her chin onto her lap. Visibility was bad enough as it was, but she couldn't stop. She took her right hand off the steering wheel and wiped her eyes. She turned on the car radio. Heard only static.

The snow stopped before she reached Leduc, and when she arrived at the southern outskirts of Edmonton a dry wind was blowing. She drove into a Husky station to use the washroom and make a phone call.

In the ladies' room, a large woman with pale white skin and a black patch over one eye was trying to get her little girl to reach up to the sink to wash. Her small fingers could barely reach the stream of water pouring from the tap. The mother rubbed soap on the child's hands, lathering her palms, her wrists, and in between each finger. Then she lifted her up closer to the tap so she could rinse.

"You never know, do you," the woman said to Hosea. "You just never know." Water splashed over the girl's skin and into the porcelain bowl. Hosea didn't answer. She examined her own splotchy face in the mirror above the sink.

"There's so much stuff out there," the woman continued. "It's all over...you can't get away from it...it gets on your skin and sticks there...then your pores soak it up...all that crud...and what happens next?....gets into the internal organs...and then...the blood!... Have you thought about this? Don't you wonder about it?"

She turned to the girl, pretty, curly haired, her blue eyes bright and curious. "Are you finished, Junie? Are you nice and clean? Let's dry your hands now." She rubbed the girl's hands with a paper towel, threw the towel into the wastebasket and headed for the exit. She bent forward, pushed the door open with her forehead, and the two disappeared.

Hosea stared after them. What's going on? Are mothers simply cracking up? She soaked a paper towel in cold water, washed her face and decided that before she did anything else she needed a cup of coffee.

In the Husky Café she chose a booth next to a window. She liked the feeling of privacy a booth gave her, a pleasant sensation of being in her own yard but surrounded by neighbours who went about their business in a quiet yet friendly way. She looked out at the grey coldness. Melting snow and slushy mud had made ragged ditches in the parking lot, and the dry wind had hardened the edges into ridges of stiff dirt. She ordered coffee and a glazed doughnut, then unfolded a paper napkin. She dug in her purse for her ballpoint pen. *Things To Do,* she printed at the top of the napkin. *Call the Letts, call Alfreda.* Often she filled a whole page with her scribbling; today this was all she had to say.

When she'd finished her coffee she went in search of a pay phone.

First she dialled the Letts – they'd want her to stay with them a night or two – but she got their answering machine. Then she called Alfreda, who told her that her mother might be coming to town this week and her cat was shedding besides. Hosea hung up the receiver and slouched against the wall. Of course, she should have called them before she left. She realized that now. Sometimes her brain didn't click into the specifics of life. She flipped through the Yellow Pages. There must be cheap lodging somewhere.

THE YWCA was situated on the corner of 100 Avenue and 103 Street. Across the street to the north was the Foster & McGarvey Funeral Chapel, and to the east, the Alano Club. A private club for ex-drunks, the Y receptionist told Hosea when she registered for the night, and a cheap place to eat when the Y dining room is closed, "which is right now," she added.

So it was here at the Alano Club that Hosea found herself sitting alone at a formica-covered table, eating a cheeseburger, drinking cold milk, and thinking of Gordon. She looked around, half expecting he would show up. You never knew. He could have decided he'd had enough and become an ex-drunk instead of a practising one. She'd decided years ago that if you came from Montana and called yourself a writer you were probably a drunk. Not that Gordon was *from* Montana. He'd only lived there a year. He was from Alberta actually. Cardston. Mormon country. But he wasn't a Mormon either. He was simply a drunk who thought he was a writer.

And where are you now? Gordon with the red beard, wide neck, broad back? Gordon with the smooth skin, the sweet words, the touch? You thought I was pretty and my hair was fine and soft, precious you said, and held the ends of it in your hand and breathed on it, and on my chin. Such a smooth little chip of a thing you said, and my neck curved under your palm and my face was easy on your chest. You funny, funny bird, you said.

"Would you like company?" The woman standing in front of her was holding a coffee cup in one hand, a red purse in the other. "Or not?" she added. "It's up to you. I sometimes like to eat alone, but then again I get really starved for conversation."

"Please, sit down," Hosea said.

"Thirty days sober," the woman said. "Never thought I'd make it this far. But one day comes and then another, and before you know it you've got thirty. Unbelievable, isn't it?"

She set the red purse on the floor under the chair, her cup on the table, and sat across from Hosea. She was a thin woman with pale skin. The heavy makeup she wore did not conceal the tiny bumps covering her face. Even in the small space below her eyebrows, the skin bubbled. But her bright red lips were smooth and her black hair shiny.

"And totally unbelievable that I'm sitting here," she continued. "I mean, two weeks ago I'dve been off by myself in some corner, hiding behind a newspaper, scared to death someone might talk to me and mad as hell if they didn't. Crazy huh?"

"Do you come here often?" Hosea asked.

"Pretty well all the time, not having a job right now,

which is a bummer. My name's Lily, by the way. And you are?"

"Hosea."

"Say that again?"

"Hosea."

"Some handle, eh? Whose idea was it?"

And Hosea told the story of how her mother, when she was pregnant, was working in a hotel in Banff, cleaning rooms, and how one day she opened up a Gideon bible to whatever page it opened to and there she saw it. Hosea. She never read far enough to know it was a man's name, much less a prophet's.

"So where are you from?" Hosea asked.

"Nowhere really. I wander around mostly. Here and there. Used to live in Ryley when I was young. Not far from here."

"Have a family?"

"Two kids. Social Services took them. That's why I'm here. I want them back. God I do. But if I don't sober up..." She folded her hands and let out a long sigh. "How about you? Any kids?"

"Three. They're with my sister. Well, two of them are. One's off somewhere. She doesn't keep in touch."

"Sounds like me," the woman said. She looked at the clock on the far wall. "Well, I have to go now or I won't make my meeting. Thirty days. They give you a red chip when you make thirty."

She leaned over and picked up her purse from under the chair. "Maybe I'll see you around."

"Sure," Hosea said. "Maybe."

The woman rose and walked away.

THEY'D HAD a pleasant supper together, the four of them sitting around the kitchen table eating spaghetti and soft Italian bread. It was summer, and the early evening was warm and rosy. Then purple blue clouds piled up on the western horizon and the rain began. Silver-beaded chains slanted down from the sky, gentle at first, then harsher until the kitchen window was streaming with water, and the yard outside – lilacs, fence, even the small garage – was hidden in the dark rain. But inside it was warm, the light glowed amber from the bamboo-shaded fixture above the table, and there was a softness about the family, a quiet gentleness.

"So what are we all doing tonight?" Hosea asked.

"Me? Nothing," Bittern said.

"Let's make popcorn and watch television and pretend it's Christmas," Doloros said.

Anxiety was quiet.

"And you?" Hosea asked.

"I don't know. I guess I'll do some laundry. I'm way behind."

"It looks like a good night to curl up with a mystery," Hosea said.

Bittern and Doloros made popcorn and snuggled in blankets in front of the TV. Hosea, in the big chair by the living-room window, sipped hot tea and looked through magazines, and Anxiety did her wash. Hosea could hear the dryer thumping in the little laundry room at the end of the hall. When the wash was done, Anxiety joined her brother and sister on the floor. She watched television, drank cocoa, joked with Bittern, tousled Doloros's hair.

And the next morning she was gone. The clean laundry she'd piled at the foot of her bed was gone. Shoes from her closet, new jeans, diary, makeup, the pink and silver comb and mirror she'd gotten from Joe – all were gone. And Anxiety was gone.

HOSEA STOOD UP, tugged at her coat, twisted her arms into the sleeves, and moved toward the door. When she passed by the grill, she saw on the television screen above it a small crowd gathered around the airplane that had crashed in Wyoming. The plane had landed in someone's front yard, on their driveway. Landed nose down and gouged out chunks of concrete.

HER ROOM AT THE Y was on the sixth floor. In it were four narrow beds, each with a thin metal rod as head-board. The headboards were flush against the wall, and the beds five or six feet apart. At the foot of each was a small metal closet. The bathroom was down the hall.

When Hosea registered, she'd paid the six-dollar fee for the dormitory room and chosen the bed farthest from the door. She'd shoved her case into the closet and laid a towel over the metal rod to reserve her space. She'd found the room empty and thought herself lucky to have the space to herself.

But now, returning from the Alano Club, she saw that the bed nearest the door had also been claimed. A canvas backpack was lying on the green blanket, and a pair of white panties hung over the metal headboard;

but whoever was her roommate was nowhere to be seen.

On the way to the bathroom Hosea passed by the lounge. She saw in a glance the large television screen, the worn sofa, the small table strewn with pop cans and magazines, and three girls slouched in overstuffed chairs, watching the screen. Only the television made any noise. She noticed that the girls were young and they all looked gloomy. One of the three was probably her roommate.

Back in her own room, the bed felt good. The mattress was thin but firm, the sheets clean, the blanket warm. She'd raised the shade on the small window between her bed and the one next to it, and a pale glow from a streetlight entered the room in a shaft of light that was comforting to her. She lay on her back and closed her eyes. Then she remembered. She hadn't called the children; she'd promised to, but forgot.

And she saw them sitting together at the kitchen table in Rocky Mountain House – Bittern and Doloros side by side, Carly opposite them, Judith and Ralph at each end. Ralph with his shaggy hair and thin lips, his funny nose and sharp chin, making comic faces and strange animal sounds. Bittern whooping with laughter, Doloros smiling, Carly feigning dismay.

She saw the woman with the bumpy skin sitting at the table in the Alano Club. "I want them back," Lily had said. "God, I do." Where were those children now? Hosea wondered.

She saw the seven-year-old girl in California tugging at her mother's arm. "Please, Mama, please? I want to fly. Get me an airplane and let me fly." And her mother says, "Yes, yes. We'll call your father." And the father says, "If that's what you want, why not? We'll set a world record." And Hosea saw them – the father, the flying instructor, the girl – in the snowy sky above Wyoming, excited and proud, speeding through morning. But suddenly the girl is shouting, "It's wrong, something's all wrong!" And the instructor is pushing her out of the way, grabbing the controls. Only it's too late. The nose of the plane jerks downward. Down down through whirling snow. *Mama Mama Mama...please, Mama.* And the father, what was he doing? Did he suddenly repent up there in the swirling madness? *My God, save her...I was wrong...have mercy.* And right then did the plane's nose smash into the concrete, hurling chunks of cement, bits of gravel, sharp flints of stone into the air above?

Hosea turned onto her side. She should try to get some sleep. In the morning she would start looking for Gordon.

A key turned in the lock, and the door opened and quietly closed, and she heard light footsteps on the linoleum floor. She lay still, listened in silence to the movements: the tearing of the velcro fastening on the backpack, crumpling plastic, the tugging and rustling of undressing and dressing. Then a deep sigh. And it was quiet.

Hosea waited several seconds before she opened her eyes. When she did she saw in the dim light a girl's form crouched on the floor beside the bed, her back to Hosea, her arms splayed out on the blanket. She was sighing, whispering very softly. Hosea strained to hear.

"Heavenly Father, Holy God, Almighty Lord." The girl's head was moving in small semicircles from side to side. She was praying. Kneeling by the bed and praying. Right there below the white panties hanging on the railing. Hosea closed her eyes. She was ashamed to be watching. But then she opened them again. And she saw the girl get up from the floor, saw her silhouette in the dim light, her thin body bending over the bed then disappearing under the covers. The girl was slender, like Anxiety, but taller.

THE FIRST TIME Gordon left was soon after Anxiety was born. Hosea had come home from the hospital with the new baby, her first. She was scared. The baby cried almost constantly. Hosea had tried to enjoy the infant, to sit on the sunny porch beside the morning glories and nurse her, to sing to her, go for walks in the park, pushing the baby in her small carriage. But she did these things without confidence, without energy. Her actions were awkward and rigid. The baby seemed to sense her mother's fear and became increasingly more nervous and discontent, vomiting, bawling, her small face turning dark red from some deep and hopeless effort she was making right there in her mother's arms. Then Gordon left. When he returned two weeks later, he explained that he wasn't able to handle the confusion: meals disrupted, sleep disturbed, wife flustered, impatient, depressed.

One day while he was still gone and the baby was crying and spitting, red faced and ugly, she laid the infant on their wide bed. The baby's legs and arms kicked and whirled above the spread. And Hosea looked down at the purplish face and in a voice full of exasperation said, "From now on your name is Anxiety."

The name stuck. Later, in school, the child's teachers refused to use that name, but most of her classmates used it freely until nearly everyone got used to it.

SHE HEARD SOFT SNORING from the other bed and pulled the blanket partway over her head. When she finally went to sleep she dreamed of her father. She was swimming in the Atlantic Ocean, halfway between Europe and North America. It was dark, the water icy cold, and she was alone. She radioed to New York to tell someone that she couldn't make it; it was too far and she was tired. If she didn't get help soon she was going to sink. And her father came to her, red faced and laughing. He grabbed her with his strong dusty arms and lifted her out of the murky water and carried her safely to shore.

When Hosea awoke, the girl was sitting cross-legged on top of her bed, digging into her backpack. Hosea could not see her face, but she saw the long straight hair, thin arms, grey white T-shirt, loose on her skinny body. The white panties were gone from the rod. The girl must have sensed Hosea's awakening. She raised her head and looked at her, a sly look, Hosea thought, a bit of a sneaky look, the look of someone who had just played a trick on you or was about to. She was not as pretty as Anxiety.

"Well, good morning, sleepyhead!" the girl said in a

voice loud and enthusiastic. "I'm just getting some break-fast and you're welcome to have some." From her pack she lifted out a loaf of McGavin's bread, a jar of jam, and a sausage ring. She laughed. "I'm travelling third-class economy as you can see." She laughed again, louder. "Actually, I've been saving for awhile for the Rose Benson weekend at the Westin Hotel. You've heard of Rose. She's a preacher on TV. From Texas. Everybody calls her the Yellow Rose of Texas. And she's wonderful! I myself came up on the Greyhound. From Bawlf, ha ha."

Hosea stood up and took her towel from the iron rod. She picked up her bath kit.

"Would you care to join me?" the girl said. "Ten dollars a session, or twenty-five for three. You won't be sorry."

"Oh, no," Hosea said. "I have business to look after. I'm kind of in a hurry. But thanks."

"No problem," the girl said.

When Hosea returned from the shower the girl was gone. But she'd left a note on Hosea's pillow: Help yourself to the food on the table. I'll be back tonight for supper. *(More bread and sausage. Ha!)*

Who was she anyway? Loud. Forward. Like an American, Hosea thought as she got dressed. Hosea didn't like Americans. She blamed the entire United States of America, especially Montana, for Gordon's behaviour. He hadn't been a run-around in Cardston. She checked her purse for keys, wallet, makeup.

In the lobby downstairs she stopped by the bulletin board and read the notices. Aerobics: Tuesday & Thursday. Makeup: Monday. Accessories: Wednesday. Self-esteem: Friday. Beside the announcements, someone had pinned a brochure announcing Sunday morning worship at the New Universal Church of Feminine Consciousness and Cosmic Awareness. "Get in touch with the Divine Feminine at the heart of the Universe. Connect with Her energy. Feel Her Power in your fingertips." In the lower corner of the board was a small poster of coloured pictures of missing children: Tara, age 10, missing since November 10, 1987. Brent, age 4, missing since October, 1990. Jonathan since 1988....

Hosea looked at the pictures and wondered why she felt nothing. No sympathy. No sadness. Her mind remembered with exact detail the morning of Anxiety's disappearance. But her heart was blank.

IT TOOK ONLY A GLANCE from the bedroom doorway to get the whole picture: the top of the dresser cleared of all its objects, the bed neatly made. For several moments she didn't move. She stood in the doorway and felt the small grey hole at the centre of her stomach slowly expand, from below her navel up into her chest and throat, then quickly out to her arms and down her sides to her legs and ankles, until there was nothing inside of her to hold her up. She sat down on the bed.

Bittern came into the room.

"Where's Annie?" he asked.

"Gone," Hosea said.

"Gone where?"

"With Joe."

"So where'd they go?"

"I don't know."

He moved to the closet and peered into its emptiness; then he opened the dresser drawers, reached his hand to the far corners of each drawer, pulled out a pink sock. "One sock. Man. She *is* gone," he said.

THE INN ON SEVENTH was only four blocks from the YWCA. Hosea decided to walk the short distance and have breakfast there. The air was clear. The sun was shining. In front of the funeral chapel, bare branches of shrubs glistened in the light.

At the Inn, she chose a booth by the window, ordered a carafe of coffee and a cinnamon bun, and got out her ballpoint pen. *What to Do* she wrote on the paper napkin. *Call Judith, go to the Cecil, the Strathcona, the Commercial.* Someone would remember him. Someone would know where he was.

He liked to sit in taverns or coffee shops and write his ideas in little scrappy notebooks. He wrote mostly about gamblers and wild women, about ex-cons in dark and smoky bars. He wrote a poem about her once – in the Commercial Hotel on Whyte Avenue. About her body, naked in an amber light. Hosea filled her cup with hot coffee from the carafe and unrolled a long strip of cinnamon bun. His favourite colour: amber.

ON ANXIETY'S FOURTH BIRTHDAY they had gone to Pancake Palace, just outside of Medicine Hat, for breakfast. Anxiety, Gordon, and Hosea. After the waiter had laid the plates of steaming hotcakes down in front of them, Anxiety examined hers carefully, her nose close to the plate, and refused even to lift her fork to them.

"Eat up," Gordon said.

"I don't eat green pancakes," she said.

"They're not green," her mother said.

Anxiety pointed to a tiny speck in the centre of one pancake. "Do you see that?"

And since it was her birthday, she got a waffle instead, with whipped cream and strawberries.

In the lobby, Hosea dialled her sister in Rocky Mountain House. No sooner had Judith answered the call than Hosea heard Bittern and Doloros arguing in the background.

"I want to, I want to," Doloros was shouting.

"I said I was going to," Bittern said.

And Judith said, "Just a minute, I have to settle something here."

While she waited, Hosea unclasped her wallet and counted her money. Four tens, two fives, some change. She'd need to fill the gas tank before she went back. She'd have to be careful with the spending.

Bittern came on the line. "Guess what?"

"What?"

"Guess."

"I can't guess."

"Guess who called."

"Who?"

"Guess."

Hosea's heart beat faster. Gordon. He must be trying

to find her. "Your father," she said. "It was your dad."

"No. Annie."

"Anxiety?"

"Annie! That's what I said."

Judith picked up the phone. "She called last night. She wondered where you were, but I didn't know so I couldn't tell her anything."

"She wondered where *I* was? *Me?*" Hosea felt her heart speeding. "Where is she?"

"She didn't say. Where are you? She might call back."

"She called?" Hosea said again.

"Yes," Judith said. "So where are you?"

"The Y. The YWCA."

THE POLICEMAN had sat at Hosea's kitchen table, pen in hand, black notepad on the blue placemat. Who is this guy? A guy. How old is he? Nineteen. Where does he work? The oilpatch. Is he abusive? I don't think so. Is she safe? The officer was a tall, lanky man. He spoke fast, got to the point. "We can find them, of course," he said. "But then what?" He stood up, stuffed the notepad and pen into his black case. "Do you have pictures?" he asked. "A recent snapshot?" Hosea gave him a school portrait of Anxiety when she was in grade eight. At the door he turned and looked at her.

"Anxiety," he said. "That's a hell of a name for a kid."

They'd found her the next day at the York Hotel in Calgary. With Joe. And when the police called Hosea, she heard her daughter yelling in the background. "I was not kidnapped. He didn't even know I was coming."

"Tell her to get home where she belongs!" Hosea shouted. "Right now!"

"Never!" Anxiety yelled back.

A policeman came on the line. "We can bring her home in handcuffs," he said. "Is that what you want? Or would you like to come up to Calgary and talk to her?"

In the end, Hosea came to Calgary, Judith drove down from Rocky Mountain House, and Anxiety agreed to stay with Ralph and Judith until things calmed down. Then Hosea drove back home.

Anxiety stayed in Rocky Mountain House for five weeks, until her sixteenth birthday, when she called her mother. "I'm going now," she said, calmly, without anger. "I'm going with Joe." And Hosea knew not to argue.

WHERE HAD HER DAUGHTER gotten her formidable will? Gordon was not one to persist in anything. And Hosea herself had waffled her way through life. But Anxiety had some bottomless source of willpower that was there right from the beginning. How hard she'd kicked against the walls of her mother's womb. Kick. Kick. Punch. Kick. And when she finally emerged – the tearing, the incredible pain.

"Look at this head," the doctor had called to someone. "The size of it." And Hosea had thought in her drowsiness that she'd delivered a monster. But no. The doctor raved on. "She'll be a stubborn one. A winner. A rare beauty." And she was a beauty. People would stop Hosea on the street to look down at the new baby in her carriage and gush at her loveliness.

As the child grew, she also became more affectionate. Even in her sleep she could sense her mother's presence hovering over the bed and would reach out her arms and pull Hosea down to her and hold her close.

Where had such love come from?

The waiter stopped at her table. "Would you like anything else?" he asked.

"No," Hosea said. "No thank you." She sipped the coffee and stared out the window at the traffic.

And where had it gone wrong?

Suddenly Hosea wanted to sleep. She wanted to undress and get into bed and sleep for a long time. She got up from the table, paid for the coffee, and walked back to the Y.

At the front desk she asked the receptionist if there had been any calls for her.

"No," the girl said. "None."

"Oh," Hosea said. She remained standing by the desk.

The receptionist looked up at her. "Was there something else?" she asked.

"Oh, no," Hosea said.

"Okay," the girl said.

"I'm going to my room now," Hosea said. "I'll be in my room on the sixth floor."

"I see," the girl at the desk said.

"My name's Hosea." She did not move from the spot.

"You're expecting a call?" the receptionist asked.

"Not really. But in case."

"I understand," the girl said. "I'll get the message to you."

Hosea took the elevator up to her floor, unlocked the door of her room. A quiet nap was all she needed. She took off her shoes, sweater, and jeans and lay down under the blanket.

ANXIETY HAD ALWAYS HATED NAPS. "Not all children take naps you know," she announced when she was five. "Christine and Scott don't take naps. Tim Hanson doesn't. Jeff Merkel never does. He doesn't have to do anything he doesn't want to do."

"That's enough now," Hosea said.

"Do kangaroos take naps? Do fish? I know dolphins take naps, but only when they want to."

"Go to sleep," Hosea said. "You're not a fish."

IT WAS MIDAFTERNOON when Hosea woke up. She lay under the blanket and tried to remember her dream, something white and moving, but nothing more came to her. Instead, she remembered the day Anxiety stepped on a hornets' nest. Kicked into it. She was three years old and playing near a cement slab that was in their backyard. The hornets had built their nest under a ridge of concrete at the edge of the slab. Anxiety had seen it there, grey and papery, and kicked it. Hosea and Gordon were in the house. They didn't hear Anxiety's screams. They didn't see the insects swarming. They didn't realize what had happened until their neighbour came to the door, holding the child in his arms. She was panting for breath, her face deep red, beginning to blister.

"Baking soda," the neighbour said. "Mix it with water."

Gordon mixed the paste and the two men daubed Anxiety's face and arms with the white mixture. Hosea tried to hold Anxiety still, but the child was wild, yelling, arms flailing. They restrained her with a sheet and drove her to the hospital.

Why was she remembering this now? She got out of bed, dressed, and walked down the hall to the bathroom.

She stopped at the lounge. A large woman was lying on the sofa, watching "The Young and the Restless." A rerun. Hosea had seen the segment before. Victor Newman's blind wife, Hope, was feeding her son, Victor Junior, in the kitchen of her farm home in Kansas. Victor himself had stayed behind in Genoa City. Hosea sat down on one of the overstuffed chairs and watched the show.

When it was over, she turned to the woman and said, "Isn't it something the way she can manage everything?"

No answer from the sofa.

"I mean being blind, and still looking after the farm, the house, and the baby? She doesn't even have a hired girl."

The fat woman kept her eyes on the screen.

"Of course, it's all made up," Hosea said.

Back at the room, she discovered the girl sitting on her bed, fumbling with a tape recorder.

The girl looked up and smiled broadly. She had a large mouth. "Bread and sausage. Remember?" She pressed a button on the recorder. "Listen to this." The tape whirred backward. "It's Rose. Listen. Her voice. I mean you've never heard such a voice. It's pure Texas. Huge. Her body just rolls when she's preaching. And that voice. Well you know Texas. Big!"

The rewinding stopped, and Hosea heard a breathy woman's voice, low and seductive.

"Well, she starts soft," the girl said. "But wait, you'll see."

Hosea lay down on the bed.

"It's about the children," the girl explained, "what happened with the children, how they tried to keep the children away. Only he said no, let them come. It's all about those children...."

Hosea sat up. "Would you mind if we didn't listen to that right now? I'm kind of tired." She lay back on the bed.

"No problem," the girl said and stopped the tape. "Are you hungry? I'm starved. I'll make sandwiches."

Hosea stared up at the ceiling. There'd been no phone call. And she hadn't even started looking for Gordon.

She turned on her side and watched the girl cutting slices of sausage onto a paper towel. She was using a pocket knife.

"You look a little like my daughter," Hosea said, kindly, her head still on the pillow.

"I do? Poor thing."

"I haven't seen her for months – or heard from her."

"Your daughter? Your own daughter?"

"She ran away with her boyfriend."

"Oh, no." The girl stopped cutting, held the knife poised in the air. "So you're here looking for her."

"No. I came to Edmonton to look for my husband."

"Your husband's gone too? Your daughter *and* your husband?"

"Both of them," Hosea said.

"Took off together!" the girl said.

"No, Gordon left a couple of years ago."

"That's awful!" the girl said. "How can you stand it?"

"We didn't get along. Our house was chaos. Angry silence, or loud yelling and fighting."

"Don't tell me! He beat you."

"No. It was words mostly. But when I got mad at Gordon, I'd hit the kids."

"You didn't!"

"Yes, I did. I hit them."

"But why? It wasn't their fault."

"I just did, that's all," Hosea said.

"So what did the kids do then?"

"Hide."

"Hide!"

"Once I found my daughter hiding in the laundry room. She was five or six, I can't remember exactly. She'd piled all the sheets and towels and shirts and jeans and underwear – all of it – in a huge stack on the floor and she was lying under the clothes."

"That is so terrible!" The girl held up both hands, fingers splayed, as if she were about to catch a falling object. "Dirty clothes? Or clean."

"Both. She dumped them all in a pile on the floor, and she was lying under the pile. And when I found her she was red-faced from crying."

"Ohh," the girl moaned, shaking her head.

She looked down at the small rings of sausage spread out on the paper towel and carefully began to place the meat on the bread.

Hosea turned to face the wall. "Can I listen to your tape now?" she asked.

"You wouldn't like this tape."

"Can I anyway?"

"You'd hate it."

"So?"

"All right, but I warned you. Here, have some bread then." She came to Hosea's bed and handed her a sandwich, then returned to her own and clicked on the recorder.

The voice was dark and husky.

What did he do what did he do what did he do? You KNOW *what he did. Lifted them up is what he did. Does that mean down? No. Does up mean down? Certainly not. And where did he lift them? In his arms, that's where. And then what? What did he do then? Says right here what he did. Laid his hands on them. On who? Who did he lay his hands on? The children. Who? Children! Say it louder.* CHILDREN, CHILDREN. CHILDREN! *That's right! You got that just right. And then what did he do? Did he beat them up with those hands? No! Slap them down? Nooo! Molest them in dirty ways?* NO! NO! NO! *So what was it he did? Says the answer right here. Right here it says. Blessed them. What? Blessed. Can't hear you. What did he do?* BLESSED THEM. *Still can't hear.* BLESSED! BLESSED! BLESSED! *That's exactly what he did. And what does that word mean? Does it mean scoff at them?* NO. *Ignore them?* NO! *Call them names? Worthless? No Good? Won't-Amount-to-Anything? Is that the meaning here?* OF COURSE NOT! *He lifted them up* ENTIRE AND COMPLETE. *His arms lifted them up, his hands lifted them, his words, his face, his thoughts, his* SPIRIT. THEY ALL DID THE LIFTING! *He* TAUGHT *them. Lifted them up. Lifted them.* LIFTED. *Oh blessed. Oh oh blessed.*

The tape stopped rolling. The girl stuffed the recorder into her pack. Hosea lay on her side clutching the sandwich. She bit hard into the bread, chewed on the crust.

When they finished eating, the girl packed up her stuff. "I won't be coming back here," she said. "I've got a ride home after the meeting."

She stood at the door and shook Hosea's hand. Large pumping movements. Up and down and again and again. And she was gone.

Suddenly the room seemed cold and empty. Hosea decided she had to get out, walk, breathe, get some air. She put on her jacket, picked up her purse, and left.

Outside, the wind had risen. Bits of debris were rolling down the street: twigs, clumps of mouldy leaves, scraps of paper. Charcoal clouds were moving over the funeral chapel. She decided she'd drive around for awhile, go over to Whyte Avenue and check out a couple of spots. Tomorrow she'd call a few places, be more methodical in her search. Then she'd drive back to Rocky Mountain House.

She backed out of the Y parking lot, drove west to 109th, then south on the High Level Bridge to Whyte Avenue.

At the Renford Inn she parked in the ramp, walked down the dusty concrete steps to the street below. She held her collar close against her neck, bent her head against the wind, and scrunched her way to the hotel entrance.

There were no customers in the restaurant. And no waiter. She'd hoped Jeanette would still be there, chattering, pouring coffee, bringing food, as she'd done in the past; but she saw no one. Then she heard a guitar and some drums, loud and pulsating, and she followed the sound down the hall to the tavern door. If Gordon were anywhere in Edmonton, this was the likely place. From the doorway she squinted into the dimness, moved slowly to the bar. The bartender was tall and wide shouldered. She hesitated, then spoke.

"Do you know a Gordon who comes here?" she asked.

"Gordon? Don't think so. Hey, Buck, you know a Gordon who hangs here?"

"You mean George?" The voice came from the other end of the bar.

The bartender leaned toward Hosea. "Are you thinking of George?"

"No," Hosea said. "Gordon."

"Gordon!" shouted the bartender.

"Don't know Gordon," the voice said. "But George,

he's here every night, should be showing up any time."

"Sorry," the bartender said.

She saw four girls sitting at a table by the window. She walked past them, glanced at their faces. Strangers. She turned quickly and walked out.

In the café she sat down at the far end by the mirrors. A skinny man in white shirt and black pants emerged through swinging doors from the kitchen. He brought a pot of coffee to her table and filled her cup.

"There used to be a Jeanette who worked here," Hosea said. "Curly hair? Friendly? Is she still around?"

"Works mornings," he said, "but she's off this week."

"Oh," she said.

She picked up a wrinkled *Edmonton Journal* from the chair next to her and spread it out on the table. On the front page was a picture of the fallen airplane in Cheyenne, Wyoming, covered with a tarp. A rough mound on the concrete.

She lifted the coffee cup, held it in both hands, and drank.

THAT NIGHT she dreamed of dolphins. She was floating in blue water watching dozens of baby dolphins sleeping under the waves, lying on their backs and snoring. Their mother was scolding them, telling them to turn over. "Dolphins always lie on their stomachs," she said. "Why?" they asked, in their high clicking voices. "So they won't snore," their mother said.

IN THE MORNING it was raining. Hosea decided to stay at the Y for breakfast. It was 10 o'clock. She'd slept later than she'd planned.

She chose a table by one of the tall windows at the far end of the coffee shop and sat down on the plastic chair beside it. She laid her arm on the tabletop, rested her hand beside a yellow daffodil in a white vase. She watched thin streams of water run crookedly down the windowpane. Heard the traffic on the pavement outside. Saw the rain splash down on roofs of speeding cars, spray up in curves from under their black tires. Across the street the funeral home wavered, grey and distant in the slanting rain.

She looked around at the nearly empty restaurant. Saw the fat girl sitting by the far wall, and two old women, one in a white sweater, one in pink, at the next table. She saw the clock on the wall above the urn, muffins in a plastic case on the counter.

Then she saw a movement in the doorway, a dark shape hovering. She leaned toward the shape and felt her heart begin to pound. And she saw her. Anxiety. Large and wet, long hair dripping water, grey coat soaked in rain. Big bellied. Huge.

Hosea sucked in her breath and stared. Anxiety didn't move, didn't speak. She just stood there. Unsmiling.

Hosea half rose from her chair, but her legs felt weak and she sat down again. She lifted her hand, beckoned her daughter with a limp wave. And Anxiety lumbered toward her mother. Hosea's breath was somewhere just below her lungs, and her heart was racing. She saw her daughter moving toward her. (That huge coat. That wetness. God.) And then she was standing by the table, solemn and dripping.

"Hi, Mom," she said.

"Oh," Hosea said. "Oh my, it's you."

"It's me all right." She gave a short laugh, nervous, more like a snort.

"It really is," Hosea said.

"Are you surprised?"

"Well, yes," Hosea said. "Yes. Of course, I'm surprised."

Water dripped from the hem of her daughter's coat, forming small puddles on the floor by her feet. Her face was rosy pink from the cold. Her body seemed to spread out, filling the aisle.

"Sit down," Hosea said. "Why don't you sit? You may as well sit down." She heard her own voice rising, getting shrill.

And Anxiety sat crooked in the chair, her belly facing out toward the restaurant, her feet sprawled in the aisle.

Hosea tried not to look at the bulging stomach. But there it was. Sticking out. Bold and rude. Even so, she could not bring herself to acknowledge it. Instead she asked, "How did you know I was here?"

"Judith. I called her yesterday. Again."

"From Revelstoke."

"Oh, no, I've been in town for awhile. A week now." She seemed impatient that Hosea didn't know this.

"I'm pregnant," she said.

"Yes, I can see that," Hosea said.

"It shows, doesn't it," Anxiety said.

And then, because Hosea really didn't know what to say next, she said, "So when did all this happen?"

"I was pregnant when I left home, if that's what you're asking."

Hosea was silent. No, that's not what I'm asking, she thought. Where have you been? is what I'm asking. Why no word? I'm asking. Did you lose your memory? I ask. Forget the street you lived on? Forget your brother's name? Your sister's face?

But out loud she said, "Is Joe with you?"

"Yes and no," Anxiety said. "He's in Kuwait."

She unbuttoned her coat, and Hosea saw her neck, a blotchy pink.

"Oh," Hosea said, "I didn't know that."

"He has a job in the oilfields. It's only for six months. He'll be sending me money. We're still together."

"I see," Hosea said and glanced down at Anxiety's stomach pressed against the rim of the table. "You're staying with friends then? You have friends here?"

"Sort of," she said. Then, "Don't you have a room here? My back's killing me. I either have to lie down or stand up against a wall."

"Yes," Hosea said. "Let's go on up." And they left the café and took the elevator to the sixth floor.

Inside the room, Anxiety struggled out of her coat, manoeuvring her arms and shoulders this way and that. She hung the damp garment over the iron bar at the head of the first bed. She stretched, yawned, rubbed her lower back with the knuckles of her fisted hand.

"Did your back bother you when you were pregnant?"

"Yes, the back's a real problem," Hosea said. She

noticed Anxiety's outfit, a nubby pink top and tights to match. It looked modern and expensive. She wore a gold chain around her neck.

Hosea sat down on her own bed at the end of the room. Anxiety waddled to the bed next to it and slowly lowered herself onto the green blanket. She sat upright, very straight, wiggled her feet out of her sneakers without unlacing them, using one foot to slide the shoe off the other.

"I hate being wet," she said.

"That's a pretty outfit," Hosea said.

"It's new. I got it here in Edmonton," Anxiety said.

"You look healthy," her mother said "You look good. You must be taking care of yourself."

"Tell me about it," Anxiety said. "I had to watch all these videos in the clinic in Revelstoke. About food and exercise and smoking and drinking. Stuff like that. I saw these skinny babies and stunted babies and fetal alcohol babies with those weird eyes. You can screw up a kid even before it's born. Did you know that? Hey, would they kill me if I laid down on this bed?"

And without waiting for an answer, she stood up, lifted the green blanket, and lowered herself again, this time lying on her back, legs stretched out, head on the pillow. She pulled the blanket up to her chin and smoothed it over her belly, a green mound in the middle of the bed.

"So what are you doing here?" she asked her mother, who was still sitting on the edge of her bed.

"Looking for your father."

"Dad!"

"Well, yes."

"You're still looking for Dad?"

"He's still my husband."

Anxiety raised her head from the pillow. "*Mother*. Pardon me for a minute here, but you two split up. Remember? I think it's time you got a new life."

Hosea sucked in her breath. Great, she thought. Just great. Miss Due-in-three-weeks-with-no-mate suddenly has the credentials for teaching me how to live.

"Go back to school or something," Anxiety said. "There's a college in Medicine Hat, isn't there?"

Hosea's anger rose. "*Me?*" she said. "*I* should go to school? You're telling me that I should go to college?" She meant for Anxiety to see her own predicament, quitting school and suffering all its worst consequences.

But instead Anxiety said, "Why not? You can read, can't you?"

Hosea felt the space between the two beds widen, the beds like small ships floating away in opposite directions. She was conscious as she drifted that she hadn't even touched her daughter – not a hug, a kiss, a handshake, not the slightest, tiniest tap of a hand on her daughter's arm or shoulder. She lay down and covered herself with the blanket. The room was chilly. Rain beat against the window.

And then, through the fog that surrounded her, through its thick haze, she heard the voice from the next bed. It cut through the greyness like thin steel.

"I've been with Dad," Anxiety said. "He lives here now. On the North side."

Hosea felt the fog pull close to her and tighten and

harden against her.

"He's changed," Anxiety said. "He's not the jerk he used to be. I think he's happy."

Hosea's voice was hoarse. "You've kept in touch with your father?"

"On and off," Anxiety said. "When Joe left for Kuwait, Dad said I could stay with him."

"I see."

"Him and Bonnie."

"Bonnie." Hosea echoed the word from a distant mountain across the continent.

"Well, you know Dad."

Hosea was silent.

"But I think this one's permanent," Anxiety said. "She's good for him, makes him laugh. A real relationship."

Hosea's least favourite word.

"Fuck relationship," she said.

"Mother. Don't be crude."

"His make-him-laugh girlfriend doesn't say crude things?"

"Of course. But she's young."

Hosea felt herself at the top of a mountain, standing on a precipice, her feet on the very edge of it, her shoes slipping on loose rock. And she heard Anxiety's voice from across the chasm.

"She took me shopping last week. Bought me a bunch of baby stuff, a layette it's called, and a receiving blanket. I didn't even know there was such a thing. And this outfit. Well, Dad paid for it, I guess."

And Hosea's feet slipped on the rock and her body

tumbled into space and her daughter's words faded, became distant, dissipated. And Hosea floated, breathless. She knew one thing: don't land. If you land you'll break into pieces. You'll be a little pile of broken bits at the bottom of the chasm.

Then something caught her, held her. She sat up. Her neck was stiff, her back rigid.

"Why have you come now?" she asked. "Is this your big Get-Even-With-Mother thing? But you've already done that. No answers to letters. No phone calls."

Anxiety didn't answer. She lay with the green blanket over her belly, her head on the pillow, her damp hair swirling up and out, over the pillow's edge. The pink smock was scrunched up over the edge of the blanket, and the gold chain had fallen in a loop away from her chest onto the pillow. Her neck was red and blotchy. And Hosea saw her there, a heap on the bed. God. She looked like a small whale. She must have gained fifty pounds. Even in that pink underwear outfit she looked huge.

Hosea hadn't landed. She hadn't broken into pieces. She was still in control, stronger than she thought. Let her daughter and Gordon both sail off into the sunset. Let the happy girl sail with them. And the new baby. She could care less.

"So why did you come?" she said again.

Anxiety turned her head slightly. Her face was flushed. Her hands lay on the blanket, fingers rigid.

"To ask you for something," she said.

Right, Hosea thought. So your father's out of cash, is he?

"I was hoping you'd be with me when the baby comes," she said.

For a moment, Hosea stopped breathing. The room was still, the darkness hovered. She stared at her daughter, saw a thin wetness seep out from the corners of her eyes.

"Me? What about...?"

"I don't want them," Anxiety said.

Hosea's back felt sore, her neck tight.

"But if you don't want to, well that's all right," Anxiety said.

The blue darkness of the long rain seeped into the room.

Suddenly Anxiety jerked upright. "Oh my God," she said.

"What? What?" Hosea said. "Is it time?"

Anxiety fell back on the bed. "It's kicking. It's really kicking. Feel it. Put your hand here. Quick, or you'll miss it. Right here."

And before she realized it, Hosea was at her daughter's side, her hand pressed on her stomach, feeling the jabs and kicks.

"It moves," Anxiety said. "Did you know that? It actually moves. And it makes noise. The doctor said so." She grabbed her mother's shoulder and pulled her down. "Listen. See if you can hear it. Try to hear it."

Then Hosea's head was on Anxiety's stomach, her ear pressed close.

And Anxiety was crying and laughing. "It's wild. It's so crazy."

But Hosea was neither laughing nor crying. She was holding onto the mattress, her eyes closed. And oh, Hosea, what are you doing here bent over this girl, your head on the smooth mound of her belly? What are you doing with your eyelids shut and your lips pressed hard? Hold on, Hosea. Hold fast.

But what could she do when her cheek was pressed like this against her daughter? When her ear was receiving even now the bumps and thuds and general chaos of the life within? And what else could she do when at this moment her daughter's arms once again came up and circled round her and held her there? Hosea let out a clumsy hiccup of a sob, and then another. And she opened her mouth and bawled.

And when her crying stopped, Anxiety lifted her mother's head with her own thin hands and raised her up and looked into her face and said, "Did you hear it?"

"Some thumps."

"That's all?"

"Some gurgling sounds."

"I want to hear it too," Anxiety said, "but my ear can't reach that far." She crouched deeper under the blanket.

She turned over on her side and yawned. "Beyond Repair. What do you think of that for the baby's name?"

"Annie!" Hosea said.

"Or I could name her after you." She smiled and closed her eyes and breathed into her pillow.

Hosea sat on the edge of the bed and watched her daughter. Ann's mouth was partly open, a bead of spit bubbled on her lower lip, and she began to snore, a soft snore like purring. And Hosea noticed things about her she thought she had forgotten: the scar on the side of her chin from a fall on her tricycle when she was three, the birthmark below her left ear, the tiny beads of sweat that formed on the bridge of her nose when she was sleeping. Hosea did not move from the bed. She laid her hand on her daughter's foot, and sat quietly looking down at her.

She thought of names for the baby. Karen, Marilyn, Sue, Kristi. And Naomi, that was a pretty name. So many to choose from. It was going to be a girl, Ann had said.

When Ann awoke it was still raining. She yawned and stretched and looked up at her mother. "Have you decided?" she asked.

Hosea rose from the bed and stepped to the window. She loved weather, especially rain, but this rain just came and came.

"Yes," she said. "Yes. I'll call Judith and let them know we're coming."

In Rocky Mountain House the sun had dropped behind the ridge of mountains. The air was cold, a blue black air left behind by the sun. The earth was still hard with frost, but in wide patches the surface ground had crumbled and become soft.

On the porch the children waited in sweaters and mitts. They'd know the whirring sound and the small clicking sounds of the car's engine. They'd know the slanted beam of its headlights, and the crackling movement of the tires on the pavement. They'd know its curved shape looming toward them out of the dark.

They sat on the steps and leaned toward the street

and waited.

They breathed in the cold air and breathed it out and watched it form small clouds in front of their faces, then disappear into the darkness.

"It's about time she came home," Doloros said.

"I guess I'll have a thing or two to say to her," said Bittern.

The Dolphins

BENEATH THE GENTLE WATER FOUR DOLPHINS sleep. They lie belly down just below the pool's rippling surface. Their smooth humps rest like quiet hills in the green waves. A dorsal fin cuts the water's edge, and one dolphin slides up, into the air above, curving himself over the others, a slick grey arch dripping water like wet crystals, shards of fluid glass. The muscled lid on top of his head pulls open. He sucks in air, pushes the lid shut, and plunges down for another snooze. A short one. Dolphins have to sleep holding their breath.

IN HER NARROW BED, under a white quilt, Emily dreams of the vessels. Thousands of glass containers that fill the shelves in rooms and corridors. Bottles, jugs, tumblers, urns, crystal cups as small as thimbles. And in one of these rooms or corridors, on one of the hundreds of shelves, hidden amidst all the glass, there is one secret vessel. In that one lies the answer. If she looks hard enough, if she is determined, if her will is strong, she will find the answer. Then she'll know. Then everything will be all right. She moves slowly down the narrow corridor.

She wakes, hears her mother in the bathroom. She's sliding open the mirrored door of the medicine cabinet, moving things around in there. Emily hears the clinking sounds. She closes her eyes, pulls the quilt over her face, and sees her mother remove a small bottle from the shelf, pry open the plastic lid with her fingernail, shake a green pill into the palm of her hand, lift her hand to her mouth. Water gushes from the tap, splashes into the porcelain sink.

She sits up in bed.

"Mother?" she calls.

"Yes?"

"I hear water running."

"I'm thirsty," her mother says.

The water stops.

"Mother?"

"Yes?"

"Did he come home?"

"Not yet. But soon he will. Go to sleep now. Everything's all right."

Those are her mother's words. That's what she always says.

"Everything's all right."

In the morning, her mother stands at the kitchen counter, fitting a pleated filter into the coffee maker.

She's wearing a purple housecoat. Her hair is uncombed.

Emily, in blue jeans, her hair brushed into one long sandy braid behind her back, pulls a chair out from the table, sits down, picks up the cereal box, examines the cartoon on the side of the box. Today's Saturday; there's no rush.

"So," she says, "will you drive us to the mall?"

Her mother doesn't answer. She's gazing into some private vision inside the coffee pot.

"You said you'd drive me and Hannah Shimizu to the mall to watch the dolphins."

Her mother stares at the bubbles rising in the plastic tube of the coffee maker, combs her tangled hair with her fingers, covers a yawn with the back of her hand.

"Well? Will you? Our report's due on the fifteenth. We've hardly gotten started. Mr. Shimizu will bring us back. So will you?"

"I said I would, didn't I?"

Emily shakes cornflakes from the white box into a blue bowl. "He didn't come home, did he," she says. It's not a question, but in her mind's eye she sees her father stumble into the house, slam against a chair. She pours milk over the yellow flakes.

"Don't worry so much," her mother says. Her neck reddens. Stiff muscles show beneath her skin. "Everything's going to be fine."

AT 1:30 EMILY AND HANNAH are at the West Edmonton Mall at the dolphin pool. They've paid their dollar and are sitting in the miniature grandstand that curves around one side. They're surrounded by noisy children, parents, grandparents, quiet lovers. On the mall's upper level, Saturday shoppers crowd behind a thick plastic railing and gaze down on the water, restless for the show to start. On the green bridge spanning the pool's far end, more shoppers gather. They're waiting for the trainer to fling open the door of his secret room beside the water, to run out onto the concrete shore and sound the whistle that will call forth the dolphins.

In front of them, through the pool's transparent wall, they see the quiet forms move slowly in the deep, and all around the moving forms, beams of yellow light shimmering, slim corridors of light flickering in the blue jade water.

Suddenly it's time. Up they leap in perfect symmetry, four dolphins arched above the pool, grey backs glistening. Then down, head first into the waves. They swim in one long smooth and flowing circle. And swiftly up higher, higher still. Crystal sparks rise after them and fall glittering to the surface. For a moment they're suspended in mid-air, beaks straight up, pointing to the steel and plastic sky high above.

"Ladies and gentlemen," the trainer calls. "Meet our four Atlantic Bottlenose dolphins, here to play, have fun, show you their tricks."

He throws an orange ball into the water. In one slippery flash the dolphin has it on the end of his beak, is pushing it forward, swiftly, so smoothly, holding it steady with his snout. He flicks it off, twists, grabs it with his flippers and around and around the pool he goes, bouncing it up and down and up again.

"Look at him look at him look at him go. See him dribble that ball down the court. He's heading for the basket," the trainer yells.

Everyone claps and someone shouts, "Oh oh see that dolphin go." The ball slips, the dolphin swirls around, nips it with his beak, and pushes it toward the basket sitting on the edge of the pool. He eyes the hoop, flips the ball with his snout and misses. On the second shot the ball circles the rim around and around, "Come on come on," and falls just outside of it. "Oh oh isn't that too bad." But on the third try the ball sails over the rim and plunks into the bucket. The crowd cheers. Someone whistles.

"Did you see that?" Hannah asks.

"My goodness," Emily says.

"A slam dunk!" the trainer yells.

And the old woman in red boots says, "My, what these dolphins can't do."

EMILY STAYS AWHILE at Hannah's house. She and Hannah are standing at the kitchen counter spreading peanut butter on slices of white bread. They're swirling the mixture into hills and valleys on each slice, letting broken pieces of nuts emerge like jagged stones on the brown surface. They laugh at their clever designs.

Hannah's mother is also at the counter, at the far end. She's stirring rice in a large bowl. One arm circles the bowl, holds it tight against her chest. With the other she mixes the rice. The counter is too high for her. Her arm sticks straight out from her shoulder, bent at the elbow like the stiff wing of a bird. She stops stirring, sprinkles vinegar over the mass, stirs again, then with her hand fans the mixture until it glistens. She does this over and over. She's making sushi for a family outing tomorrow at the Devonian Gardens.

Mr. Shimizu is sitting at the kitchen table in the centre of the room. He's reading the paper and drinking coffee from a thick mug. The Devonian Gardens is his idea; he's a botanist. He's wearing sweatpants and an old sweater. Sits easy, seems to feel at home here, to like it here, in the kitchen drinking coffee and reading, not saying much of anything. Emily notices these things. Upstairs, Hannah's brother and his friend whoop and thump at some game or other.

Hannah leans toward Emily and says in a low voice, "My parents don't know anything about dolphins."

"Mine neither," Emily says. "Well, I've told my dad one or two things."

Suddenly Hannah turns and moves to the refrigerator across the room. She moves in an arc, around her father sitting at the table. She stands with her back against the fridge, her hair sharply black against the white door.

"I would like your attention," she says. She stands straight, her hands resting on her narrow hips. She stands like Mr. Murray, the sixth grade science teacher.

"Today I will teach you about dolphins," she says.

Her father looks up from the table. "A lesson on Saturday?" But his eyes smile. Her mother looks up too, but she doesn't stop working the rice.

"We recognize the intelligence of dolphins by what

they do," Hannah says. "One. They make friends. That's important. Two. They play and have fun. Not like some people I know – I won't mention names. Three. They take good care of their children. You may want to think about that for awhile." Mr. Shimizu makes a face at Hannah, but he's enjoying the speech, Emily can tell. "Four," Hannah continues, "they come to the aid of other dolphins in their time of need. They've even been known to help creatures not of their own species. Like humans. There's another, but I can't remember."

"They mourn the death of loved ones," Emily says.

"Yes," Hannah says. "They feel sorrow." She looks intently at her father, then at her mother. "In conclusion, these are the signs of intelligence."

Mr. Shimizu claps. Mrs. Shimizu stops stirring and wipes her forehead with the palm of her hand.

"I know something about dolphins," she says.

"What," Hannah says. "What do you know?"

"In winter, in the north, in Hokkaido, Ainu fishermen stand on the shore and look out to the sea. The water's cold and black, and they stand there on the rocks and call out. *'Iruka kujira,'* they say."

"What's that?" Hannah asks.

"And sometimes," her mother continues, "these fishermen can see one of them way out there, alone, lost, left by the others, jumping up and down like they do, in that icy water."

"What does it mean, *iruka kujira?*" Hannah asks again, but her mother still doesn't answer. Hannah goes to her, leans her chin on her mother's shoulder, speaks loudly into her ear. *"Mother.* You can't just not tell us. What does it mean?"

"It means dolphin," her mother says. "Dolphin whale."

"That's it? That's all it means?" Hannah says.

But her mother doesn't answer. She's standing alone on a rock somewhere in Japan, looking out.

HANNAH'S ROOM is full of stuff – shelves of dolls, games, furry animals; a dressing table with photographs on it and little bottles of perfume, a long-handled mirror, a crystal bell. Hannah clears a space on the dresser. Emily puts the plate of bread down. She picks up an old brown photograph in a silver lace frame.

"It's my grandfather," Hannah says. "My mother's father."

"He looks young,"

"He *was* young." She turns on the red lamp suspended over her pine Ikea desk. "He died of leukemia."

"Really," Emily says.

"After the bomb. A long time after. He lived in Nagasaki." She adjusts the light to shine closer to the clippings and coil notebooks that litter the desktop.

"Some blew up, some burned up, some just blistered all over. My grandfather got leukemia. Where do you want to sit, on the bed or on the chair?"

Emily sits cross-legged in the middle of the bed, on a pink quilt, ruffled and rippling like a small sea, Hannah on the chair by the desk. "I'm glad this war is over," Emily says. The War in the Persian Gulf ended only short weeks before. "I don't think it did much good."

"Not for people anyway," Hannah says.

"Especially not for little children."

"Mothers either for that matter."

"Are there dolphins in the Persian Gulf?"

"I guess."

Hannah leans forward and raises her head. *"Iruka kujira,"* she calls. She reaches to the dresser for a slice of bread. "I told you, didn't I? My mother knows nothing about dolphins."

EMILY TAKES the long way home, following the Mill Woods ravine. The evening sky is overcast but strangely bright. A harsh light. It has an edge to it, like tin. It lies sharp on stones and dirt, on mouldy scraps of paper stuck on branches, on dead leaves packed in ditches. Scattered flakes of snow drizzle down on her. She buries herself in her jacket.

She thinks of the Shimizus at the Devonian Gardens tomorrow. She sees them walk among the trees and shrubs, stop to look at branches, to examine small buds. They comment, ask questions, make jokes. They don't hurry. Then she sees them sitting on a bench outside. They pass around the box of sushi and everyone takes and eats. Mrs. Shimizu pours tea from a tall thermos into small cups without handles. They hold the cups in both hands, their hands like bowls. And everyone's there, not somewhere else. They take time, don't always look at their watches. Some families are like that.

WHEN SHE GETS HOME, the car is not in the driveway. Her mother must still be shopping. She walks around to the back, digs in her pocket for the key, but the door is unlocked. She pushes it open and climbs the four steps into the back hall. The light is on. She removes her jacket, hangs it in the hall closet, and opens the door to the kitchen. She stops. Her breath freezes in her chest.

Her father is sitting at the kitchen table.

He sits rigid, chin on chest, one arm stretched over the formica top, one hand holding an empty glass. Nothing else is on the table, just one thick empty glass. Emily knows that somewhere in the house – on a ledge in the basement, behind some books in the bookcase, on a closet shelf – his bottles are hidden. She knows her mother will find them, will gather them up in green plastic bags and carry them to the alley. She will do this at night when no one can see her.

Emily watches her father. Maybe if she moves behind him lightly, ever so softly, as quiet as a robin's feather, her feet hardly touching the floor, she can get to the corridor and to her bedroom at the end of it, without his notice.

"Hold it. Just hold it right there."

He turns in his chair and, barely lifting his head, raises his eyes and looks at her. His face is wrinkled, the whites of his eyes lined with pink threads. He's wearing a brown bathrobe, open at the neck, and his neck is very thin.

"No greeting? No salutation?"

"Hi, Dad," Emily says.

"Hi, Dad? Is that it? Hi, Dad? I'm your father, remember. Honour your father, don't forget. Sneaking behind me, creeping like a scared caterpillar." His Adam's apple swims and bulges under the loose skin of his neck. He leans back in the chair. Emily shifts slightly.

"Hold it."

She breathes in thin strips of air.

"What's going on? Where's your mother? Who's in charge around here anyway?"

Emily shrugs. He lets go of the glass. It sits alone in the centre of the table. "Hey." He raises his hand to her, a limp benediction. "Can you answer the questions of eternal life?"

She's stuck. She knows her father's drinking pattern: first religion and poetry, then anger, more like rage, finally a whimpering self-pity. The last is worst.

"Where did you come from? Why are you here? Where are you going?" He says the words slowly, over-articulates. He eyes her slyly. "Well? Answer me."

"I've been to the dolphin show," she says, "and I live here."

"Damn," he says. "I forgot about that. Oh, I *am* sorry, *very very* sorry. Truly I am. I do repent."

"It's all right," she says.

"The living womb of the sea of creation and I forgot. Come here. Give your father a kiss. Apollo was a dolphin, you know, when he carried poor damned souls to the land of the dead. Did you know that?"

"It was me who told you."

"Come. Right here. One kiss." He curls his finger, inviting.

Emily goes to him and bends over him. His skin is

yellow. She touches his forehead with her lips. It feels damp and cold.

"You're my dolphin," he says. His eyes are wet.

She turns to go.

"Hold it. Stay right where you are." His hands clutch the table's edge. He lifts himself up, lets go of the table, stands alone, stretches tall. "They're whales you know." Slowly he slides back into the chair. "Stunted whales. Runts. Not in the big league. No leviathan."

His eyes slits, he gazes at Emily standing quiet in front of the refrigerator.

"Canst thou draw out leviathan with a hook? Tie a rope around his tongue and pull him out? Well? Canst thou?"

"No," she says.

"Canst thou put a hook in his tongue and a chain on the hook and swing him around in the deep?" His voice rises. The veins on his forehead stand out.

"Canst thou pierce his skin with barbed irons?" He coughs, gurgling, and wipes his mouth with the back of his hand.

Emily leans hard against the refrigerator door. Her hands are fists against her thighs.

"Hey, I asked you a question, Miss High and Mighty. Canst thou?"

"I said no, Dad. I already said no."

"Hold it. No talking back, like Job, right? Getting God all riled up."

He shakes his head, puzzled. "But God didn't know, did he? The Heavenly Father such a refuge e'er was given just didn't know. He *thought* he knew, but he was mistaken. That's the problem right there. Mistaken. Isn't that the whole problem? Isn't that the trouble? That's it, isn't it?"

He sits up, makes his hand a gun, and points it at his daughter. "Ra-a-a-a-a-a-a-a-a-a-a," he croaks. He bends his head back. "Ra-a-a-a-a-a-a-a-a-a," he shouts to God somewhere above the roof. "Have you heard the latest?" he says. "We can fill his skin with iron. We know how to do that now. We can crush his huge whale heart and smash his liver to bits." He tries to raise the gun, to point it up, to wave it in the face of God, but his hand falls limp onto the table.

Emily is quiet, unmoving, watching.

He looks at the empty glass in front of him. His voice turns to crooning. "Don't cry," he says to God, now floating just above the glass. "Don't cry," he says, and strokes the rim with his finger. "Hey, fathers make mistakes too, you know, they're not perfect, they have their weaknesses. But we try our best, don't we?" He sucks in his breath, makes small whimpering sounds, then large ragged sobs, his body shaking.

Suddenly he's up, his arm extended, his hand clutching the glass. He aims it at her. Emily ducks. The glass smashes against the fridge door, falls in chunks, pieces, powdery crystals onto the tile floor. He walks slowly, only a little crookedly, very carefully, into the living room.

"Fathers are a piece of shit." He groans, falls into the sofa, and snores almost immediately.

For now it's over. Emily can breathe.

IN THE ALLEY, she stands beside the back gate. She has emptied the dustpan of shattered glass, replaced the lid on the aluminum garbage can that leans against the fence. She is holding the empty pan in her hand and looking down the alley at the houses: at the roofs and doors, fences and gates, at the windows letting out the light from inside, at Bornemans' next door, whose little kids run naked in the yard in the summer rain, at Hallesbys', where Sarah is probably right now practising her cello for church tomorrow, at the house at the end of the alley, with the huge kennel in the backyard, where sometimes dogs howl in the middle of the night. The sky has darkened. The rim of a narrow moon hangs below a grey cloud. The wind settles into quiet ripples about her, and Emily turns back to her own house.

THE FRONT DOORBELL RINGS. Emily doesn't answer. She's setting the dustpan on the floor in the kitchen closet. It rings again. She sits down on the edge of the chair beside the table in the darkened room. There's a knock on the back door, loud and persistent, then a voice.

"Anyone home?" it says.

"Are you there?" it says.

Gladness. Comfort. Hope. Richard is back. Emily rushes to the back door to welcome him in.

"How the hell are you?" he says, his big hand on her shoulder. In the dimness she looks up to where his face is, brown and shiny, to where his welcome eyes are, his smile.

"Hi, Richard. When did you get back?"

"Thursday," he says. "Can I sit down? Aren't the

lights working? Did you blow a fuse or something?"

Emily flips the switch by the refrigerator. The room glows. They sit at the table, facing each other.

"So. What's new?" he asks.

"Not much."

"Where's Papa Sam and Mary?"

Emily jerks her elbow toward the living room and Richard strides into the room, his long feet gliding over the tiles.

Richard is a friend of her father. In the old days they were together often. They'd stay up nights singing, talking, drinking. Later, fighting. Then Richard disappeared for a year and when he came back two years ago he was different.

He returns from the living room. "I put his leg up," he says. "You can't sleep very well with one leg dangling. Where's the coffee?"

He goes to the counter, pulls out the filter from the coffee maker, empties the soggy grounds into the sink. He rummages on a shelf for a clean filter and fresh grounds.

"So did you like Australia?" she asks.

"Did I *like* it? Do I like blue skies? Do I like strawberries and cream? Do I like a warm bed in winter?"

"You've got a tan. Did you see any dolphins? Me and Hannah Shimizu are doing a report on dolphins."

"Is that so?" he says. "Well, I'm sorry to say I didn't see the dolphins. I heard a story about one though."

"What *did* you see?"

"Fish." He plugs in the coffee maker and sits down across from her. "Water and fish. I learned to dive with one of those tanks on my back and a mask on my face. Get this – in the *Pacific. Ocean.* Deep, eh? And I saw fish. Huge, tiny, fat, skinny, pink, purple, polka-dotted, fish with spikes on them, honest-to-god, like nails sticking out all over, and little yellow fish that looked like flat canaries, really cute, and blue fish and silver. I'd hang there in the water, tons of it, thousands and millions of tons on all sides." He leans toward Emily, his eyes intent and personal. "Water's so powerful you know. And there I'd be, suspended in all that power. And the fish would swim up to me, right up to my goggles, and they'd look in at me with those bulgy eyes, and they'd say hi Richard, and I'd say hi fish, and then they'd take off, who knows where." He gets up from the chair.

What's the story?" Emily asks.

"Story?"

"About the dolphin."

"Well." He pours himself a cup of coffee and sits down again. He holds the cup in both hands. "It's about this dolphin called Opo, not in Australia, in New Zealand actually. People used to go out in the ocean and swim with her and touch her. She even let children ride on her back. They all loved her. But one day someone found her in a coral pool near shore. She was dead. And when the village people heard, they became very sad. And that evening at dusk, some Maoris dug a grave by the town hall and carried the dolphin there and buried her. And they covered her grave with flowers." He sips the coffee. "That is a true story," he says.

Emily sits very quiet. She looks toward the living

room, then at Richard. "Why can't he stop?" she says. "You did."

He stands up and moves to the counter to refill his cup. "It's a mystery to me," he says.

For a moment she considers his words.

"I think it sucks," she says finally.

EMILY IS HOME FROM SCHOOL. She sees her mother in the living room, looking out the big window, staring at something beyond the ravine. The television is on, her mother's favourite afternoon soap, "The Young and the Restless," but she's not watching it.

Katherine Chancellor, in living colour, is flicking her fingers about her face in little circles, long jewelled fingers glittering near her eyes, her cheek, her chin. Kay Chandelier, Emily's father calls her, but her mother loves her. She loves her fancy house, everywhere huge bouquets of flowers in crystal or gold vases. She loves her maid Esther in her tidy uniform, and Katherine's own expensive clothes in colours to match the flowers, never the same outfit twice, and her hair graceful and stylish, even when she's sleeping, even when she's walking in a strong wind.

Emily throws her books on the chesterfield.

"Get in the car," her mother says. "Your father's at the Grey Nuns."

THE NARROW BED. The square table. The ice water in a green glass. The metal dish, pewter kidney turned inward. The high pole. The bottle strapped to the pole. The tube from the bottle dangling down, onto the bed, onto the blue sheet, onto his hand resting there, into the silver needle, the needle flat, visible under the skin, slim outline on a blue vein.

And Richard on a chair at the foot of the bed watching the form in front of him: the feet and knees smooth hills under the sheet, the chest a little field, the penis a small stone. Emily stands by the high window. She looks at her father's face. His eyes are closed. The skin is tight over the cheekbones.

Her mother pushes the door open and backs into the room with a tray holding two cups of coffee and a can of Coke. She sets the tray on the bedside table, then goes to the window. She lays her hand on Emily's arm, and they move together to the bed. And the three of them sit on the chairs by the bed. They linger there in the semi-darkness, sipping, talking in low tones, their voices strangely clear, melodic in the stillness.

He opens his eyes and looks at them.

"Everyone's here," he says.

He looks at her.

"Hi, Emily," he says.

"Hi, Dad."

EMILY DREAMS again of the vessels. She's standing in a long tunnel. Its walls from floor to ceiling hold the shelves filled with glass. She's waiting for the right container to reveal itself to her, to empty its secret to her. Then gradually, almost imperceptibly, the shelves begin to loosen from the wall, to dip, lean, bend. Pitchers, bottles, tumblers, cups are falling one by one, softly, slowly. They turn in the air, circle, glide, and finally land. Pieces of amber glass, and jade, and ruby red, rise like fountains before her, then fall in piles everywhere, glittering heaps on the tunnel floor.

And she's standing by a streetlight on a road she doesn't know. It's evening. A small rain is falling. From the house at the end of the street a woman walks toward her. She's old and wearing boots that glisten. Emily knows that when the woman reaches her she will stop for a minute under the light. They will look at each other. Emily will say hello, and the woman will say hello. Emily will say it's a nice rain isn't it, and the woman will say yes it is.

And in that instant, that one swift and slippery moment, circled in light, washed in rain, Emily knows exactly what she needs to know. She knows nothing. She knows everything.

IN THE ATLANTIC, north of the Hebrides, a mother dolphin nudges her calf through purple water into white spume on the ocean's surface. With her snout she pushes the calf into the cold clear air above the spray. The infant muscles on the baby's head stretch open, and the dolphin takes her first breath.

In the Mediterranean, off the coast of Tripoli, two dolphins swim close together. They nuzzle each other with their beaks, caress with the soft tips of their flukes. She opens herself to him, a thin crevice in her slick body. And he is there, twisting himself around her. They turn and swirl in the foam. They dip and glide and together plunge down into the ancient sea.

On a windy shore in New Zealand, a dolphin lies stranded. His pearl grey neck and white belly blacken on the stones. In the ocean a family calls. Their whistling clicking cries speed through the rolling depths, the crashing surf. Where have you gone? Oh. Oh. Where?

At the mall in Edmonton, the dolphins are playing. They're swimming around in circles, being friends, having fun, taking care.

The Day I Sat with Jesus
on the Sundeck and a Wind Came
Up and Blew My Kimono Open
and He Saw My Breasts

WHEN AN EXTRAORDINARY EVENT TAKES place in your life, you're apt to remember with unnatural clarity the details surrounding it. You remember shapes and sounds that weren't directly related to the occurrence but hovered there in the periphery of the experience. This can even happen when you read a great book for the first time – one that unsettles you and startles you into thought. You remember where you read it, what room, who was nearby.

I can remember, for instance, where I read *Of Human Bondage*. I was lying on a top bunk in our high school dormitory, wrapped in a blue bedspread. I lived in a dormitory then because of my father. He was a religious man and wanted me to get a spiritual kind of education: to hear the Word and know the Lord, as he put it. So he sent me to St. Paul's Lutheran Academy in Regina for two years. He was confident that there's where I'd hear the Word. Anyway, I can still hear Mrs. Sverdrup, our housemother, knocking on the door at midnight and whispering in her Norwegian accent, "Now, Gloria, it iss past midnight, time to turn off the lights. Right now." Then scuffing down the corridor in her bedroom slippers. What's interesting here is that I don't remember anything about the book itself except that someone in it had a club foot. But it must have moved me deeply when I was sixteen, which is some time ago now.

You can imagine then how distinctly I remember the day Jesus of Nazareth, in person, climbed the hill in our backyard to our house, then up the outside stairs to the sundeck where I was sitting. And how he stayed with me for awhile. You can surely understand how clearly those details rest in my memory.

The event occurred on Monday morning, September 11, 1972, in Moose Jaw, Saskatchewan. These facts in themselves are more unusual than they may appear to be at first glance. September's my favourite month, Monday my favourite day, morning my favourite time. And although Moose Jaw may not be the most magnificent place in the world, even so, if you happen to be there on a Monday morning in September it has its beauty.

It's not hard to figure out why these are my favourites, by the way. I have five children and a husband. Things get hectic, especially on weekends and holidays. Kids hanging around the house, eating, arguing, asking me every hour what there is to do in Moose Jaw. And television. The programs are always the same. Only the names change: Roughriders, Stampeders, Blue

Bombers, whatever. So when school starts in September I bask in freedom, especially on Monday. No quarrels. No TV. The morning, crisp and lovely. A new day, a fresh start.

On the morning of September 11, I got up at seven, the usual time, cooked Cream of Wheat for the kids, fried a bit of sausage for Fred, waved them all out of the house, drank a second cup of coffee in peace, and decided to get at last week's ironing. I wasn't dressed yet but still in the pink kimono I'd bought years ago on my trip to Japan, my one and only overseas trip, a five-hundred-dollar quick tour of Tokyo and other cities. I'd saved for this while working as a library technician in Regina, and I'm glad I did. Since then I've hardly been out of Saskatchewan. Once in awhile a trip to Winnipeg, and a few times down to Medicine Lake, Montana, to visit my sister.

I set up the ironing board and hauled out the basket of week-old sprinkled clothes. When I unrolled the first shirt it was completely dry and smelled stale. The second was covered with little grey blots of mould. So was the third. Fred teaches science in the junior high school here in Moose Jaw. He uses a lot of shirts. I decided I'd have to unwrap the whole basketful and air everything out. This I did, spreading the pungent garments about the living room. While they were airing I would go outside and sit on the deck for awhile since it was such a clear and sunny day.

If you know Moose Jaw at all, you'll know about the new subdivision in the southeast end called Hillhurst. That's where we live, right on the edge of the city. In fact our deck looks out on flat land as far as the eye can see, except for the backyard itself, which is a fairly steep hill leading down to a small stone quarry. But from the quarry the land straightens out into the Saskatchewan prairie. One clump of poplars stands beyond the quarry to the right, and high weeds have grown up among the rocks. Other than that, it's plain – just earth and sky. But when the sun rises new in the morning, weeds and rocks take on an orange and rusty glow that is pleasing. To me at least.

I unplugged the iron and returned to the kitchen. I'd take a cup of coffee out there, or maybe some orange juice. To reach the juice at the back of the fridge my hand passed right next to a bottle of dry white Calona. Now here was a better idea. A little wine on Monday morning, a little relaxation after a rowdy weekend. I held the familiar bottle comfortably in my hand and poured, anticipating a pleasant day.

I slid open the glass door leading onto the deck. I pulled an old canvas folding chair into the sun, and sat. Sat and sipped. Beauty and tranquility floated toward me on Monday morning, September 11, at around 9:30.

FIRST HE WAS A LITTLE BUMP on the far, far-off prairie. Then he was a mole way beyond the quarry. Then a larger animal, a dog perhaps, moving out there through the grass. Nearing the quarry, he became a person. No doubt about that. A woman perhaps, still in her bathrobe. But edging out from the rocks, through the weeds, toward the hill, he was clear to me. I knew then who he was. I knew it just as I knew the sun was shining.

The reason I knew is that he looked exactly the way I'd seen him five thousand times in pictures, in books and Sunday School pamphlets. If there was ever a person I'd seen and heard about over and over, this was the one. Even in grade school those terrible questions. Do you love the Lord? Are you saved by grace alone through faith? Are you awaiting eagerly the day of His Second Coming? And will you be ready on that Great Day? I'd sometimes hidden under the bed when I was a child, wondering if I really had been saved by grace alone, or, without realizing it, I'd been trying some other method, like the Catholics, who were saved by their good works and would land in hell. Except for a few who knew in their hearts it was really grace, but they didn't want to leave the church because of their relatives. And was this it? Would the trumpet sound tonight and the sky split in two? Would the great Lord and King, Alpha and Omega, holding aloft the seven candlesticks, accompanied by a heavenly host that no man could number, descend from heaven with a mighty shout? And was I ready?

And there he was. Coming. Climbing the hill in our backyard, his body bent against the climb, his robes ruffling in the wind. He was coming. And I was not ready. All those mouldy clothes scattered about the living room, and me in this faded old thing, made in Japan, and drinking – in the middle of the morning.

He had reached the steps now. His hand touched the railing. His right hand was on my railing. Jesus' fingers were curled around my railing. He was coming up. He was ascending. He was coming up to me here on the sundeck.

He stood on the top step and looked at me. I looked at him. He looked exactly right, exactly the same as all the pictures: white robe, purple stole, bronze hair, creamy skin. How had all those queer artists, illustrators of Sunday School papers, how had they gotten him exactly right like that?

He stood at the top of the stairs. I sat there holding my glass. What do you say to Jesus when he comes? How do you address him? Do you call him Jesus? I supposed that was his first name. Or Christ? I remembered the woman at the well, living in adultery, who'd called him Sir. Perhaps I could try that. Or maybe I should pretend not to recognize him. Maybe, for some reason, he didn't mean for me to recognize him. Then he spoke.

"Good morning," he said. "My name is Jesus."

"How do you do," I said. "My name is Gloria Johnson."

My name is Gloria Johnson. That's what I said all right. As if he didn't know.

He smiled, standing there at the top of the stairs. I thought of what I should do next. Then I got up and unfolded another canvas chair.

"You have a nice view here," he said, leaning back against the canvas and pressing his sandalled feet on the iron bars of the railing.

"Thank you," I said. "We like it."

Nice view. Those were his very words. Everyone who comes to our house and stands on the deck says that. Everyone.

"I wasn't expecting company today." I straightened the folds of my pink kimono and tightened the cloth more securely over my knees. I picked up the glass from the floor where I'd laid it.

"I was passing through on my way to Winnipeg. I thought I'd drop by."

"I've heard a lot about you," I said. "You look quite a bit like your pictures." I raised the glass to my mouth and saw that his hands were empty. I should offer him something to drink. Tea? Milk? How should I ask him what he'd like to drink? What words should I use?

"It gets pretty dusty out there," I finally said. "Would you care for something to drink?" He looked at the glass in my hand. "I could make you some tea," I added.

"Thanks," he said. "What are you drinking?"

"Well, on Mondays I like to relax a bit after the busy weekend with the family all home. I have five children you know. So sometimes after breakfast I have a little wine."

"That would be fine," he said.

By luck I found a clean tumbler in the cupboard. I stood by the sink, pouring the wine. And then, like a bolt of lightning, I realized my situation. Oh, Johann Sebastian Bach. Glory. Honour. Wisdom. Power. George Fredrick Handel. King of Kings and Lord of Lords. He's on my sundeck. Today he's sitting on my sundeck. I can ask him any question under the sun, anything at all, and he'll know the answer. Hallelujah. Well now, wasn't this something for a Monday morning in Moose Jaw.

I opened the fridge door to replace the bottle. And I saw my father. It was New Year's morning. My father was sitting at the kitchen table. Mother sat across from him. She'd covered the oatmeal pot to let it simmer on the stove. I could hear the lid bumping against the rim, quietly. Sigrid and Frieda sat on one side of the table, Raymond and I on the other. We were holding hymn books, little black books turned to page 1. It was dark outside. On New Year's morning we got up before sunrise. Daddy was looking at us with his chin pointed out. It meant be still and sit straight. Raymond sat as straight and stiff as a soldier, waiting for Daddy to notice how nice and stiff he sat. We began singing. Page 1. Hymn for the New Year. Philipp Nicolai, 1599. We didn't really need the books. We'd sung the same song every New Year's since the time of our conception. Daddy always sang the loudest.

> *The Morning Star upon us gleams;*
> *How full of grace and truth his beams,*
> *How passing fair his splendour.*
> *Good Shepherd, David's proper heir,*
> *My King in heaven, Thou dost me bear*
> *Upon thy bosom tender.*
> *Near–est. Dear–est. High–est. Bright–est.*
> *Thou delight–est still to love me,*
> *Thou so high enthroned a–bove me.*

I didn't mind actually, singing hymns on New Year's, as long as I was sure no one would find out. I'd have been rather embarrassed if any of my friends ever found out how we spent New Year's. It's easy at a certain age to be embarrassed about your family. I remember Alice

Olson, how embarrassed she was about her father, Elmer Olson. He was an alcoholic and couldn't control his urine. Her mother always had to clean up after him. Even so, the house smelled. I suppose she couldn't get it all. Anyway, I know Alice was embarrassed when we saw Elmer all tousled and sick-looking, with urine stains on his trousers. Sometimes I don't know what would be harder on a kid – having a father who's a drunk, or one who's sober on New Year's and sings "The Morning Star."

I walked across the deck and handed Jesus the wine. I sat down, resting my glass on the flap of my kimono. Jesus was looking out over the prairie. He seemed to be noticing everything out there. He was obviously in no hurry to leave, but he didn't have much to say. I thought of what to say next.

"I suppose you're more used to the sea than to the prairie."

"Yes," he said. "I've lived most of my life near water. But I like the prairie too. There's something nice about the prairie." He turned his face to the wind, stronger now, coming toward us from the east.

That word again. If I'd ever used *nice* to describe the prairie, in an English composition at St. Paul's, for example, it would have had three red circles around it. At least three. I raised my glass to the wind. Good old St. Paul's. Good old Pastor Solberg, standing in front of the wooden altar, holding the gospel aloft in his hand.

In the beginning wass the Word,
And the Word wass with God,

And the Word wass God.
All things were made by him;
And without him wass not anything made
That wass made.

I was sitting on a bench by Paul Thorson. We were sharing a hymnal. Our thumbs touched at the centre of the book. It was winter. The chapel was cold – an army barracks left over from World War II. We wore parkas and sat close together. Paul fooled around with his thumb, pushing my thumb to my own side of the book, then pulling it back to his side. The wind howled outside. We watched our breath as we sang the hymn.

In thine arms I rest me, Foes who would molest me
Cannot reach me here. Tho' the earth be shak–ing,
Ev–ry heart be quak–ing, Jesus calms my fear.
Fires may flash and thunder crash,
Yea, and sin and hell as–sail me,
Jesus will not fai-ai-ail me.

And here he was. Alpha and Omega. The Word. Sitting on my canvas chair, telling me the prairie's nice. What could I say to that?

"I like it too," I said.

Jesus was watching a magpie circling above the poplars just beyond the quarry. He seemed very nice actually, but he wasn't like my father. My father was perfect, mind you, but you know about perfect people – busy, busy. He wasn't as busy as Elsie though. Elsie was the busy one. You could never visit there without her having to do something else at the same time. Wash the leaves of her plants with milk or fold socks in the basement while you sat on a bench by the washing machine. I wouldn't mind sitting on a bench in the basement if that was all she had, but her living room was full of big soft chairs that no one ever sat in. Now Jesus here didn't seem to have any work to do at all.

The wind had risen now. His robes puffed about his legs. His hair swirled around his face. The wind was coming stronger now out of the east. My kimono flapped about my ankles. I bent down to secure the bottom, pressing the moving cloth close against my legs. A Saskatchewan wind comes up in a hurry, let me tell you. Then it happened. A gust of wind hit me straight on, seeping into the folds of my kimono, reaching down into the bodice, billowing the cloth out, until above the sash, the robe was fully open. I knew without looking. The wind was suddenly blowing on my breasts. I felt it cool on both my breasts. Then as quickly as it came, it left, and we sat in the same small breeze as before.

I looked at Jesus. He was looking at me, and at my breasts, looking right at them. Jesus was sitting there on the sundeck looking at my breasts.

What should I do? Say excuse me and push them back into the kimono? Make a little joke of it? Look what the wind blew in? Or should I say nothing – just tuck them in as inconspicuously as possible? What do you say when a wind comes up and blows your kimono open and he sees your breasts?

Now there are ways and there are ways of exposing your breasts. I know a few things. I read books. And I've learned a lot from my cousin Millie. Millie's the black sheep in the family. She left the Academy without graduating and became an artist's model in Winnipeg. And she's told me a few things about bodily exposure. She says, for instance, that when an artist wants to draw his model he has her either nude and stretching and bending in various positions so he can draw her from different angles, or he drapes her with cloth, satin usually. He covers one section of the body with the material and leaves the rest exposed. But he does so in a graceful manner, draping the cloth over her stomach or ankle. (Never over the breasts.) So I realized that my appearance right then wasn't actually pleasing, either aesthetically or erotically, from Millie's point of view. My breasts were just sticking out from the top of my old kimono. And for some reason that I can't explain, even to this day, I did nothing about it. I just sat there.

Jesus must have recognized my confusion, because right then he said, quite sincerely I thought, "You have nice breasts."

"Thanks," I said. I didn't know what else to say, so I asked him if he'd like more wine.

"Yes, I would," he said, and I left to refill the glass. When I returned he was watching a magpie swishing about in the tall weeds by the quarry. I sat down and watched with him.

Then I got a very, very peculiar sensation. I know it was just an illusion, but it was so strong it scared me. It's hard to explain because nothing like it had ever happened to me before. The magpie began to float toward Jesus. I saw it fluttering toward him in the air as if some vacuum were sucking it in. When it reached him, it flapped about on his chest, which was bare now because the top of his robe had slipped down. It nibbled at his little brown nipples and squawked and disappeared. For all the world, it seemed to disappear right into his pores. Then the same thing happened with a rock. A rock floating up from the quarry and landing on the breast of Jesus, melting into his skin. It was very strange, let me tell you, Jesus and I sitting there together with that going on. It made me dizzy, so I closed my eyes.

And I saw the women in a public bath in Tokyo. Black-haired women and children. Some were squatting by faucets that lined a wall. They were running hot water into their basins, washing themselves with white cloths, rubbing each other's backs with the soapy washcloths, then emptying their basins and filling them again, pouring clean water over their bodies for the rinse. Water and suds swirled about on the tiled floor. Others were sitting in the hot pool on the far side, soaking themselves in the steamy water as they jabbered away to one another. Then I saw her. The woman without the breasts. She was squatting by a faucet near the door. The oldest woman I've ever seen. The thinnest woman I've ever witnessed. Skin and bones. Literally, just skin and bones. She bowed and smiled at everyone who entered. She had three teeth. When she hunched over her basin, I saw the little creases of skin where her breasts had been. When she stood up the wrinkles disappeared. In their place were two shallow caves. Even the nipples seemed to have disappeared into the small brown caves of her breasts.

I opened my eyes and looked at Jesus. Fortunately, everything had stopped floating.

"Have you ever been to Japan?" I asked.

"Yes," he said. "A few times."

I paid no attention to his answer but went on telling him about Japan as if he'd never been there. I couldn't seem to stop talking about that old woman and her breasts.

"You should have seen her," I said. "She wasn't flat-chested like some women even here in Moose Jaw. It wasn't like that at all. Her breasts weren't just flat. They were caved in, as if the flesh had sunk right there. Have you ever seen breasts like that before?"

Jesus's eyes were getting darker. He seemed to have sunk farther down into his chair.

"Japanese women have smaller breasts to begin with usually," he said.

But he'd misunderstood me. It wasn't just her breasts that held me. It was her jaws, teeth, neck, ankles, heels. Not just her breasts. I said nothing for awhile. Jesus, too, was not talking.

Finally I asked, "Well? What do you think of breasts like that?"

I knew immediately that I'd asked the wrong question. If you want personal and specific answers, you ask personal and specific questions. It's as simple as that. I should have asked him, for instance, what he thought of them from a sexual point of view. If he were a lover, let's say, would he like to hold such breasts in his hands and play on them with his teeth and fingers? Would he now? The woman, brown and shiny, was bending over her basin. Tiny bubbles of soap dribbled from the creases of her chest down to her navel. Hold them. Ha.

Or I could have asked for some kind of aesthetic opinion. If he were an artist, a sculptor let's say, would he travel to Italy and spend weeks excavating the best marble from the hills near Florence, and then would he stay up all night and day in his studio, without eating or bathing, and with matted hair and glazed eyes, chisel out those little creases from his great stone slab?

Or if he were a patron of the arts, would he attend the opening of this grand exhibition and stand in front of these white caves in his purple turtleneck, sipping champagne and nibbling on the little cracker with the shrimp in the middle, and would he turn to the one beside him, the one in the sleek black pants, and would he say to her, "Look, darling, did you see this marvellous piece? Do you see how the artist has captured the very essence of the female form?"

These are some of the things I could have said if I'd had my wits about me. But my wits certainly left me that day. All I did say, and I didn't mean to, it just came out, was, "It's not nice and I don't like it."

I lifted my face, threw my head back, and let the wind blow on my neck and breasts. It was blowing harder again. I felt small grains of sand scrape against my skin.

Jesus, lover of my soul,
Let me to thy bosom fly.
While the nearer waters roll,
While the tempest still is nigh.

When I looked at him again, his eyes were blacker still and his body had shrunk considerably. He looked almost like Jimmy that time in Prince Albert. Jimmy was a neighbour of ours from Regina. On his twenty-seventh birthday he joined a motorcycle gang, the Grim Reapers to be exact, and got into a lot of trouble. He ended up in maximum security in P.A. One summer on a camping trip up north, we went to see him, Fred and the kids and I. It wasn't a good visit, however. If you're going to visit inmates you should do it regularly. I realize this now. Anyway, that's when his eyes looked black like that. But maybe he'd been smoking pot or something. It's probably not the same thing. Jimmy LeBlanc. He never did think it was funny when I'd call him a Midnight Raider instead of a Grim Reaper. People are sensitive about their names.

Then Jesus finally answered. Everything seemed to take him a long time, even answering simple questions.

But I'm not sure what he said because something so strange happened that whatever he did say was swept away. Right then the wind blew against my face, pulling my hair back. My kimono swirled about every which way, and I was swinging my arms in the air, like swimming. And there right below my eyes was the roof of our house. I was looking down on the top of the roof. I saw the row of shingles ripped loose from the August hailstorm. And I remember thinking – Fred hasn't fixed those shingles yet. I'll have to remind him when he gets home from work. If it rains again the back bedroom will get soaked. Before I knew it I was circling over the sundeck, looking down on the top of Jesus' head. Only I wasn't. I was sitting in the canvas chair watching myself hover over his shoulders. Only it wasn't me hovering. It was the old woman in Tokyo. I saw her grey hair twisting in the wind and her shiny little bum raised in the air, like a baby's. Water was dripping from her chin and toes. And soap bubbles trailed from her elbows like tinsel. She was floating down toward his chest. Only it wasn't her. It was me. I could taste bits of suds sticking to the corners of my mouth and feel the wind on my wet back and in the hollow caves of my breasts. I was smiling and bowing, and the wind was blowing in narrow wisps against my toothless gums. Then quickly, so quickly, like a flock of waxwings diving through snow into the branches of the poplar, I was splitting up into millions of pieces and sinking into the tiny, tiny holes in his chest. It was like the magpie and the rock, like I had come apart into atoms or molecules, or whatever we really are.

After that I was dizzy, and I began to feel nauseated. Jesus looked sick too. Sad and sick and lonesome. Oh, Christ, I thought, why are we sitting here on such a fine day pouring our sorrows into each other?

I had to get up and walk around. I'd go into the kitchen and make some tea.

I put the kettle on to boil. What on earth had gotten into me? Why had I spent this perfectly good morning talking about breasts? My one chance in a lifetime and I'd let it slip through my fingers. Why didn't I have better control? Why was I always letting things get out of hand? Breasts. And why was my name Gloria? Such a pious name for one who can't think of anything else to talk about but breasts. Why wasn't it Lucille? Or Millie? You could talk about breasts all day if your name was Millie. But Gloria. Gloria. Glo-o-o-o-o-o-ri-a in ex-cel-sis. I knew then why so many Glorias hang around bars, talking too loud, laughing shrilly at stupid jokes, making sure everyone hears them laugh at the dirty jokes. They're just trying to live down their name, that's all. I brought out the cups and poured the tea.

Everything was back to normal when I returned except that Jesus still looked desolate sitting in my canvas chair. I handed him the tea and sat down beside him.

Oh, Daddy. And Philipp Nicolai. Oh, Bernard of Clairvaux. Oh, Sacred Head Now Wounded. Go away for a little while and let us sit together quietly, here in this small space under the sun.

I sipped the tea and watched his face. He looked so sorrowful I reached out my hand and put it on his wrist. I sat there a long time rubbing the little hairs on his wrist with my fingers; I couldn't help it. After that he put his arm on my shoulder and his hand on the back of my neck, stroking the muscles there. It felt good. Whenever anything exciting or unusual happens to me my neck is the first to feel it. It gets stiff and knotted up. Then I usually get a headache, and frequently I become nauseated. So it felt very good having my neck rubbed.

I've never been able to handle sensation very well. I remember when I was in grade three and my folks took us to the Saskatoon Exhibition. We went to see the grandstand show – the battle of Wolfe and Montcalm on the Plains of Abraham. The stage was filled with

Indians and pioneers and ladies in red, white, and blue dresses singing "In Days of Yore From Britain's Shore." It was very spectacular but too much for me. My stomach was upset and my neck ached. I had to keep my head on my mother's lap the whole time, just opening my eyes once in a while so I wouldn't miss everything.

So it really felt good having my neck stroked like that. I could almost feel the knots untying and my body warmer and more restful. Jesus too seemed to be feeling better. His body was back to normal. His eyes looked natural again.

Then, all of a sudden, he started to laugh. He held his hand on my neck and laughed out loud. I don't know to this day what he was laughing about. There was nothing funny there at all. But hearing him made me laugh too. He was laughing so hard he spilled tea on his purple stole. When I saw that, I laughed even more. I'd never thought of Jesus spilling his tea before. And when Jesus saw me laughing like that and when he looked at my breasts shaking, he laughed harder still, till he wiped tears from his eyes.

After that we just sat there. I don't know how long. I know we watched the magpie carve black waves in the air above the rocks. And the rocks stiff and lovely among the swaying weeds. We watched the poplars twist and bend and rise again beyond the quarry. And then he had to leave.

"Goodbye, Gloria Johnson," he said, rising from his chair. "Thanks for the hospitality."

He leaned over and kissed me on my mouth. Then he flicked my nipple with his finger, and off he went.

Down the hill, through the quarry, and into the prairie. I stood on the sundeck and watched. I watched until I could see him no longer. Until he was only some dim and ancient star on the far horizon.

I went inside the house. Well, now, wasn't that a nice visit. Wasn't that something. I examined the clothes, dry and sour in the living room. I'd have to put them back in the wash, that's all. I couldn't stand the smell. I tucked my breasts back into my kimono and lugged the basket downstairs.

That's what happened to me in Moose Jaw in 1972. It was the main thing that happened to me that year.

Acknowledgements

Some of these stories have appeared previously: "The Day I Sat with Jesus on the Sundeck and a Wind Came Up and Blew My Kimono Open and He Saw My Breasts" in *Cutbank* (Montana); *Grain* (Saskatchewan); *Best Canadian Stories,* Oberon, John Metcalf and Leon Rooke, eds.; *3x5,* NeWest Press, Douglas Barbour, ed.; *Canadian Short Fiction,* Oxford University Press, Margaret Atwood, ed.; *The Oxford Book of Stories by Canadian Women in English,* Rosemary Sullivan, ed.; *From Timberline to Tidepool,* Owl Creek Press, Seattle, Washington, Rich Ives, ed.; *The Gates of Paradise,* Macfarlane Walter and Ross, Alberto Manguel, ed.; *Myths and Voices,* White Pine Press, New York, David Lampe, ed.; as well as publications by European Education Publishers Group, Arhus, Denmark, Tina Bundgaard and Johannes Andersen, eds.; Iwanaami Shoten Publishers, Tokyo, Japan; and Alianza Editorial, Madrid, Spain.

"Mother's Day" appeared in *New Canadian Writers,* Doubleday, and in *3x5*; "The Ground You Stand On" in *NeWest Review* (Saskatchewan), and as "Hang Out Your Washing on the Seigfried Line" in *3x5*, and *Alberta Bound,* NeWest Press, Fred Stenson, ed.; "Haircut" and an excerpt from "A Song for Nettie Johnson" in *Other Voices,* Edmonton; "The Dolphins" in *The Road Home,* Reidmore Books, Fred Stenson, ed.; "Hosea's Children" in *Intersections,* The Banff Centre Press, Edna Alford, ed.

I would like to acknowledge the financial assistance of the Alberta Foundation for the Arts, the Canada Council, and Noboru Sawai, during the writing of these stories.

Thank you to my intricately precise and ever encouraging editor, Edna Alford. And to friends who have read these stories and who, by their thoughtful criticism, have also helped to make them better: Ruth Krahn, Theresa Shea, and Merna Summers.

Several of the songs that appear in this collection deserve particular acknowledgement: "Mid Pleasures and Palaces," by John Howard Payne (1792-1852); "A Lamb Goes Uncomplaining Forth," by Paul Gerhardt (1607 - 1679); "The Morning Star" by Philipp Nicolai (1566 - 1608); and "The Holy City," by E. Weatherly (1848 - 1929); and "Jesus, Priceless Treasure," by Johann Franck (1618 - 1677).

 PHOTO: MARILYN TUNGLAND

ABOUT THE AUTHOR

GLORIA OSTREM SAWAI has been a fiction writer, teacher, playwright, and one time actor and theatre director. Her short fiction has been published in anthologies in Canada, the United States, England, Spain, Denmark and Japan; and her plays have had professional productions. This is her first book-length collection of short stories.

Born in Minneapolis, she spent her childhood in Saskatchewan. As an adult, she has lived in Japan, the US and Canada. She attended high school at Camrose Lutheran College in Camrose, Alberta, received a BA degree from Augsburg College in Minneapolis, and an MFA from the University of Montana. She has taught creative writing at the Banff School of Fine Arts, the Saskatchewan School of the Arts, and at Grant MacEwan College in Edmonton, where she now lives.